Prime Yuth
Operation Turbulence

Prime Youth: Operation Turbulence

Copyright ©2025 by Ethan Cooley

ISBN: 979-8-9994157-1-4 (hard cover)

ISBN: 979-8-9994157-0-7 (paperback)

ISBN: 979-8-9994157-2-1 (ebook)

Contact Info: www.eecooley.com

Cover Art: Addison Hofer (Instagram: @addoodly)

Cover Typography: Darnell Drake Jr. (Instagram: @dj_who_draws)

Editor: Kim Autrey

First Edition

To the fans who wait

Part 1

After Action Report 799-547 – Complex Red 2
Operation Name: Recruit Ceremony (Group 1)
Date: ███████
Time: ███████

The following account has been compiled from
security footage from Complex Red 2 and Youth who
participated in the operation. [This is an
abridged compilation. For the unabridged account
refer to After Action Report 79-547]

    The first group of recruits to be brought in
for *Operation Growing Allegiance* were Calvin Fritz,
Megan Nall, Thomas ████████, Dakota ██████, Sydney
████, and ████████████. Upon arrival, Calvin
Fritz quickly expressed doubt in the legitimacy
of the school (Complex Red 2). After former
General Edward could not ease any of Calvin's
concerns, the General ordered the last arriving
recruit, ████████████████, not to be shuttled to
Complex Red 2 but instead to Complex 2; where ██
would receive the same offer of joining the Youth
as the other recruits from Group 1 did.
    Former General Edward quickly realized
Calvin's doubts were not eased by anything the
staff at the school told him and swiftly offered
all the recruits the contract to join the Youth
[Note, this was done 6 weeks earlier than
scheduled]. Calvin did not sign the contract and
showed open distrust to the Youth and their cause.
The other recruits signed but slowly started
believing Calvin the more he brought his concerns
to his fellow recruits. Former General Edward
ordered Calvin to be sedated and removed from the
group to ensure no more doubt was sewn.
    After two weeks of being closely monitored and
with life support on standby, Calvin was awoken

from sedation. During these two weeks, the remaining recruits were given formal combat training. No one showed any sign of doubt or distrust toward the Youth, that is until Calvin was returned to the group. In the less than one day between when Calvin was awoken from sedation to the Allegiance Ceremony, he had managed to turn all but one of the recruits against the Youth.

With the help of a fallen youth, Calvin was able to escape the Allegiance Ceremony. Former General Edward escorted the remaining recruits to safety while a manhunt for Calvin and the fallen youth was conducted across the Complex. After a full day, and finding no one, former General Edward decided to give the remaining recruits one last opportunity to join the Youth by finishing the Allegiance Ceremony. The recruits were escorted across campus where their parents, who had been flown in, waited to make the recruits rethink their decision not to join. But Calvin and the fallen youth came back, conducting an attack on the Youth to kidnap the recruits and their parents.

During this attack, Sydney, the only recruit never to show any doubt in her allegiance to the Youth, was the only one not to assist when the recruits attempted to overpower former General Edward. The Former General called for Sydney to be escorted and flown away to Complex 3 to ensure her safety for her loyalty to the Youth. Then upon delivering the recruits to their parents, Calvin and the fallen youth kidnapped the recruits and their parents, attempting to flee the Complex. The Youth gave chase and were able to rescue all the recruits's parents except for Megan Nall's mother. Her, the remaining recruits, and the fallen youth fled the Complex. A chase ensued which crossed outside the Complex's borders.

2

[The continuation of this account can be found in After Action Report 79-548]

Getting cut in the stomach easily ranked as the worst time of my life so far, next only to being stuck in a freezer. Because every tiny movement made me feel like I was on fire and wanted to throw up, not a great combo. At least I had Megan to talk to. She sat on the floor in front of me while I lay on the front seat of the van.

"Calvin, are you listening?" said Megan, breaking me from my thoughts.

"I thought I was."

"You thought you were?"

"I… was…" I started before being saved by Thomas.

"Where did you get those?"

I pulled myself up to see over the seat back, immediately regretting it and clenching my teeth. Megan put a hand on my shoulder, and I did my best to smile back.

"Why do you ask if you already know the answer?" said Dakota, shoving a handful of crackers into his mouth.

"I don't know," said Thomas, "but it doesn't matter. We need to save our food. We don't know how long we'll be out here." He tried to grab the bag, but Dakota pushed him away.

"You are not stealing my food," said Dakota, fending off Thomas.

"You already stole it so I'm just returning it."

"How can I–hey!" The Youth, or Renegade now as I called them, in the seat behind Thomas and Dakota, grabbed the bag of crackers. The Renegade still had his helmet and suit on. Dakota tried grabbing them back, but the Renegade was too quick. He closed the crackers up and put the box in the back of the van.

With his hand still outstretched, Dakota said, "What am I going to eat now?" The Renegade grabbed Dakota's hand and twisted it. "Ow, ow, ok, ok, I get it." The three of us laughed as the Renegade let go of Dakota's hand.

"Try not to hurt them yet, Cody," said our driver.

"Yet," said Megan and I at the same time.

"If you want us to train you, I will more than gladly let Cody hurt you. For training purposes."

"We just want to get our parents and get out of here," said Thomas. "I don't plan to stick around and have you train us."

Our driver chuckled. "You still don't realize what you're involved in now?"

"What do you mean?" asked Thomas.

"You have Edward after you," said our driver. "You won't be out of this until you put an end to him."

As much as I wanted to agree with Thomas, I also agreed with our driver. The way Edward acted back at the school, I had a feeling he would be after us for a while. Or until he found the next group of kids to kidnap and brainwash.

"We lost a van," said our driver. "Get ready, Cody."

"Which one?" I asked. After meeting up, we all took off in intervals. That way, if the Youth caught up to one of the vans, they wouldn't be able to take out all of us. And it would give the others time to prepare.

"The one behind us," said our driver.

We all turned around to see little black dots in the distance.

"You think that's them?" asked Megan.

Cody bent over and grabbed something from beside him.

"Everyone strap in," said our driver. I strapped myself into the seat, and Megan hopped up and sat next to her mom in the seat behind me.

Cody climbed to the front and laid a long case on the floor in front of me. He hinged it open and assembled a sniper rifle from inside.

"Sweet. When do I get my gun?" asked Dakota as he and Thomas peered over the seat in front of them.

"You aren't going to kill them, are you?" asked Megan's mom.

"Once they start shooting water guns at us, come talk to me," said Cody.

"You are not—" said Megan's mom before being cut off by her daughter.

"Mom, just let them help us."

"This is not—"

"Shut your mouths!" yelled our driver.

I could hear some engines approaching us and tried sitting up to see out the window when Cody put his hand on my shoulder. "Stay below the windows, helmets on," he said to everyone before opening the window in front of me. It hinged open inside the van, allowing Cody to stick his sniper out with ease.

I said a prayer in my head as I grabbed my helmet from the floor and shoved it on. Cody fired a shot, which was greatly muted by the helmet. I heard something crash behind us as Cody fired again. The van jerked suddenly, and I grabbed onto the seat to keep from sliding around. We swerved back and forth a couple of times before we heard a spray of bullets hit the right side of the van and a giant hiss of air.

Cody turned around and fired a shot off toward the front of the van, shooting left-handed this time. The driver swerved a bit before running into something, our car jumped in the air and went off the road. Our driver was able to dodge one tree before running head-on into another one. Everyone screamed and yelled as I flew forward, sliding out of the seat belt as the van spun and flipped over, landing on its right side.

By some miracle, I was still alive, but Cody had fallen on top of me. I could barely breath, and I tried shoving Cody off me, only to have my body scream at me to stop.

"Calvin!" cried Thomas as he unbuckled himself and fell on the window below him with an "oof." He crawled over to me and helped shove Cody off me enough so I could breathe. I sucked in a deep breath and coughed, which made me feel even worse.

"We need to get you out of here," said Thomas shoving Cody even further off me. As he was doing so, Cody stirred and sat up, immediately looking back and forth and climbed up the front seats to get to the still open window he had just shot out of. A burst of gunshots came from our driver who had one foot on the side of the front passenger seat and the other on the dash; his head sticking out of his window firing his gun.

The others started to stir as Thomas got an arm under me and helped me up. I screamed as he picked me up, which woke everyone else up.

"Calvin!" cried Megan.

"I'm coming," said Dakota.

"What happened," asked Megan's mom with blood running down from a gash on her head.

Dakota slid out of his seat and came over to help me up while Megan helped her mom out of her seat.

Thomas and Dakota were able to get me upright, and without them, I wouldn't have been able to stand.

"Cody!" yelled Dakota. "We're gonna lift him up to you."

Cody fired a round, and the spent cartridge hit Dakota's helmet and fell to our feet. "Stay inside!" he looked down and yelled at us.

"We need to get out of here!" yelled Thomas.

A second later, the firing ceased from both Cody and our driver. "All clear!" yelled our driver as he hopped back down into the van. He knelt in front of me and put his hands together for me to stand on.

"You need to help us get you out of here, Calvin," said my driver.

"I'll try," I said stepping up onto my driver's hand.

He counted down quickly, "Three, two, one." I pushed with all my strength, and with the help of Dakota and Thomas, was able to reach up and grab Cody's hand. I screamed as Cody pulled me up and through the window. I grabbed something on the underside of the van and held it to keep myself from falling back down.

"Keep going," said Cody, but I didn't have the strength.

"I can't," I cried. At that, he grabbed the waist of my suit in one hand and wrapped the other around my chest and pulled me up. I grimaced as the suit pulled right where my stomach was cut. Cody hauled me up and placed me next to the window. I grabbed onto the underside of the van again, so I didn't slide off.

I tried looking through the windows at everyone, but they were too tinted. Cody put his hand through the window and brought up Megan's mom. Cody also had to grab her by her belt and pull her through the window. After Cody set her down, she climbed over and sat next to me. "Are you alright?" she asked. I just shook my head.

Megan came up next, and she was able to get herself through without any help. "Are you alright, Calvin?" she asked, putting a hand on my shoulder.

"Do I look alright," I said, annoyed.

Megan hesitated a moment before replying, "I'll help you down. Come on, Mom." Megan slid down to the edge of the Van and jumped off. Her mom followed her. "Just slide down, and we'll help you down, Calvin!" yelled Megan as Thomas came through the window.

"Let me help you," said Thomas, grabbing my hand, and I slid down the side of the van. Megan and her mom both reached up and helped me down, then laid me on my back.

Megan's mom took my helmet off as her daughter knelt next to me and took her helmet off, flipping her hair out of her face. As she did that, the sequins on her dress caught the light and blinded me.

"What?" she asked.

"I'm surprised you're getting your dress dirty," I said, grinning.

"We are long past keeping this clean, Calvin."

Dakota hopped down and joined the circle surrounding me.

"Looks like you need a new bandage," said Dakota, leaning over and pointing to my now completely red bandage.

"Is there any in the van," said Megan, pointing to the back of the van.

Thomas and Dakota ran over and forced the back doors open. "Don't get distracted by any of the food back here," I heard Thomas say.

"I can't believe you think that low of me," said Dakota, pulling crates out and searching through them.

"It's not hard when all I've seen you do is eat and sleep," said Thomas. We all chuckled, even Megan's mom.

"What do you want to bet he'll come back with some food stashed away in his pocket?" I asked Megan.

"I wouldn't be surprised if he just brings an entire box with him."

"Head's up!" yelled Cody, throwing a backpack on the ground next to us. "Med kit's attached to the front."

Megan's mom grabbed my left hand as Megan went to get the med kit. "You'll be alright, Calvin."

"I hope so."

"If you've survived this much, I don't know what can stop you."

"Thank you," I said as Megan came back over with the med kit. She pulled it open and looked through everything.

"We found one!" Megan yelled at Thomas and Dakota.

"Are there any scissors?" asked Megan's mom.

"Here." She handed her mom a pair, and she started cutting my bandages off.

"Should I ask how bad it is?" I said as Megan's mom started peeling the wet bandages off.

"Don't worry about it, Calvin," said Megan before her mom could reply. Must be pretty bad if no one wanted to tell me. The two of them continued pulling bandages and wrapping off while Cody and our driver threw more backpacks onto the ground next to us.

Once all my bandages were removed, Megan went searching through the med kit again.

"That'll make a great scar, Calvin," said Dakota, leaning over me with his helmet off.

"Not if we can stitch it," said Megan's mom.

"Where's the fun in that?" said Dakota.

"Can you all hold him down," said Megan.

"Hold me down?" I asked.

"Just hold him down, please," said Megan. "Thomas, hold his arm. Dakota, grab his legs."

"Stop, no one is holding me down," I said sitting up. "What are you doing Megan?"

"It's better if you don't know," said Megan, pushing me back down, but I pushed her arm off me.

"Tell me, Megan," I said, staring at her.

We locked eyes a moment before she responded, "I was going to clean out the wound. I knew it would hurt, so I didn't want you to know."

"Don't clean it out," I said. "Just put a bandage on it and be done."

"Why are all men like this," Megan's mom muttered under her breath.

"We don't have time for this," said Cody, grabbing something from the med kit and kneeling next to Megan. "Mason, hold him down," he said, pointing beside Megan's mom. Without saying anything, Megan pushed me back down and held my arm down.

"No, no, no, we are not doing this." I tried getting out of Megan's grasp. When she realized she was losing, she put her knees and all her weight on my arm. Mason, our driver, did the same thing. I tried wiggling out, but in my state, nothing was happening.

"Cover his mouth," Cody told Megan, who quickly complied. I shook my head back and forth, but Megan still managed to cover my mouth.

9

Cody opened a bag and poured a white powder out, and before I knew it, I felt like there was acid eating at my stomach.

Even with my mouth covered, my scream pierced the air. Mason shoved his hand on top of Megan's as my whole body tensed up. Someone grabbed my legs as they flailed, and all I could do was close my eyes and scream.

I never heard it, but Cody said "done" after dumping an entire packet of what he called miracle powder on my stomach. The feeling of my stomach being eaten by acid was the powder mixing with my blood and exposed flesh and cauterizing it. Something about a chemical reaction. All I know is it was the worst pain I had ever experienced.

The next thing I remember was being dragged over in front of a tree next to our pile of gear. I was propped up against a tree, and my helmet laid next to me. Thomas squatted next to me and shook my arm. "Calvin. It's all over now."

"Why do I still feel like crap then?" I asked.

Thomas smiled and opened the top of a canteen. "I don't want to know what you're feeling, but I think that describes it perfectly. Here, drink some water." He handed me the canteen, and I guzzled it.

"Thank you," I said, wiping my mouth with the back of my arm and handing the canteen back to Thomas. "Where's Megan and her mom?" I asked, only seeing Cody and Mason going through some crates from the back of the van.

"They're changing in the van," said Dakota, looking through the front window of the van.

"I hope you're not doing what I think you're doing," I said to Dakota. Thomas followed his gaze and immediately turned back, staring at Dakota. When Dakota didn't move, Thomas took his finger and turned Dakota's helmeted head toward him.

"No," said Thomas. The two stared at each other for a moment, then Dakota looked down at me. I shook my head.

"Fine," said Dakota, throwing his hands up, "I'll do it for the Christian boys."

"Thank you," said Thomas and I together.

"Did we find some extra clothes in the back?" I asked, seeing some clothes next to both Thomas and Dakota.

"They gave us suits like yours," said Dakota, unfolding his and looking over it. "Look at this," he said, pointing to different parts of the suit. "It's got bullet proof armor, a heating and cooling pack, these cool gloves and boots, it looks sweet." He had his helmet on, but I knew Dakota was smiling behind it. "I can't wait," he said, scooping up the suit and running off.

Thomas leaned over to see where Dakota ran off to. "Guess he's alright changing out here."

"I would only do it if I had to," I said.

"I like my privacy, too," said Thomas.

"Can we get some help!" yelled Megan from inside the van. Thomas and I turned as Mason got up on top of the van.

"I'll be right back," said Thomas, grabbing his suit and running over to help Mason.

I laid my head back against the tree and held my hand over my stomach, getting a sharp sting in return. This was not going to make things very easy going forward. I doubted I could even walk on my own.

I looked around and realized I didn't even know where we were. Every time I'd ask Mason, he refused to say anything, explaining their radios were still connected to the Youth mainframe; but he informed me that my suit and helmet, along with Thomas, Megan, and Dakota's, were not connected. All I knew was that we were surrounded by a forest that was just as cool as the sea off Rhode Island.

As I looked around, I spotted Mason as he pulled off the heating and cooling unit from the back of Cody's suit. The two reversed roles and threw the assemblies far into the woods. I hoped that meant the Youth couldn't track us anymore.

Some smoke caught my eye from something behind our van, closer to the road we had run off. It wasn't much, but it came from a vehicle of some kind, but what that vehicle was was far from recognizable. Then I saw among the crash a Youth helmet, with a body connected to it. I know that they were shooting at us, but it made me almost sick looking at a dead body, and that body being a kid's made it all the worse. Maybe Megan's mom was right about not killing them. I'm just glad it wasn't me that killed them.

Dakota came back around the tree and broke me out of my thoughts. "How does it look," he asked, showing off the suit with his helmet on. Without the red helmet, he would have looked just like a Youth, a very muscular Youth.

"I like it," I said, still thinking about the destruction in front of me.

Dakota followed my gaze.

"Oh," he said, "I didn't see that."

After a moment of silence, I said, "We should bury them."

"Why would we do that?" asked Dakota, spinning around. "They're our enemy?"

"They're kids." My eyes narrowed looking up a Dakota. "And whether they're our enemy or not doesn't matter. You bury the dead."

"They tried to kill us, Calvin," said Dakota, pointing to the crashed vehicle. "The Youth can bury them if they want, but I'm not."

"If you died," I asked Dakota, "would you prefer to be buried and have a cross or sign to signify that you are the person buried there, or would you rather have the crows and insects eat you until you're just a skeleton?"

"I mean," Dakota hesitated, "when you put it that way, I'd rather be buried, but not by my enemy. That's just humiliating."

"It's respectful," I said, crossing my arms and looking back toward the van as Megan and her mom walked up. Megan's mom had a bandage over her head. They both had on Youth suits, Megan carried her helmet at her side and set it down as she knelt next to me.

"Doing better?" she asked.

"I'm fine," I replied.

Megan looked down and rubbed the back of her head. "Sorry about earlier," she said, looking back up.

I had completely forgotten about earlier. "Don't do it again," I said, looking at the ground.

"At least you're not bleeding," said Megan.

I uncrossed my arms and looked down at my completely white bandage.

"Oh my," said Megan's mom. I looked up, and she had a hand over her mouth as she looked at the destruction Cody and Mason had caused.

Megan turned around and slowly stood up.

"Have none of you seen dead people before," said Dakota, crossing his arms.

None of us replied. I wanted to yell at Dakota for his snarky and inappropriate comment. But Cody walked up before I could say anything.

"Everyone, grab a pack and get ready to leave," said Cody, holding two empty ammo boxes, and walked over to the dead Youth, pulling them from the wreckage.

"What are you doing," yelled Megan's mom. Without replying, Cody started pulling stuff off the Youth's suit.

Mason walked over and stood next to Megan's mom. "Really, Cody," he said, putting his hands on his hips.

Cody pulled another Youth from another wreck I hadn't seen and did just like before. When he was done, he brought over full ammo cans.

"Cody," said Mason again, stepping in front of Cody and stopping him.

"You'll thank me later," said Cody, pushing past Mason.

We all turned and stared at Cody as he took the ammo boxes and attached them to his backpack.

"I'd like to bury them if we have time?" I asked, looking up at Mason. I knew with the Youth still on our tail, we didn't have too many luxuries.

Mason looked at me for a moment before replying, "We don't have time to bury them, but we can at least cover them with a tarp."

"We need to get moving, Mason," said Cody, hefting his backpack on. He clipped the waist belt together and grabbed his sniper that was standing up against the van. As he walked past our group, he stopped in front of Mason and looked at him. "That is unless you'd rather meet the Interrogators." Cody slapped Mason on the arm and took off into the forest, parallel to the road and in the same direction we had been traveling.

"We cover them and leave," said Mason, running over to the crates from the back of the van. I could see everyone still tense. If the Interrogators were anything like what Edward put me through, I didn't want to be here any longer than I had to.

Mason ran back over with two black tarps when we heard Thomas yell from the van, "Can I get some help!"

"Be quick," said Mason, handing Megan the tarps and running over to help Thomas out of the van. Megan stared blankly at Mason and didn't move.

Dakota walked up and took the tarps from her, making his way over to the Youth. "This isn't that hard," he said as he reached the first Youth.

"We should put their helmets on a stick or something," I said as Thomas walked over. "Can someone help me up?" Both Thomas and Megan grabbed my hands and slowly pulled me up. "Let me try and stand on my own."

"Are you sure?" asked Thomas.

"Just let me try." They both slowly let go of me, and to my surprise,

I was able to stand up. But continuing to stand up was something else entirely. I could do it, but it made my stomach feel even worse. I took a step and immediately grabbed for Megan and Thomas, who caught me as I started to fall.

"You don't walk unless someone carries you," said Megan.

"That won't be hard to follow," I said.

Dakota had laid the tarp over the second Youth as Mason was driving a stick into the ground and put the Youth's helmet on top of it.

It wasn't very pretty looking, but at least we gave them the respect they deserved.

"I'll grab our bags," said Megan, giving me time to shift my weight fully onto Thomas before letting me go.

"You think the Youth will catch us?" asked Thomas quietly, so no one else could hear.

"Are you going—" I took a breath, exhausted already from standing up — "going to let them catch you?" I asked.

Thomas took a moment before replying, "I won't make it easy." We both grinned.

"One for you, Thomas," said Megan, walking up, dragging three backpacks behind her. "Do you think you can carry one?" she asked me.

"I can barely carry myself," I replied.

"I can carry his," said Dakota, walking past and grabbing one of the bags.

"Thank you," I said as everyone got their bags on. "Could you grab my helmet?" I asked Dakota as he walked by it. He handed it to me and grabbed Thomas's helmet.

"Catch," he said, tossing Thomas his helmet.

"Thanks," he replied, catching it and putting it on.

I pulled up my balaclava and shoved my helmet on.

"Everyone ready?" asked Mason, turning around to look at all of us; we all had helmets except Megan's mom. With no complaints, Mason turned around, and we followed. Both Thomas and Megan carried me into the forest, everyone else keeping pace with us. I was concerned that Cody had disappeared, but at least I knew he wouldn't go down without a fight. I just hoped I would be able to put up even a fraction of what he could. I took one last look at the van and the covered Youth beside it. What in the world had I gotten myself into?

<u>Crimson Platoon Helmet Log [Video and Audio]</u>

Youth: YT1 [Gen. Edward], YT3, YT4, YT7, YT9, YT12, YT45
Location: ██████████████████████
Date of Transcript: ████████
Time of Transcript: ████████████████████

<u>Transcript</u>

Secure Channel ZR17 Activated
Users on Channel: YT1, YT3, YT4, YT7

   Gen. Edward steps out from the forest to the middle of the road.
   Gen. Edward: What's the status of the roadblock?
   YT3: [Over Radio] We're only three-quarters of a mile out sir. There's one lady who refuses to move back and has repeatedly tried going around

us or run us over.

Gen. Edward: As long as there aren't any witnesses, you have permission to terminate subject.

YT3: [Over Radio] Copy, sir.

Gen. Edward walks over to three fallen youth. Each handcuffed behind their backs and kneeling in a line just off the road with their helmets off. Three Youth surround them.

Gen. Edward: What have they said?

YT7: Nothing yet, sir.

Gen. Edward squats down in front of the fallen youth.

Gen. Edward: You have one chance to tell me what the other traitors plan to do with the recruits they brainwashed.

The fallen youth don't say a word.

Gen. Edward stands up, takes a step back, and kicks one of the fallen youth in the face. Gen. Edward stands over the fallen youth and puts his foot on his chest.

Gen. Edward: You want to tell me now or wait until you've been in the Black Room for a week.

fallen youth 2: We don't know where they are. I swear. We were never told.

Gen. Edward: How unfortunate.

Gen. Edward stands and motions to the Youth surrounding the fallen youth.

Gen. Edward: Get them back to base and throw them with the other fallen youth awaiting the Black Room.

fallen youth 1: We don't know anything, please.

Gen. Edward: Unless you want to tell me what I want, speaking is pointless.

The Youth haul the fallen youth off to the nearby van. Gen. Edward walks back toward the wrecked van. A group of Youth are looking through the contents of the trunk spread out around them.

Gen. Edward: What have you found?

YT9 looks up at Gen. Edward.

YT9: Nothing yet, sir. Just equipment and rations.

Gen. Edward: Your squad doesn't leave until every inch has been searched. Tow it back to base when you're done.

YT9: Yes, sir.

YT12: [Over Radio] General, I've got an update on the fallen youth, sir.

Gen. Edward: On my way.

Gen. Edward makes his way over to the Forward Command Van. Its back doors are open, and the General steps inside. YT12 and YT45 sit in front of the wall of monitors and dials. The General leans against YT12's chair and looks at his monitors. YT12 points to a monitor.

YT12: Four vans of fallen youth have all stopped here, at safe house 8-24-1.

Gen. Edward: What about the fifth van we sent our scouts after?

YT12 points to a different monitor.

YT12: All four of our scouts were taken out.

Gen. Edward: Why are there no signals for the fallen youth from that van.

YT12: We lost their signals about five minutes ago, sir.

Gen. Edward slaps YT12 on the helmet.

Gen. Edward: And you didn't tell me.

YT12: You were interrogating the prisoners when I found out, sir.

Gen. Edward grabs YT12 by the collar and drags him out of his seat, throwing him out of the van.

Gen. Edward: You're on prisoner watch now. [To YT45] Get someone more competent in that chair.

Gen. Edward points to the now empty chair.

YT45: Yes, sir.

Gen. Edward hops out of the van.

Gen. Edward: Cougar Squad and Dynamo Squad. Proceed to safehouse 8-24-1. My squad, take the bikes, we have some fallen youth to find.

Gen. Edward runs over to a group of three OR bikes [off road].

YT4: Are we waiting on Cory, sir?

Gen. Edward: ETA, Cory?

YT3: One mike out.

Gen. Edward: Cory will catch up with us.

Crimson Squad mounts the OR bikes and takes off toward the last known location of the fallen youth signals.

End Transcript

"You sure you don't need a break?" said Thomas through the radio in my helmet for what felt like the hundredth time. Both him and Megan carried me. Thomas on my right, and Megan on my left. And at this point, they were dragging me more than they were carrying me.

"I'm fine," I said breathless. We hadn't stopped since we left the van. And I was trying not to slow our pace down, but I could tell Mason was getting nervous. He kept looking behind us more and more the farther we went.

"Don't you think we'd hear them long before we saw them?" asked Dakota.

"Nothing wrong with being overly cautious, especially without Cody," said Mason.

"He hasn't contacted you?" I asked.

"Not yet."

I was liking Cody less and less. Even if we were being slow, he never should have run away from his team.

"Do you need a break, Megan?" asked her mom.

"I'm fine mom. Thanks."

"You should take a break," I said.

"I don't need a break, Calvin."

"What if I say I'd like to talk to Dakota?"

"I don't know why you're letting me stop you."

"Dakota, could you give Megan a break?" I asked.

Dakota looked at me, carrying my bag on his shoulders. "She'll have to carry your bag," he said glancing at Megan.

"It'll just be a minute," I said.

"I can help you Megan," said her mom jogging from behind us and grabbing my bag from Dakota.

"Are you sure?" asked Dakota not letting her take it.

"I can carry it, come on, Megan," she said waving her over.

Megan let go of me and helped her mom take the bag as Dakota came over and replaced her.

"So, what did you want to talk about?" asked Dakota right away.

"Why did you cover the Youth?" I asked.

Dakota didn't answer for so long that I thought he hadn't heard me. When I was about to ask again, he said, "Because no one else was going to do it. And it got us out of there quicker."

I took a second to craft my response. "But you had just told me earlier that you would never bury a dead Youth?"

"Putting a tarp over someone and burying someone are two completely different acts."

"You're still respecting the dead though. I though you said that would be humiliating?"

Dakota shifted his backpack before replying. "I did what I had to, alright," said Dakota quieter than before. And at that I dropped the topic. But I'd definitely be bringing it back up. Hopefully when we weren't being chased by a psycho maniac teenager.

"Thanks for carrying me," I said. Dakota gave me a small nod. "You, too, Thomas."

"Of course," replied Thomas. "I'm surprised you didn't say it earlier."

"When you're running for your life, things like that tend to go by the wayside. Sorry."

"No need," chuckled Thomas. "I was just pointing it out to you."

I looked over at Megan and her mom as they readjusted the bag. They walked side by side carrying it.

"Want to take the bag from them?" I asked Dakota.

"Gladly," he replied quickly and immediately let me go. I didn't realize I had made Dakota so upset with my question.

When Megan came over and took over for Dakota I asked, "happy to be back?"

"Yes, that bag was awkward to carry."

"I just think you didn't want to be away from me."

"Well in your condition, yes. Someone should always be with you."

"Did you catch that, Thomas?" asked Dakota.

"Catch what?" asked Thomas.

"What Calvin did."

"He's talking to Megan?" said Thomas very confused.

"I don't know what you're implying?" said Megan before Thomas could figure out what Dakota was trying to get to.

"I'm just trying to help him out," said Dakota holding a hand up.

"I don't understand, what do I need help with?"

"Youth, Run!" Yelled Mason spinning around and grabbing my bag from Dakota. "Carry Calvin and run," he told Dakota, sprinting off.

"Let the fun begin," said Dakota, rubbing his hands together.

"Does he really need to carry me?" I asked, trying to walk faster.

"The decision's been made," said Dakota, scooping me up. I screamed as he hefted me in front of himself.

"Can you carry me any other way?" I asked. "I look like a bride."

"It's this or a fireman carry," said Dakota "I don't think you want that." In a fireman carry my stomach would be right on his shoulder. I'd deal with the embarrassing carry if it saved me some pain.

I looked behind me for the Youth and didn't see anything. But everyone else was in a dead sprint. I was surprised to see Megan's mom keeping up with us. "Where are they at?" I asked Mason.

"Just run," he said between breaths.

As we weaved around the trees, Mason led us further into the forest, away from the road. Dakota nearly tripped and almost dropped me in the process. Then I heard engines, several of them, approach behind us.

"Don't stop!" yelled Mason, as he dropped my bag next to a tree and got down on one knee.

"What are you doing!" I screamed over Dakota's shoulder as Mason looked down the barrel of his rifle. He never replied, unless you count firing a gun an answer. Then I saw it. A group of motorcycles approaching us. Mason fired at them as they barreled toward us.

"What are we gonna do, Calvin?" asked Thomas.

"Unless we-we have any weapons, keep running."

"You went pretty long without stuttering there," said Dakota.

"I know right," I said, smiling.

"Focus you two," said Thomas, throwing his hands up. "Do we have any weapons?"

"I have some guns in my bag," said Dakota.

"Do you know how to use them?" I asked.

"I wouldn't suggest it if I didn't."

The Youth were almost on top of Mason. I turned around and found a couple of trees that would make some good cover. "There," I pointed and Dakota followed. He set me down against a tree, and my head immediately reeled back as I gritted my teeth.

"Sorry," said Dakota.

"You can't help it. So, what do we have?" I asked as Dakota ripped his bag off and opened it up. Everyone else ran around and knelt by us.

"One rifle and one pistol," said Dakota, pulling out pieces of the rifle and assembled it.

"Give me the pistol," I said, sitting up on my knees.

"Calvin you can't—"

"Do you know how to shoot a gun?" I interrupted Megan.

"You're in no condition to."

Dakota handed me a case, inside was a pistol and some mags. I loaded one in and turned around, grunting and moaning the entire time; praying I didn't freeze up like I did last time I tried shooting the gun.

"You can barely move, Calvin," said Megan, putting a hand on my arm. I ignored her and brought the pistol up. I could see Mason, and he was still firing at the bikes as they fired back. An instant later, his body jerked back, he fell on his back with his arms splayed out and dropped his gun.

"Mason!" I yelled, "Mason!" He lay there sprawled on the ground.

Dakota opened fire, and I followed, only to shoot a pepper spray ball that landed in front of a bike, which harmlessly ran through the cloud of smoke.

"Crap, not this gun," I said, looking at it and back at the case.

"Calvin said a bad word," said Dakota as he fired.

"Crap is not a bad word," I said, taking another shot at the approaching bikes.

"God is not happy with you right now," said Dakota.

"How about crapola, crud, turd. Any of those work better for you?" A spray of bullets was coming toward us as it ripped through the trees to my left. I shoved Megan's head down, throwing my body over hers. When I looked up, Megan's mom was on top of her daughter, and a Youth stood in front of me, pointing his gun at me. "Drop it," he yelled.

I complied, slowly setting it in front of me. Behind me I could hear more yelling, but I didn't dare turn my attention away from the Youth in front of me. Megan and her mom both sat up, and Megan's mom yelped when she saw the Youth in front of me.

"Hands in the air, all of you!" the Youth yelled.

"Please don't hurt my daughter," said Megan's mom, her hands shaking as she put them on her head.

"Ow," said Thomas behind me. I wanted to look behind me. But I didn't know how this Youth would react with his gun pointed at me.

Then someone grabbed the back of my collar, shoving me down on my stomach. I screamed as a knee slammed into my back, and my hands wretched behind me. "Get off me!" I screamed.

"You're hurting him," pleaded Megan.

I continued to scream while my hands were handcuffed, and I was pulled up by the collar, again. forced to sit on my knees. My helmet was ripped off my head and thrown in front of me; and thanks to my balaclava, my glasses stayed on. Megan was thrown down on her stomach next to me when her mom got up and charged the Youth who now had his knee in her daughter's back.

"No you don't," said the Youth in front of us, grabbing her by the waist and pulling her away.

"Get your hands off her!" screamed Megan, as she squirmed under her captor.

"Don't—" started Megan's mom before the Youth holding her put his hand over her mouth. He pinned her to the ground and handcuffed her.

Dakota was forced to his knees next to me, and still fighting as he went down. The Youth slammed the butt of his rifle into the back of Dakota's helmet.

"Don't resist," I whispered to Dakota.

"A little too late for that," said Dakota, as his helmet was ripped off and thrown in front of him.

"Well now you'll know so it doesn't happen again."

"Quiet," said a Youth walking up from behind us, the same one that had pointed his gun at me. That made two Youth total.

I noticed another Youth standing a ways off. It looked like he was talking to someone, but I couldn't hear him. Then he messed with something on the right side of his helmet and pressed a button before coming over to us.

"Welcome ladies and gentlemen," said Edward, holding his hands behind his back as he walked up. I immediately leaned back, wanting to get as far away from him as possible. But I still kept my eyes on him, not wanting to take him out of my sight. Funny how someone can make you want to run away and also garner your undivided attention.

"I hope you all enjoyed your little game," continued Edward, "but fun time is over." Edward looked over at Thomas who was kneeling across from me. Edward snapped and pointed his finger toward the end of the line next to Megan's mom. "Get him in line with the others." The Youth behind Thomas pulled him up by the collar and shoved him over in line. We were all helmetless, bound, and with a psycho maniac now in charge.

"Relieve them of their packs. They won't be needing them anymore." The two Youth started cutting everyone's backpacks off, while leaving us handcuffed. The packs were then thrown into the pile of helmets.

We sat there in silence as Edward looked up and down the line of us. "Go get the other," he said, and one of the Youth ran off, dragging back who I assumed was Mason, dropping him in front of Edward. Edward knelt and pulled the Youth's helmet off, freezing at the sight of Mason before throwing his helmet furiously into the forest. "I expected more from you, Mason."

So that was Mason. He had crew cut black hair and olive skin. I was glad to see he was still alive, but that didn't mean anything. He could still be injured. And I'm sure being shot didn't feel good, bullet proof armor or none.

Edward handcuffed Mason's hands and picked him up in a fireman carry. "Get them all up to the road."

"What about the bikes, sir?" asked a Youth.

"We'll come back for them." Edward headed for the road, which wasn't too far away, and I'm glad it wasn't. The Youth forced us all up and had us walk to the road. I barely made it a single step before falling over. One of the Youth came over and pulled me up, only for me to fall when I took my next step. He picked me up in a fireman carry all the way to the road. At first I screamed as his shoulder dug into my stomach, which turned into a moan with every step the Youth took.

When we got to the road, he threw me down next to the others. I landed hard on my shoulder and groaned as I rolled onto my back. Megan started to move toward me when a Youth pointed his gun at her. "Back on your knees." Megan reluctantly complied.

A Youth walked up and stared down at me. "If only you knew how much trouble you caused me," said Edward

"You seem pretty mad right now. Would you like me to get back to you," I said, smiling. Dakota chuckled. Edward looked up, and with his pointer and middle finger out, pointed twice to the line. All the Youth pointed their guns at the line as Edward stepped on my stomach. I screamed and struggled as my handcuffed hands were crushed underneath me. Edward leaned over and put his arm on his knee, putting even more pressure on my stomach as he stared at me.

"Quit it!" yelled Thomas.

"Stop, please," pleaded Megan.

My screams continued to fill the air as Edward looked back and forth between Thomas and Megan. He took his foot off me, and I sucked in a breath, panting. Edward stepped over me and motioned to the Youth holding Thomas and Megan who were brought and knelt in front of Edward. He stared at the two for what felt like an eternity. "We unfortunately didn't get to cover this in your training as our time was cut short, but if you ask me to stop any form of punishment I'm giving to an enemy, I do the same to you."

I saw Megan gulp, lean back, and look away from Edward. He knelt down and grabbed Megan by the chin, forcing her to look at him. Thomas tried shoving Edward only to receive a back hand that sent him reeling.

"Get your hands off my daughter!" yelled Megan's mom.

"Ms. Nall," said Edward, keeping eye contact with Megan. "You can do nothing in this situation."

Ms. Nall began looking queasy. That's something a parent should never have to hear. Something that they never ever want to hear.

"As I was saying," said Edward, letting go of Megan's chin, who whipped her head back and away from him. "Since you are not in the same condition as subject oh-oh-one here, I will have to modify what I do for you." Edward flipped open a case on the side of his belt and pulled out a set of shurikens. "Three shurikens to the stomach should be sufficient."

Megan squirmed backward, but didn't get very far as Edward grabbed

E.E. Cooley

the front of her suit and pulled her back. He dragged her up as she screamed and tried to escape. Ms. Nall also tried getting up, only to be stopped by a Youth. "Hold her against the tree," said Edward, the other Youth running up and holding her.

"Wait!" I yelled as Edward took a few steps away from Megan and turned around, who thrashed and screamed still against the Youth holding her. When he didn't respond, I yelled "I'll take their punishment!"

"What?" cried Megan. "No, Calvin!"

"I can't do that to you, Calvin," said Thomas.

Edward and I locked eyes. Like the predator locking eyes with the prey.

"No one's asked for this before," said Edward, sounding genuinely stunned. "Why?" he asked, walking over to me.

"You don't need to hurt them."

"I know that idiot, why?"

I took a minute to figure out why I was doing this. "Bear one another's burden, and so fulfill the law of Christ. Galatians six two."

Edward knelt in front of me and whispered while pointing the shurikens in my face, "One day you'll be worshipping me, Fritz. Hold him down." He looked up, and two Youth held my arms and legs before he threw the shurikens into my stomach.

4

Two Youth dragged me by the arms, which were still handcuffed behind
me. I wasn't in any position to resist, nor did I want to. But they were smart
to be cautious. Had I been alone it would have been a different story. I was
dragged in the back of the line, with everyone else handcuffed like me,
walking single file. Edward walked to the side of the group, leading us
further through the trees by the side of the road where we were all made
to kneel, those of us that could. I was thrown on my back, landing with a
dull groan escaping my mouth.

"You've already hurt him enough," said Megan, glancing at the Youth
that dropped me.

"Quiet," one of them said without looking at her.

Edward walked up to the two Youth who dragged me and said, "When
the van gets here, go back and collect their gear."

"Yes, sir!" they both replied.

I readjusted myself to keep the handcuffs from digging into my wrists.
But doing so caused my stomach to flare up. I sat up to look at my bandage
and lay right back down as soon as I saw the fresh blood consuming my
bandage. Every move I made sent a fire through me. I was constantly
praying we would survive this and the new holes in my stomach would

heal.

I looked over at Megan, trying to do anything to distract myself from the pain. I could see her looking at me out of the corner of her eye. She was definitely concerned, and looked like she was ready to pounce at the next Youth that even bothered glancing in her direction. She looked to her left down the road, and a second later, I heard a car engine. We didn't have to wait long for a black van with an extended top to pull up, screeching to a stop next to us. Before it had fully stopped, a Youth jumped out of the passenger door, immediately yanking Megan up, dragging her, kicking and screaming, toward the back of the van.

"Please don't hurt her," pleaded Ms. Nall. Edward grabbed her by the hair and pulled her, following Megan.

"Get your hands off her!" I heard Megan yell, but couldn't see her.

The two Youth who dragged me here ran past into the forest. I heard Thomas struggling and turned to see him being picked up by a Youth. One by one we were all taken into the van, me last. Two Youth grabbed me by the arms and dragged me toward the back of the van. I did my best to hold back a scream to no avail. Maybe someone would hear my screams and rescue us.

At the back of the van, I was hauled up backward and sat on a bench. There were two benches, one on either side of the van. Everyone was strapped in with one seat in between each other. I was placed on the right bench closest to the front, with Thomas on my left. Everyone had their hands strapped above their head against the wall. A strap was also put over everyone's stomachs and legs, keeping everyone from moving even an inch. After I was strapped down, in the most pain yet, Edward walked up into the van and stood over me. All I could see was a faint reflection of myself in his helmet visor. Without a word, he took my stomach strap and tightened it even more. I grunted and threw my head back against the wall as I shut my eyes.

"I am gonna sock you so hard in the face when I get the opportunity," said Thomas.

Edward did the strap up even tighter and walked out of the van, slamming the back doors shut, leaving us in complete darkness.

We all sat there, my heaving breathing breaking the silence

"Are you ok, Calvin?" asked Ms. Nall.

"I'm alive," I managed to get out.

"You didn't have to do that, Calvin," said Thomas quietly, almost ashamed.

"I did Thomas. The last thing I want is to see you hurt."

"And I don't want to see you hurt any more."

"I care more about getting you out of this unharmed."

"Don't know how well that's working out now, Calvin," said Dakota.

"Shut your mouth, Dakota," said Megan, frustrated.

"Megan," said her mom taken aback.

The van became silent once again.

"Don't suppose anyone has a light?" asked Dakota.

"Let me think for a second," said Megan, sarcastically. "We're all strapped down in this van, so even if we did have a light, we have no way of using it. So no, Dakota, we don't!" she yelled at him.

"Calm down, Megan," said her mom.

"We are right back where we started!" yelled Megan. "After everything we did, we're back in Edward's hands again."

"We still have everyone else."

"Everyone else?" asked Megan. "No one is coming back for us."

"You don't know that," I said. "The Renegades could be getting ready to attack Edward and free us."

"Who are the Renegades?" asked Thomas.

"It's what I've been calling the kids who saved us."

"You've named 'em?" asked Dakota.

"It's just a name so I can differentiate them from the Youth."

"He's using big words now," said Dakota.

"Again, with the teasing and the joking," said Megan. "We are about to die, and you're just going to town over there."

"Joking makes me calm," said Dakota. "Maybe you should try it."

"I would slap you so hard right now if I could." I could hear Megan pushing against her restraints.

"Megan," cried her mom.

"Hey," said Thomas, "leave him alone. If it makes him calm then let him."

"See," said Dakota, "someone appreciates my humor."

"I never said that," said Thomas.

"I take back my compliment."

"Why are all boys so immature," said Megan

"Whoa!" cried Thomas and Dakota. They both started arguing with Megan.

When it didn't seem like they would stop, I yelled, "Enough!" The whole car became dead silent. "I understand this isn't the situation we expected to be in, nor is it the one that we want to be in. But we are not dead, nor do I see Edward wanting to kill us anytime soon. So pull yourselves together, come up with some ideas to get out of here, and start acting like the mature young adults I know you are."

Everyone stayed silent as the van started up, and we rolled away.

"Sorry, Calvin," said Thomas, quietly.

"It's alright," I replied.

After a moment, Thomas asked, "How ya feeling?"

"Like crud," I said, looking at Dakota, at least I think I was.

"I think turd would have been better used there," said Dakota.

"I feel like a turd?" I asked. "I don't know. Doesn't sound right."

"I'd say you meet all the requirements of being a turd except smelling like one."

"I take my previous statement back, Megan," said Thomas. "You have full permission to slap him."

"Calvin, what happened to be the 'mature young adults,'" said Megan, "'cause this doesn't look like it."

"It's a boy thing, just go with it," I said

Megan exhaled. "My last moments are going to be me sitting with a bunch of guys talking about turds. What a great way to send me out, Calvin."

"Megan, we don't—" The van stopped and we all lurched forward.

"Why did we stop," asked Thomas.

<u>Cougar Squad Helmet Log [Audio and Visual]</u>

Youth: YT12, YT17, YT21, YT34, YT67
Location: ████████████████████
Date of Transcript: ███████████
Time of Transcript: ███████████████

<u>Transcript</u>

Secure Channel ZR26 Activated
Users on Channel: YT12 YT17 YT21 YT34

    YT12 stands up in the front of the troop transport van, holding on to the storage nets above the seats as he addresses his squad.
    YT12: Orders just came in. The fallen youth are hold up in one of our safe houses. This is a classic pincer attack. Dynamo Squad will attack from the north, Phantom Squad will attack from the

south, and we'll attack from the east. The general wants them alive, so non-lethal rounds only once we're inside the house. Make sure you grab a gas mask. Any questions?

YT17: How many targets are we looking at?

YT12 sways back and forth as the van hits a bump.

YT12: Last confirmed count was nine. But I did get word of some removing their trackers. So expect more. Any other questions?

None of the Youth reply.

YT12: Get ready then.

Cougar Squad gets up and changes out their gear, replacing half of their pistol ammo with non-lethal rounds and replacing their S-16 with a PS-S12.

YT21: [To YT34] I wish we were bagging and tagging.

YT34: Same here. They don't deserve to live after what they've done.

YT21: Without the Youth, they wouldn't be as well off as they are.

YT34: Without the Youth, most of them would already be dead.

YT21: I know I wouldn't be here without them.

YT34: And we're all glad for that.

YT34 slaps YT21 on the shoulder. They both grab a gas mask pouch and attach it to the back of their belt.

YT67 [Van Driver]: Approaching drop point! Awaiting confirmation to engage.

YT12: Everyone mic-drop.

All of Cougar Squad mic-drop.

YT67 presses a button on the center console and all the lights inside the van turn red. The squad stands in a line facing the back doors.

YT12: Red light, standby.

Everyone lurches as the van stops. YT21 grabs

the door handle, everyone hunches forward, waiting in the silence. After 17 seconds, the lights turn green. YT21 shoves the double doors open.

YT12: Go, go, go!

YT21 hops out of the van, followed by YT34, YT17, and YT12. Cougar Squad runs around the van toward safe house 8-24-1, stopping behind some trees near the house.

YT12: Do not shoot to kill, fire on my mark.

Cougar Squad, behind the cover of trees, raise their R-32's at the safe house.

YT12: Mark.

Cougar Squad fires through the window wall lining the east side of the safe house. The fallen youth scramble around inside, a couple overturn tables for cover. YT21 ducks behind his tree as a fallen youth returns fire.

YT21: Are you sure we can't kill them?

YT12: Cut it! Dynamo Squad is moving up. Give them covering fire.

Transcript Continues

——

Dynamo Squad Helmet Log [Audio and Visual]

Youth: YT18, YT24, YT97, YT105, YT124
Location: ███████████████
Date of Transcript: ████████
Time of Transcript: ████████

Transcript

Secure Channel ZR14 Activated
Users on Channel: YT18, YT24, YT97, YT105, YT124

Dynamo Squad finishes putting on their gas masks and sprint toward safe house 8-24-1. YT24 runs over and throws a PSG [Pepper Spray Grenade] through the shattered windows on the east side of the safe house. It explodes into a white cloud and sends the fallen youth scattering. Cougar Squad stops firing, allowing Phantom Squad to break through a door on the south wall. YT24 and YT105 pull out their PS-S12's, scanning the room for any remaining fallen youth. YT18 throws a PSG into the kitchen. A fallen youth, spraying water on his face from the sink, spins around and kicks the PSG away. The PSG explodes moments after the fallen youth kicks it, making him fall to his knees.

YT18 sweeps the room with his PS-S12 drawn. After crossing through the dining room, YT18 meets YT24 with his PS-S12 drawn.

YT18: Open the door and I'll throw one in.

YT18 motions to the door in front of him, then pulls out a PSG.

YT24 grabs the door handle.

YT24: Ready?

YT18: Ready.

YT24 opens the door halfway, YT18 throws the PSG down the stairs and YT24 immediately closes the door. YT18 draws his PS-S12 as YT24 counts down from five on his fingers. At zero, he opens the door fully. YT18 charges down the stairs. He stops at the bottom of the stairs and throws his last PSG down the hallway. Several people can be heard screaming and coughing from down the hall. YT18 waits 4.9 seconds after throwing the PSG to enter the hall.

3 fallen youth are on all fours, reeling from the effects of the PSG. A fallen youth fires at YT18 from the last door at the end of the hallway. YT18 ducks into the room on his right, firing 2 rounds as he does so.

YT24 leans out from the stairway and fires three rounds from his PS-S12, a cloud surrounding where the fallen youth was.

After 6.3 seconds of the fallen youth not returning fire, YT18 motions back to YT24 to advance. The two run toward the end of the hall. They stop, pressed up against the wall, next to the door where the fallen youth was last seen. YT24 throws a PSG into the room, entering the room 2.3 seconds after the PSG detonates. The fallen youth is on his knees, helmet off now, reeling from the effects of the PSG. The fallen youth raises his rifle toward YT24, who kicks it out of the fallen youth's hands and forces him to the ground.

YT24: Clear!

YT24 handcuffs the fallen youth. YT18 does the same with the fallen youth in the hallway. YT24 then investigates a table in the center of the room. He finds multiple Youth suits with the covers off their electronics housing.

YT24: They were definitely trying to get rid of their trackers.

YT18: All the fallen youth try, did you expect any different.

YT24: It's been a while since we've had a manhunt. Following trackers gets boring after a while.

YT18: Following trackers keeps our casualties down.

YT24: One of the costs of being a Youth.

YT18: We're done here. Let's get these traitors upstairs.

YT24: Right behind you.

End Transcript

"We've been stopped for a while," said Thomas. "I wonder what's going on?"

"As long as we're in here nothing good," said Megan matter-of-factly.

"We'll get out of this, Megan," I said.

"You keep saying that, Calvin, but I don't see how in the world that's going to happen!" Megan snapped at me.

"Enough, Megan," said her mom.

"Am I the only one who sees how hopeless this is?"

"Megan!" I yelled. "Quit it with the constant negativity. We're all scared. You need to find another way to deal with your fear that doesn't negatively affect the rest of us."

Megan was silent for a long time, as were the rest of us. In the silence I was reminded that I hadn't prayed for Megan's fear. I had completely neglected God in this moment of reprieve, or for the past couple of hours. So, as I was praying for forgiveness and that Megan wouldn't let her fear control her, the back doors opened. I looked away from the blinding light as Youth poured in, unstrapping those nearest to the door and taking them out first.

"Where are you taking us?" said Megan nervously as two Youth unstrapped her, not replying.

"You want us in the van, or you don't," said Dakota. "Make up your mind," which swiftly got him shoved out of the van, falling face first in the dirt.

Two youth unstrapped me and dragged me to the van doors, handing me off to two other Youth outside the van. They dragged my limp body around the van. I barely had enough energy to look up as we followed the others toward a house. Its windows were completely destroyed on one wall, furniture was overturned inside, and the wood wall behind the windows was splintered beyond recognition.

In front of the house on the dirt parking area were several Youth surrounding several other Youth, who must have been the other Renegades, were on their knees and handcuffed. They were hacking and coughing with something coming out of every hole in their face; just like the kids I shot on the roof yesterday.

The Youth brought us and knelt us down with the other captured Renegades. As the Youth let go of me, I fell to the side against Thomas.

"Get up," whispered Thomas, trying to push me back up.

"I can't" I wheezed.

"Get up," said a Youth, walking in front of us holding his rifle.

"He can barely walk," said Thomas.

"Sitting's not walking," said the Youth.

"Ah!" I yelled as someone from behind grabbed my hair and pulled me up.

"Quiet," said whoever was behind me.

I looked down at the line of prisoners and saw a Youth start walking down it, squatting in front of a Renegade next to Megan.

"Hello, Marcus," said Edward.

His voice was still the same, but that didn't mean it wasn't ten times creepier now after what he did to me.

Marcus continued to hack and couldn't reply.

"A very noble effort from you indeed. It honestly surprised me when it happened. But I knew it wouldn't last. And it looks like even some of your friends abandoned you, too." Edward looked down at us, his gaze staying on me for an uncomfortable amount of time.

Marcus spat on Edward, and Edward grabbed Marcus's throat, shoving him backward onto the ground. The two Renegades next to Marcus tried shoving Edward off when two Youth pulled them away.

"After your interrogation, you will have only two options. Join or die," said Edward. He let go of Marcus and stood up, walking down and squatting in front of Megan's mom. "How are we doing today, Ms. Nall? Enjoying the situation we're in?"

Ms. Nall just shook her head and looked at the ground.

"Let's hope for both our sakes that your daughter isn't so closed lip. Because after I do what I have planned for her, I'll ask her the same thing as your friend over there, join or die. Her answer will decide your fate." Edward took his gloved hand and lifted Ms. Nalls chin up, and she closed her eyes. "Never been afraid of someone have you?"

Ms. Nall starts breathing heavier.

"Get your hands off her!" yelled Megan, scrambling up before two Youth pounced and held her back. Megan tried to break free to no avail. Edward continued looking at Ms. Nall while Megan screamed at Edward. The Youth holding Megan shoved her to her knees while a third Youth brought over a bag and put it over her head, the same ones they put over our heads before. The ones that blocked out all light and sound as her screams were suddenly cut off.

"You have nothing to be afraid of," continued Edward as he combed Ms. Nall's hair out of her face with his other hand. "That is if you all make yourselves useful to us." He looked back down the line at us.

"House is clear sir," said a Youth girl, walking up behind Edward. "No sign of the missing one."

Edward released Ms. Nall and slowly stood up, walking further down the line and stopped in front of Thomas. Edward glanced at me before staring down at Thomas. "Look at me," said Edward. Thomas immediately complied. "Where's the last one?"

"The last one what?" said Thomas very quickly.

"The last one of your group."

"I don't know."

"Would you like to go back to the Black Room?"

"I don't know where they are. I promise," said Thomas, leaning back. A Youth walked up behind him and stopped him leaning back anymore. Thomas frantically turned back and forth between the Youth and Edward. "He ran off ahead of us. I promise I don't know where he went."

"He? Thank you for your help, Thomas. With some time, you would have made a great Youth. The offer still stands?"

"Don't listen to him, Thomas," I said.

Edward snapped his head toward me, staring at me for what felt like ages. "Subject oh-oh-one."

"Fritz is the quickest of all the names you've called me," I replied.

"You're not worthy of a name after what you've done," said Edward, leaning over me. "You on the other hand would have made a commendable Youth. I won't make the mistake of recruiting a religious freak like you again."

"If I were you, I would be scared of Jesus freaks," I said, smiling.

Edward punched me in the stomach, and I doubled over. The Youth holding my hair let go, and I fell face first in the dirt. Edward paced back in front of us a couple of times before screaming, "Where is he?"

Cody finished tying the R-32 to a tree pointing toward the Youth surrounding the Renegades. He wore his sauna tarp around him, covering as much of his body pointed toward the Youth as possible. He took a stick and shoved it into the trigger well, tying the stick to a rope. That rope was connected to a big stick, that was tied to two more R-32's, tied to trees facing the Youth.

Cody checked the sights of all the rifles one last time before pulling the stick back and forth. The rifles all fired together, sending the Youth scrambling. Cody continued pulling the stick until all the rifles ran out of ammo. While the Youth returned fire toward the rifles and moved the Renegades behind whatever cover they could find, Cody sprinted away toward his sniper setup far away from where he just was. Under some leaves and sticks next to a tree were Cody's sniper, backpack, and R-32.

He took off the sauna tarp and slid behind his equipment, immediately shoving the leaves and sticks off. As he laid prone behind his sniper, he pulled the sauna tarp over his back and head, leaving just enough room to use the scope while covering the rest of him.

With the Youth frantically shooting back at where he just was, Cody took out some of the Youth in the back of the pack, all unknown to them thanks to the suppressor on the end of the sniper, making Cody nearly invisible.

After the Youth broke into the tree line, where Cody just was, he scanned the front of the house, finding a few Youth watching over the Renegades. Using the rest of his magazine, the Youth were all taken out, never missing a single shot.

Cody replenished his magazine, flipped the safety, and strapped his sniper to the left side of his backpack. He shoved his sauna tarp into its side compartment on the opposite side, threw the backpack on, and grabbed his R-32, sprinting toward the Renegades. Staying low, he made his way behind any cover he could find until he made it to the first group of Renegades.

Cody grabbed the handcuff key from his belt and freed the group of five Renegades, directing them toward weapons and their pile of helmets near the door of the safe house. In less than five minutes, all but Calvin's group had been released.

"Are you sure that's Cody?" Thomas asked Mason, who had just woken back up. We were all glad to see him alright as we huddled together behind a van, still handcuffed as a Youth ran from group to group releasing the Renegades.

"I am positive, Thomas," said Mason, trying to unlock his handcuffs using a key he got off a dead Youth. Megan's mom had some heavy words as the Youth started falling one by one. Mason even yelled at her to keep quiet. She hadn't spoken a word since.

"Got it!" said Mason, unlocking one of the cuffs. I was pretty impressed he was able to do that. He took the other one off and started helping the rest of us.

Cody sprinted over to our group and started unlocking the rest of the cuffs.

"Thank you," I said to Cody as he took off my cuffs, laying back against the van, dreading the moment I'd have to get up. I put a hand against the bandage, and it came away covered in blood. I don't really know what I was expecting. The six places Edward threw the shurikens into my stomach all blended into one. It was a miracle I was even awake, let alone breathing.

"Thank you," said Thomas next to me as he rubbed his wrists. "You think we'll make it out of this?" Thomas leaned over and whispered to me.

"I plan on it."

"Here," said Megan, wearing her blue (or teal for you people that like specifics) helmet. She dropped my green helmet in front of me and Thomas's orange helmet in front of him.

"Thanks, where did you get these?" I asked.

"Pile by the house." She pointed behind her as she peeked around the van. "They're coming back," she said, ducking behind the van.

"They won't kill us," I said, putting on my helmet.

"I doubt that" she said, cocking her head to the side.

"They had plenty of opportunities to kill us in the forest. Edward needs to bring us back alive."

"They know where Cody is now, so what's stopping them from killing us all now," said Megan, stepping closer to me.

"Everyone in the van!" yelled Mason, waving us over toward the back of the van.

"Time to go," said Thomas as he and Dakota both got up.

"I feel a chase coming on," said Dakota all giddy as he and Thomas picked me up. Megan helped her mom up and made their way to toward Mason.

"On three," said Thomas under my right arm, Dakota on the opposite. "One, two, —

I never heard the three as I screamed. It didn't help it sounded like it all bounced back at me inside my helmet. I didn't even attempt to walk, so they dragged me toward the door.

"Almost there, Calvin," said Thomas as we rounded the corner of the van. One of the back doors was opened, and Thomas jumped in, pulling me up.

"Lay him on the floor," I heard Megan's mom say. Several hands helped me down to the floor.

"We have to stop this bleeding," said Megan, standing over me, looking through the shelf above the seats.

"With what?" I heard Thomas say as I rolled my head over to the opposite side of the van. He, too, was looking through the shelves.

"We need Ash," said Mason, stepping over me. "He's not going to make it. Did you see her on your way to us?"

"She can transfer vans if he makes it out of this. Close the door!" yelled Cody.

"He's going to die, Cody," said Mason as calm as ever.

Gravel peppered the bottom of the van as we took off, everyone grabbing onto something as they all nearly fell over.

"Today's gonna be a fun day," said Dakota, hanging onto a strap from the roof.

"This is the exact opposite of fun!" yelled Thomas.

"This doesn't make your heart beat a little quicker?"

"It's being overworked right now."

"Enough you two!" yelled Megan, "find something to help Calvin."

Ms. Nall eased my helmet off and gently laid my head on the floor of the van. "We'll find something for you soon, Calvin."

"Under the seats," said Mason, kneeling next to my head.

"I need you up here, Mason!" yelled Cody.

"And we're the only one that can save him right now."

Megan knelt across from her mom with a first-aid kit in her hand as Mason knelt down next to Ms. Nall and started cutting my bandages off. "Hold him down," said Mason. Now everyone was around me and held down a part of my body.

"Don't tell me—" I started before Mason interrupted me.

"We have to stop the bleeding, Calvin." Mason tore open a miracle powder pack and poured it on my open wounds. My screams filled the van as I squirmed under everyone's grasp.

"Son of a motherless goat!" I screamed as Mason pulled my stab wounds together and taped them together, placing gauze over them.

"What did you say?" asked Dakota, nearly laughing

"Almost done," said Mason, lifting my back up. "Start wrapping." I was finally able to open my eyes to find Megan wrapping another bandage around my stomach. I wanted to know what her face said under her helmet.

"That's good," said Mason, cutting the bandage and tucking the end under a strand. He sat me down as several dull thuds came from the back doors of the van. We all looked back.

"Mason!" yelled Cody

"What was that?" said Ms. Nall.

"Non-lethal rounds," said Mason, grabbing a rifle attached to the back of the passenger seat. "Something I won't be using." He opened the left side window inward, sticking his head out, and firing off several rounds.

"Don't say it, Mom," said Megan.

"I wasn't going to say anything," said Ms. Nall.

"You looked like you were."

I had so many questions I wanted to ask and comments to say. But my mouth didn't want to cooperate. My stomach was on fire, I wanted to throw up, and I had a massive headache starting. The van swerved, and everyone leaned toward the left side of the van, Ms. Nall falling into her daughter, her hands barely missing my stomach as they shot for the floor.

"Two bikes got past!" yelled Mason.

As the van leveled out, I closed my eyes and leaned my head over on its side.

"Calvin," said Megan, grabbing my face with her gloved hands and moving my head back up. "Stay with us."

"Don't die on us now, man," said Dakota, "the fun's just beginning." I grinned as my vision grew blurry, and I couldn't keep my eyes open. I couldn't think, I couldn't concentrate on anything, everything was jumbled in my mind. My head fell over again, and Megan picked it back up, this time holding my head up with both hands.

"Calvin, look at me... Look at me, Calvin!" yelled Megan.

"You can make it, Calvin," said Ms. Nall.

"Calvin, don't die on me," said Thomas.

"Calvin, Calvin." Megan was starting to choke up. She turned her head and screamed, "Mason, we're losing him!"

Mason continued to fire as dull thuds came every now and then against the van. The last thing I remember was Megan lifting her visor, and the fear in her eyes was unmistakable.

"Calvin! Calvin!" screamed Megan as she checked Calvin for a pulse. "His heartbeat is dropping."

"Give me a minute," said Mason, firing at a Youth van pursuing them. The van they were in was similar on the exterior to the one they escaped from the school in. This one, however, was a troop carrier van. The sliding side door had been removed so a bench could line both walls of the van, leaving only the back double doors to enter the back. Shelving occupied the space under the benches as well as above the benches, with straps on the ceiling for those that stood. A window was placed between the driver and passenger seats before the benches started. These windows were bulletproof and opened inward, exactly like the ones in their previous car. This allowed Mason to keep the majority of his body safe behind the armor of the van walls. At max capacity, the troop carrier could fit twelve in the back, four on each bench, and four standing in between them, two window gunners, a driver, and a passenger, for a total of sixteen.

These same vans were the ones chasing the Renegades. Youth sticking out both windows. And the van that was immediately behind them was making it very difficult for Mason to hit anything. With bulletproof windows, hitting the front window was next to pointless. So, Mason took a PSG and threw it at the van, exploding on the windshield. The white cloud swept around the van into the faces of the two gunners. They both pulled back into the van, giving Mason enough time to get a couple shots on the wheels. And after six shots, he managed to puncture a hole in the left front wheel, causing the van to veer off the same way.

"He's dying, Mason," screamed Megan.

"There has to be something we can do?" said Ms. Nall.

Thomas was frozen staring at Calvin.

"We already fixed him, why is he still dying?" asked Megan, staring helplessly at Calvin.

"So, he's a robot now," said Dakota

"Quit it, Dakota!" Megan snapped her head toward him.

"When you said fix it just—"

"Shut your mouth!"

"Megan," said her mother taken aback.

"Why is no one helping him? He's dying!"

There was a loud crash as the van behind the Renegades wrecked. Mason put the rifle back behind the passenger chair and raced over to Calvin, checking his pulse.

"He's lost too much blood." Mason changed his radio dial to the Renegade open frequency, one that none of the Youth were on. "Ash, this is Mason, do you copy? Ash, this is Mason, do you copy?"

"This is Ash, copy."

"Ash, we have a potential casualty if you don't help him soon. I think he's lost too much blood. Are you able to do a blood transfusion?"

"Are any of their squad members present?"

"Yes."

"Once we deal with these Youth on our tail, I can hop over to your van. Give us a minute."

"Copy."

"How are we going to do a blood transfusion if we don't know our blood types, let alone his?" asked Megan.

"You all have the same blood type," said Mason, bracing himself against the bench as the van swerved.

"This day keeps getting crazier," said Dakota. "What's next, we're all from the same family?"

Thomas wanted to say "technically yes," but couldn't focus on anything other than Calvin's nearly lifeless body.

"What do we need?" Megan asked Mason.

"Ash will have everything. There's nothing more I can do here."

Everyone inside lurched forward.

"What was that?" asked Thomas.

"It's him or us Mason!" yelled Cody.

Mason looked back and forth between Cody and Calvin before getting up and grabbing the rifle from behind the passenger seat again.

"You can't let him die!" cried Megan.

"There's nothing more I can do Megan."

"You know, if someone gave me a gun, I could help out," said Dakota.

More thuds hit the side of the van, getting closer and closer to Mason.

"Keep it steady!" cried Mason.

Cody slammed on the brakes, everyone bracing themselves from flying forward while Megan pulled Calvin to keep him from sliding forward. The Youth van chasing them tried to swerve out of the way so as not to crumple the back of the Renegade van, and anyone in it. They veered off to the right, missing one tree right off the road only to hit another, stopping the van dead in its tracks.

"Ash, how's that tail coming?" asked Mason, pulling his head back inside the van.

"Eliminated."

And with that, the chase was over. The closest Youth were all back at the safe house finishing catching some of the Renegades that couldn't get away with the others.

Dakota stood up and braced himself between the overhead shelving as he looked out the front windshield. "I found our tail," he said, pointing to two motorcycles on the road with their Youth riders thrown off. The van jumped as Cody ran over the bikes. Everyone inside cried as they flew around.

"You're going to kill Calvin driving like that!" screamed Megan.

"Don't say anything, Cody," said Mason, just as Cody was about to rebuttal Megan's statement.

"Get ready for a transfer," said Cody, catching up to Ash's van, coming off another road that connected in front of Cody's van.

"Ash, decrease speed so you can transfer to us," said Mason.

Ash's van slowed down, and Cody went as fast as he could through the forest-lined road.

"How is this going to work?" asked Dakota as Ash's van came into view.

It started to rain as the back doors of Ash's van burst open, revealing eight Renegades all packed inside. Ash made her way to the door as Cody sped up, bumping bumpers with Ash's van. Ash jumped onto the hood and climbed to the roof. Mason opened his door, and Ash climbed down into the passenger seat. Ash's old van sped up, and the Renegades closed the doors.

Ash knelt beside Calvin as she examined him. "He's definitely lost too much blood. Which one of you is the calmest right now."

Both Thomas and Megan looked over at Dakota. "Oh no, you are not sticking a needle in me."

"You will if it saves Calvin," said Ash, taking off her backpack and opening up pockets all over it.

"Nobody's —" Dakota started before Megan charged at him. Ash darted up and grabbed Megan before she connected with Dakota.

"Doing that won't keep him calm," said Ash, tensely.

"I'll do it," said Thomas.

Megan stopped struggling against Ash and turned around. "You will?" she asked.

"Yeah, I'll do it," Thomas said, perturbed. "What do you need."

Ash let go of Megan "Take off your suit so I can get to your arm."

Thomas quickly unzipped his suit so he could slide his right arm out. Megan and Dakota stood opposite him as Ash readied her needle.

Dakota shook his head and threw his hands up, turning away and walking toward the front of the van.

"Keep it steady, Cody," said Ash, sticking the needle into Thomas's arm.

"Do you know what you're doing?" asked Thomas.

"You ask me that after I stick the needle in your arm?"

"Just answer the question, please."

"I've done this more than I should have."

"That's not answering the question."

"She just did, Thomas," said Megan.

"I'm looking for a straight answer. A yes or no. That's it," said Thomas, adamantly.

"Yes, Thomas. Now hold still please." Ash attached a tube to the needle.

Megan sat next to Calvin. The wait and helplessness agonizing. There was nothing she could do but watch as life slowly drained out of Calvin.

"Where are we going?" Dakota asked Cody, leaning toward him.

"Do you know if the others were able to remove their trackers?" asked Mason, looking at Cody.

"Don't risk it," said Cody.

"You'll find out then," said Mason, looking at Dakota.

"I thought escaping the Youth would mean we were done with secrets; I'm not liking this Mason," said Dakota.

"Get used to it then."

The dirt road met a paved road, and the whole van jumped as it went over the edge. As soon as he got control, Cody floored the van. Both Renegade vans racing down the road through the forest.

"He'll be alright, Megan," said her mother, scooting closer to her.

"You don't know that!" screamed Megan. "None of us do."

"Would you calm down, honey. Ash is saving him."

Megan slammed her visor shut, crossing her arms and looking at Ash. "How much longer?"

"He's not going to die, I promise you that," said Ash, watching her bag fill with Thomas's blood.

"She always keeps her promises, Megan," said Mason.

That reassured Megan, if only slightly. But it was enough for her to take her mind off Calvin and onto Dakota. She took a deep breath, her shoulders rising and falling as she looked at the back of Dakota. "Do you really not like needles?" she asked.

Dakota's silent reply was all she needed to know.

"It's not that bad," said Thomas.

"Nothing should be going in your body. Bad things happen when they do."

"What about food," said Ash with a smile under her helmet.

Dakota hesitated a moment before replying, "Not all foods are good. My point still stands."

"You don't intentionally eat bad food," said Thomas.

"Yet, some food can make you sick."

"You're grasping at straws here," said Ash.

"The fact that I can still grab some proves my point."

"You know you can turn around when you talk to us," said Thomas.

"I guess I—" Dakota started to turn around but stopped and faced forward. "Oooh, you sly dog."

"Their back on our tail," said Mason, breaking up the fun. The small moment of reprieve now lost. Megan immediately looked back at Calvin then up at Thomas.

"How much longer?" asked Megan.

"Still need more," said Ash, "What's our ETA?"

Bullets flew past the van, a few hitting it. The tires squealed as Cody yanked the wheel, sending everyone flying across the van. Ash braced herself and kept Calvin from sliding too much on the floor.

"What was that for?" yelled Mason, when out the window they passed a crashed van. "We're the last ones," said Mason, solemnly.

"Last ones of what?" asked Dakota.

"We're all that's left of the force that rescued you." Mason went behind the passenger seat and pulled open a drawer underneath it. Inside was a grenade launcher with six grenades, all in a foam insert.

Ash had enough blood and hung Thomas's blood bag from the ceiling, a tube going into Calvin's arm, when she noticed Mason load the grenade launcher. "Hold up, Mason."

Mason stuck the launcher out the side window and launched a grenade at the Youth behind them. It landed just in front of the van and exploded a second later, the front of the van jumping into the air and engulfed in flames. It skidded to a stop sideways on the single lane road, sitting between trees near and around the road that made it impossible to go around.

"There," said Mason with a smug grin under his helmet. "That should give us some time."

The van was silent a moment, everyone but Cody stared at Mason, when Ash finally asked, "What was that for?"

"To get them off our tail."

"And alert all the local law enforcement now because of a massive car explosion and potentially a forest fire."

"And when did you suddenly become worried about our collateral damage?"

"Because we're bringing far more innocents into this than necessary."

"That's what you signed up for, Ash. We all did."

"I didn't sign up to get innocent lives killed."

"The Youth are not innocent, Ash."

"We don't have to kill every single one we come in contact with."

"Well, sometimes that happens."

"It doesn't have to though." Ash got right up into Mason's face. The two of them staring each other down, both ready to pounce.

"You have a patient to attend to," said Mason coldly as he stood back from Ash and walked back to the passenger seat. Ash spun around and huffed as she went to check on Calvin.

Cody didn't say a word as he drove through the forest and to a train station. The Youth doing everything they could to clear the road and regain the ground they'd lost.

Paige was dragged limp across the wood-paneled hallway by Interrogator Youth, a boy and girl, who spent all night interrogating Paige. Each of the Interrogators wore all white; a slim white coat, pants, shoes, and gloves. The girl had her hair up in a bun while the boy had a crew cut. Blood covered both Interrogators from head to toe.

Paige wore her undersuit, a black formfitting shirt and shorts, which were torn and ripped, revealing the aftermath of her interrogation. As the group approached the double doors at the end of the hallway, the Interrogators push them inward, revealing Johan behind his custom-made walnut desk, sitting in his complementing green leather rolling chair. He didn't look up from his papers as the Interrogators dragged Paige across the dark green carpet and dropped her in front of his desk. Paige groaned as the Interrogators stood at attention.

Johan stacked his papers and stood up. "Wait outside," he said as he walked around his desk. The Interrogators left as Johan leaned back against the front of his desk, crossed his arms, and looked down at Paige. "Look at me."

Paige's initial instinct was to say "I can't," but she knew you never say that as a Youth, not unless you want to be yelled at by your squad

Sergeant, possibly beaten by the rest of your squad mates if the Sergeant allowed, and given the agua-pan diet for a week. And she didn't know what saying it in front of the General would lead to, but she didn't want to find out. So, she tried sitting up, her whole body on fire and screaming for her to stop. She gritted her teeth and groaned but could barely push herself up, even with the adrenaline coursing through her that the Interrogators injected into her before dragging her down here.

She slumped back to the ground and tried sitting up again. This time not able to move at all.

"If you can't comply with my orders, you are more than welcome to ask for help," said Johan. The last time Johan suggested asking for help was during the Mainframe Compromise. The Youth that asked for help were never seen again. Paige tried sitting up again only to fall just as before.

Johan grabbed Paige by her mangled hair and lifted her head up as he squatted down in front of her. "Do you understand how disappointed I am in you?" asked Johan. Paige looked him square in the eye and coughed up as much respect and dignity as she could in her current condition.

"No sir," she said hoarsely and started coughing. Johan looked away until she stopped coughing.

"I can't trust you anymore."

"You still can," said Paige, bursting into another coughing fit.

When she stopped, Johan said, "Just because the Interrogators say you're with us doesn't mean I don't have my doubts." Johan grabbed Paige's shoulder and flipped her over on her back. She sucked in a breath and closed her eyes. When she opened them, Johan was staring down over her. "Even if Edward's plan didn't make any sense, that's no excuse to disobey your General. Because now, I don't know if you'll follow my orders."

"I would never disobey your command, sir," said Paige without coughing.

Johan stood up, pointed a finger at Paige, and yelled, "You disobeyed Edward, and you could just as easily disobey me!" He stormed back around his desk and pressed a button underneath the top of the desk.

Outside the double doors, a small green light flashed and a chime sounded, alerting the Interrogators to come inside. They stood behind Paige awaiting orders.

Johan stood with his clenched fists pressed into his desk and leaned over to look down at Paige. "Take Private Paige to medical to get patched up. You're to stay there until you're deemed combat ready. Get why-tee-two out of here." He waved her off like a dog and sat down, looking again at the stack of papers from before.

She had just been demoted from Sergeant to Private. She had worked so hard to get where she was with Edward. Now, all those years of work gone. She'd have to do it all over again, and even more just to get back to where she was. And this was the first time anyone had referred to her by her Youth number in a long time.

The Interrogators picked Paige up and dragged her out of the room. All Paige could think about was all the time that was wasted. She felt like a failure, a failure that would forever be seen as a failure. No matter what she did, no matter how hard she worked, no matter how far she climbed the ladder, she would forever be a failure in the eyes of every Youth, and Johan would never forgive her.

The rain beat on top of the van, making a deafening sound inside. Megan sat on the ground next to Calvin while everyone else was in a seat. Without any sedatives, Calvin came in and out of consciousness as the new blood worked its way through his body. None of it he would remember.

"Alright everyone," said Mason, "we're approaching the town. Grab your bags and be ready to ditch. And no visible weapons, hide everything under your ponchos, we don't need to be stopped by security."

Even though the train station they were headed to was under control of the YOUTH, Mason didn't want to take any risks or be slowed down by a misunderstanding by security. The Youth could be anywhere behind them.

Everyone got up and grabbed a backpack from above the seats, pulling out the black poncho that matched their combat suits. Buttons down the side allowed for it to be closed or worn loosely, but Mason advised everyone to button as many buttons to cover the packs and gear underneath it.

"Everyone ready?" asked Mason, throwing his hood on over his helmet.

"Let's do this," said Dakota, ready to pounce.

Ash and Dakota grabbed Calvin under his arms. Hoisting him so he looked like he could still walk. Ms. Nall held her daughter's hand as Cody slammed on the brakes in front of the train station. Thomas opened the back door, and everyone but Cody jumped out, who before the doors fully closed, floored the van, screeching the tires and flying down the road.

Everyone at the station flew up the steps to the ticket booth. Mason found an empty booth and pulled out a silver coin stamped with the Youth insignia. "Eight," he told the ticket lady, who without a word handed Mason eight silver tickets.

"I'll wait for Cody," said Mason, handing the tickets out to everyone.

"Follow me," said Ash, taking lead of the group. At the sight of their silver tickets, the group was waved through security, getting several looks from the passengers in the security line.

Pushing their way through the unusually large crowd for how small the station was, they waved their tickets and were immediately allowed on the train. Several passengers in the line yelled and argued with the door attendant, one even pushing Thomas who stumbled and nearly fell.

"Hey!" yelled Dakota, stopping and turning toward the man who shoved Thomas.

"Not now, Dakota, get on," said Ash, pulling Calvin toward the train. The train attendant stepped in front of the man before he tried to charge at Dakota, allowing everyone to get on board uncontested.

Once inside, Ash led everyone to the back of the car, yelling and pushing aside passengers as they passed through two cars before coming to a locked door for the next car. Ash pulled out a silver coin identical to the one Mason used, waving in over the door lock. The door slid open, and they passed through to the YOUTH car. Looking like a completely different train once inside, the recruits took a moment to marvel at everything.

"To the last car," said Ash, leading Dakota to the next door. They passed through the tactical car, the bunk car, the armory car, and into the medical car. "Throw him on the bed and start taking his suit off," Ash pointed to the closest bed as she let go of Calvin and ran to a cabinet opposite the bed, pulling out various vials and liquids. By the time she came back to the bed, Dakota had one of Calvin's suit arms off. Ash pulled the rest of the suit off Calvin, pulled down to his waist, and got him hooked into all the necessary machines.

"What else can I do?" asked Dakota, looking helpless.

"Get everyone secured in the Tac car, the first car we came into."

"On it." Dakota ran out of the car, only to be stopped by the armory car like a kid in a candy store.

"On our way," said Mason over the radio. "Cody's on his way. I'm getting this train started."

"Copy that," said Ash.

The recruits back in the Tactical car, or Tac car as the Youth called it, stared in amazement at their surroundings. A wall of monitors and consoles filled one side of the car. On the opposite side was bench seating, and a kitchen sat in the corner.

"I'm gonna go see Calvin," said Thomas, taking his poncho and backpack off, setting it on one of the tables.

"Let's stay here," said Ms. Nall, grabbing her daughter's shoulder. Megan stared at the consoles and took a step toward them when Cody burst through the door. He pressed several buttons on the consoles before the monitors above flared to life with the Youth logo. Setting his rifle against the console, Cody took his poncho and backpack off, laying them on the floor next to him. All the monitors came to life, and each one was filled with something different. Cody blew a radar up over all the monitors, and red dots started appearing, each was getting closer to the center of the screen as the radar passed over them.

"Three mikes before the Youth arrive," said Cody, shifting the radar to half the screens, filling the others with various programs, and a few with security camera feeds.

"Train is starting," said Mason through the radio.

"Let's sit down Mom," said Megan, guiding her mother to a seat.

"What's going on?" she asked.

Forgetting her mother didn't have a helmet, she filled her in.

As Thomas ran through the cars, he stopped as he found Dakota in the armory. "Look what I found," he said, turning around from a shelf full of rifles. "Which one should I choose?"

"The one you know how to use," said Thomas, passing the isles of weapons upon weapons. Entering the medical car, Thomas found Ash finishing up with Calvin. "How's he doing?"

"He's stable," said Ash, taking off rubber gloves, "so long as we make it out of this."

Thomas cautiously walked up to Calvin, leaning against the side rails of the bed. "Hey, Calvin—"

"Cody, turn Megan off the radio please?" asked Ash. A moment later, doing the same with Thomas, pressing buttons on his statscreen so he wasn't broadcasting his conversation with Calvin to everyone in the squad, but still able to pick up transmissions.

"There's a lot going on," said Thomas, chuckling. "Too bad you're not here to see it. I'll have to tell you about it later." Thomas hesitated a moment before continuing. "I hope you trust them, Calvin, 'cause I'm still a little nervous. I think they'll have gained my trust when you come out of this." He grabbed Calvin's hand. "I hope I didn't waste my blood for nothing."

"Come on," said Ash, turning Thomas's radio back on and showing him how to do so. "Let's get back—" The train shook as it eased out of the station, making Thomas and Ash stumble.

"What was that?" asked Thomas.

"We're moving. Now, let's—"

"The Youth are outside the station," said Cody.

Dakota walked in from the armory, kitted out with as much gear as his suit could hold. "Let's make sure we escape this time," he said before loading his rifle.

The Youth pulled up in front of the train station, the back doors of the vans flew open and Youth poured out. They ran up the stairs when the security guards pulled their guns on the Youth.

"Put your weapons down!" one yelled.

"Youth clearance code 1156," yelled Cory over the now screaming passengers, cowering on the ground as he held his rifle at the guards.

They hesitated a moment before lowering their weapons. "How can we help, sir?" one asked.

"Let us through." Cory lowered his weapon as he led the Youth forward. The security guards pushed everyone in line out of the way. The Youth filed through the three terminals and onto the platform.

The last train car left the station as Cory ran after it. He stopped with the Youth behind him at the end of the platform, the train now past and picking up speed. One Youth raised his rifle toward the train when Cory stopped him.

"Not in front of people. They'll think we're terrorist. We need them to think we're the good guys."

"I thought we were the good guys?" asked the Youth.

"Perception is key." Cory heard an engine approaching and turned around. When he looked down the tracks cpposite the train, he saw a Youth on a motorcycle running parallel to the track. Some of the Youth started cheering as the Youth passed.

"Quite cheering, you idiots, and cortinue the pursuit," said Edward as he rode by.

"Move, move, move," yelled Cory as he pushed the Youth behind him, and Edward continued to chase the train.

11

"Motorcycle approaching!" yelled Mason through the radio.

"Protect Calvin," said Ash, throwing off her poncho and pulling her rifle off her backpack.

A thud came from the back wall as Dakota moved behind another medical bed, his rifle trained on the door. Ash stood behind the supply cabinet, and Thomas knelt in front of Calvin's bed.

"Do not fire unless fired upon," said Mason through the radio. "There's too many civilians on this train."

The sound of screeching metal came from the back door, and a moment later, the door cracked open.

"That's not good," said Thomas.

Ash had her rifle raised at the door when it opened, and something was thrown inside.

"Look away!" yelled Ash as a stun grenade was thrown into the room. Harsh light illuminated the room followed by loud pops that continued for several seconds. Their helmets prevented most of the sound from overwhelming them, but it still wasn't pleasant to hear.

Thomas was blinded by the light, on all fours as he waited for his vision to return. Dakota didn't get the full effect of the light but was still slightly blinded and unable to discern his surroundings with the loud pops.

Using her training, Ash was able to block out the sound. Swinging around after the light went off, only to find Edward charging toward her. He slammed into Ash, ripping the gun out of her hand before she could escape his hold. Edward pulled out a knife as Ash fought without a weapon, blocking and dodging the knife strikes before Edward grabbed her arm, wrenching it behind her back, and slamming her head into a bed frame. She slumped over as Edward whipped around, grabbing the barrel of Dakota's rifle, and bringing it up away from his head as two shots were fired. Pushing off the bed, Edward yanked the rifle out of Dakota's hand, bringing it around, and slamming the stock into Dakota's head, falling onto an empty medical bed. Pushing himself up off the bed, Dakota managed to right himself and brought his sidearm out, dazed but able to level it at Edward who ducked behind the bed.

Pulling out three shurikens, Edward blindly threw them over his head. One hit Dakota in the arm, one stuck into his chest armor, and the other stuck into his helmet. Dakota stumbled back and tried removing the shuriken from his arm, only to cut his hand before getting it out. He let out a yell as he charged at Edward, losing his sidearm at some point, and running with his fists swinging. Edward dodged them easily, toying with Dakota a moment, grinning beneath his helmet, before dodging a punch and returning two in its place. With a knee to the gut, Edward shoved Dakota backward, stumbling and running into Thomas still on the floor. He fell on top of Thomas, trapping him underneath

As Edward took in his surroundings, Mason ran through the door, rifle trained on Edward a moment before taking a shot. Edward ducked and threw another stun grenade. Mason kicked the grenade and closed his eyes as it detonated. By the time he opened his eyes and had his bearings again, Edward charged to disarm him. Edward pushed Mason into the wall, the rifle stuck between both their hands. Edward kneed Mason who pushed off the wall and slammed Edward into the foot of a bed frame. Edward kneed Mason again in the groin, ripping the weapon from his hand, and shoved him back into the wall. Ash started to stir, but Edward kicked her in the head, and she slumped back again to the floor.

Mason charged forward throwing punches, forcing Edward to let go of the rifle. The two fought toward the back door when Edward was able to land a punch to Mason's stomach, sending two more before Mason pushed himself away. Edward took a step forward when a bullet crossed between the two of them. Mason staggered backward as Edward quickly whipped around, pivoting toward where the shot came from, only for Cody to shoot Edward in the chest, sending him reeling backward and out the open train door.

Mason slowly hobbled toward the door seeing the body of a Youth on the train tracks disappear as the train gained more speed. "Who was that?" he asked Cody. Without a word, Cody turned around and headed toward the armory. "Where are you going!" Mason yelled.

"Sealing the door," Cody replied as he walked out the car.

Mason shook his head. He struggled but managed to get the door closed. As he turned around, Ash began to stir. Mason knelt and helped her sit up. "What's hurt?"

"My head," she said, reaching a hand up to her helmet.

"Do you think you have a concussion?"

"Not with these helmets. Whoever that was just had a strong arm."

"Yeah…" Mason looked up at Dakota helping Thomas sit up. "Careful of that shuriken in your helmet Dakota."

"There's one on my—AH." Dakota whipped his hand back, a fresh cut across his hand. Mason let out a sigh before getting up and helping remove both remaining shuriken on Dakota.

"Sorry I wasn't much help," said Thomas as Dakota pulled him up.

"You didn't miss much," mumbled Dakota.

"Is everyone accounted for?" asked Mason.

"Where are Megan and her mom?" asked Dakota.

"Still in the Tac car." Mason glanced at Calvin, and a sigh of relief went through everyone when his heart monitor beat normally. "Let's head there and give Calvin some time to rest."

Cody walked back in carrying a portable welder and headed to the back door. "Make it quick, Cody," said Mason, leading everyone out of the medical car.

On their way to the Tac car, they passed through the armory and through the bunk room, with a bathroom and shower on the far end, and finally into the Tac car. Megan and her mom were ecstatic to see everyone as they were filled in on what had happened in the medical car.

"I think it was Edward who attacked us," said Mason. "Not many people can beat me in combat, and only Edward would go alone into a situation like he just did."

"How do we know if he's dead?" asked Megan, anticipation behind her words.

"We probably won't know for a while."

Megan was clearly disappointed with the answer, slumping into the bench seat as her mom followed.

"So, what's the plan now," asked Thomas.

"Give me a second," said Mason, heading to the console under the wall of monitors. He pressed several buttons as the screens changed above him, eventually pulling up a prisoner list. Less than a minute of searching brought up a mug shot of Thomas's parents.

"Mom…" Thomas inched toward the monitors, taking his helmet off, and tucking it under one arm. "They look horrible."

"Don't be surprised," said Mason, pulling up a map on a different monitor. "The Youth don't like those who defy them. But here's where they are, Complex 4."

"Where is that at?" asked Dakota.

"North Dakota. Near Devil's Lake. We'll be there in about a day and a half."

"What about the Youth who were following us?" asked Thomas.

"If that was Edward we shot out the train, then I don't think they'll be after us for a while. And if they do, it will be a far smaller force than what was at the safe house."

"Are we safe then?" asked Megan's mom.

"For now, yes. Once we get to Complex 4, that's a different story.

Rescuing your parents won't be easy. But you better get some sleep, you'll need all the energy you can get."

"Will someone stand guard in case of another attack?" asked Dakota.

"Me, Cody, and Ash will stay up. We'll work out the plan and get everything prepped."

"Sound good to me," said Dakota, stretching. "Hopefully those beds are comfy."

"They're better than nothing," said Ash.

"That's all I need."

Mason and Ash began preparations for the assault on Complex 4 as everyone followed Dakota off to the bunk car. Megan's mom held an arm around her daughter the entire way, very glad to have a moment of reprieve.

Dakota flipped the overhead lights cn, a dull white making the gray and black interior even more sterile and lifeless. The only color came from the white sheets and pillow. Bunk beds lined the right side of the car as everyone claimed one. Dakota immediately grabbed the first bed while Thomas took the second one. Megan took a top bunk of the third while her mom claimed the one underneath. Storage drawers sat under the bottom bunk, containing changes of clothes and plenty of empty space. Dakota began unloading all his gear into the drawers before falling face first into bed, dropping his helmet on the floor next to him. Thomas perfectly arranged his helmet and shoes on the floor next to him, and by the time he was finished, Dakota was out cold.

"I thought we could chat, Megan, but I am so tired all of a sudden," said Megan's mom, helping her daughter out of her combat suit.

"I am, too," said Megan with a yawn.

"Hey," said her mom, grabbing her shoulders. "I'm proud of you. You were very brave today, or these last few days. It's felt like a lifetime since we've been at that school."

"It definitely has. I didn't do much though, Mom."

"You were brave in the face of danger. You kept going even when you were scared for your life. If your father were here, he'd be very proud of you."

Megan looked away from her mother, slowly removing her hands from her shoulders. "I need to get some sleep," she said without looking at her mother and climbing the ladder to her bunk.

"Your father still loves you, Megan," said her mother, reaching out but not touching her daughter.

Megan disagreed as she laid on the bed, not bothering to get under the covers. And within a few minutes, she was fast asleep. Her mother let out a quiet sigh as she got into bed and was out just as fast.

Thomas was the only one still awake as he neatly folded his combat suit, setting it in his drawer. After realizing this, he shut the light off, basking the room in darkness. Very little light came from the high-hanging widows on both sides of the car. Climbing into bed, Thomas was relieved to be in something comfortable. His body ached and desperately needed to rest. The rain bouncing off the car was a soothing sound that helped Thomas fall asleep, but only for a few minutes.

Immediately, Thomas dreamt of his time in the Black Room, recalling the horrible things that happened in that room while he was still at the school. He desperately tore himself from the dream, waking with a gasp. This happened again and again for what seemed an eternity for Thomas. After the fourth eternity, Thomas had had enough. He got up and quietly made his way to the medical car.

When he entered, a small grin spread across his face as he saw his best friend breathing. There was a chair next to Calvin's bed, and Thomas gingerly sat down, trying his best not to wake Calvin.

Relief flooded over him as he looked upon his friend that wasn't dead. Alive, in fact, because of his actions. Looking back, it didn't make any sense to Thomas how he had the strength to do a blood transfusion. It was truly a miracle.

Thomas took some time to look back over everything that had happened since he waved goodbye to his parents at the airport, finding time and time again a miracle. Not getting killed by the Youth, the Youth not killing their parents, escaping from the school, Calvin surviving the fall through the skylight, finding some ex-Youth that were helping rescue everyone's parents, and someone who was able to patch Calvin up. Why they were all still alive, Thomas didn't know, only God did. He just hoped that God still had some more plans for him so he could stay alive.

As he thought back to their time before the Youth, Thomas reminisced on all the fun adventures and shenanigans that Calvin and him had over the years. From sledding during the big snowstorm, pulling all-nighters playing their favorite video games, all the silly youth group games they played, and the tons and tons of laughs they shared. Thomas did his best to hide his laugh as he thought about the time they were driving one of their parents' cars around a parking lot after church one day, and Calvin decided to hit the brakes. He had hit them too hard and sent both of them flying forward, both of them slamming their heads into the dash with Calvin hitting the horn. They both laughed, and Calvin forgot to keep his foot on the break. Just as they were about to hit the curb, he slammed on the brakes, and again they both flew forward. The car horn always made Thomas laugh the hardest. What felt like a lifetime ago still made Thomas crack up to this day. More of those stories came to his mind, and in the laughter and joy, Thomas fell asleep slumped over in the chair, finally able to get some uninterrupted rest.

I woke up and wished I hadn't. I was sore all over and had a headache. When I rubbed my face, something pulled at my arms. Tubes and wires dangled from my hands and arms, leading to a box next to me. I took a deep breath when someone stirred next to me, finding Thomas sitting in a chair.

"Hi," he said, rubbing the sleep from his face.

"Where am I?" I asked, trying to look around, unable to find much in the dark room.

"That's a long story," said Thomas before recounting their adventures while I was unconscious.

"Is Edward alive then?" I asked

"We don't know. Depends on if he got shot in his armor or not. But still, falling out of the train had to hurt."

"I bet…" my thoughts drifted to what would happen if Edward was dead, but for some reason, that felt wrong to think about. He could still be alive for all we knew. And even if he was dead, the Youth would probably still come after us. Especially after wrecking some of their vans. "So, you really gave me your blood to save me?" I ask.

"Yeah," said Thomas, hesitantly, like he'd rather that fact not be known.

"Thank you, Thomas," I said, unsure what else to say.

Thomas just nodded his head.

"So where are we going?" I asked.

"I'm not sure. I fell asleep soon after we were away from the station."

"And how long ago was that?"

"Oh, not very long, four or five hours ago" said Thomas almost distant, rubbing his eyes again.

"I didn't wake you up, did I?" I asked, embarrassed if I had.

"No, no. You didn't wake me. I...I actually couldn't sleep, so I came in here."

"Why is that?"

"Every time I close my eyes, I see it..." whispered Thomas.

"See what?"

"The room they put me in."

"That who put you in?"

"The Youth. Who else do you think." Thomas started raising his voice.

"Calm down. Was this when they took you while we were locked in the girls' room?"

Thomas nodded his head.

"I assume you-you don't want to tell me what you saw?" I asked.

Thomas shook his head, "No. No. No, no, no." He leaned over and put his head in his hands.

"Alright." I reached my hand out toward Thomas "Second Timothy one verse seven: For I have not been given a spirit of fear, but of power, love, and a sound mind. Lord, I don't know what Thomas has gone through, but we both know that you do. You also know exactly what Thomas is feeling, and I rebuke this fear that has overtaken Thomas, that is preventing him from sleeping. I ask that your overwhelming peace would come upon him, and that this fear would all be removed, that it would be utterly destroyed in Jesus's name.

"And I ask that whatever these thoughts are that are creeping into his head and causing this fear, that they would be erased from his mind. That these would not hinder him again. That when he goes to sleep, he would lay his head down and be able to fall asleep peacefully and with no trouble. In Jesus's name I pray, amen."

Thomas's breathing was more controlled now. "You'll make it through this," I whispered to him.

"You really think that's going to help?" asked Mason, walking through the door, light pouring in from the outside covered his face in shadows.

"Yes," I said, perturbed but careful not to let it come through my answer.

"If that's what you think."

"Mason," said a girl, pushing him aside, making her way toward me.

"Either way," said Mason, perturbed, "we're glad to see you up."

"Yes...very much so," said the girl, pressing buttons and checking readings on the boxes attached to my wires and tubes.

"I don't believe we've met?" I asked the girl.

"I apologize, the name is Ash." She stuck out her hand and we shook. Her grip was a lot stronger than I expected it.

"Calvin," I said. "But I assume you already know my name?"

"I've heard it plenty of times, yes."

"Have you now. And what do you do?"

"I'm the only medic for the time being," Ash said, returning to the readings on the box next to me.

"So, this is all your handiwork?" I asked, examining my arms.

"Sure is, but you'll be free from them soon, don't worry."

It was odd she used the word free, but before I had time to question it, I flinched a moment when a Youth in full armor walked into the room.

"That's just Cody," said Mason.

"Is there anybody else out there?" I asked, straining to look around the corner.

"Just us. Everyone else is asleep," said Mason, taking a step to lean against the foot of my bed. Ash stepped back from the boxes and stood by Mason. The two of them updated me on what had happened, filling in any gaps in my memory.

"Before we go any further," I asked slowly, "why-why are you guys helping me."

No one moved for a long moment. Everyone looked at the floor, except Cody who just stared at me through his helmet. Then Ash spoke up, "Because we used to have parents before we were taken."

"Used to?" I asked.

"We never got a nice talk and a summer to decide like you guys did. I was told my mom didn't want me, but I looked into it and found out she was murdered just after I was taken by the Youth."

"Didn't your dad want you?"

"Didn't have a dad."

I fidgeted with my hands a moment before asking Mason, "What about your parents?"

"The Youth switched up my parents. I had already seen a family while in a foster home for a few months while the adoption papers were going through. The day they were supposed to take me, someone else came for me. I didn't realize it at the time because I was so young. They brought me back to Complex 2 in Rhode Island, and I've been there since."

"How old were you when that happened?" I asked.

"Four, same for him," Mason pointed to Cody, "and Ash."

"If they just steal kids, why did the Youth cho-choose us?"

"Do you watch the news?" asked Cody.

"No one would know to look there, Cody," replied Mason.

"It's pretty obvious to me."

Mason took a breath. "At the end of April, we had exhausted all we could from the foster system. The news was covering it as foster numbers at record lows. They were praising the YOUTH for helping take in so many kids. We ran the system so dry that many foster houses had to close and combine with others."

"They took every child from the foster system?" I asked.

"Not everyone. They don't take anyone older than five years old, the older a child gets, the harder it is to rewire their brain."

"To brainwash them," I said.

"Basically. There're other avenues in which new kids are brought in, but the foster system was our biggest. Their biggest," Mason corrected. "And that's when you came in."

"So, what did they see in us?"

"Did Edward show you your file during your meeting with him."

"You mean the-the interrogations? Yeah. He had been tracking me for at least two years."

"We started searching for potential older recruits when, after crunching the numbers, we found we would run the foster system dry."

"I'd compliment that strategy if what you guys did wasn't so horrible."

"Which is how most people looking in would see it."

"So, help me figure this out. What exactly is it that you do. Because all I got from Edward is basically stopping evil people."

"It's really hard to say," Mason shrugged his shoulders, "we just follow orders."

"You don't know at all?"

"...I do," Mason hesitated, "I just don't want to overwhelm you."

"I'm just trying to figure out if-if I can trust you."

"We want to stop the Youth, Calvin," said Ash. "We don't want them to do what they did to you and the other recruits."

I sat there doing my best to digest all the information. But having just woken up from blood loss was making my head start to spin.

"Why don't we tell you our plan," said Ash, "and show you that we want to stop the Youth."

"Actions do speak louder than words."

"Not all the time," added Thomas.

"Most of the time, though," I said, looking over at him. He had definitely recovered since I prayed with him. He was looking much better. "Let's just start with where we are again?"

"Here, let's get him a map," said Ash, leaving the room and returning with a large rolled up map. She turned on a light above me, revealing a map of the entire United States. "The safe house we were at was in central Tennessee." Ash pointed on the map as everyone gathered around. "We left the station here and are making our way across this line. We'll make out way up here to Devil's Lake in North Dakota."

"What's at Devil's Lake?"

"Nothing good," said Thomas.

"Where your parents are," said Mason.

"You know where our parents are?" I asked, excitedly

"How long till we get there," asked Thomas.

"A little over a day if all goes well. The hard part will be getting through the stations. We can't stop."

"Why would we not stop at the stations?" I asked.

"We can't afford to," said Ash. "I can guarantee you the Youth have sent squads to all the train stations along this route. It's not like we have multiple paths."

"So, what's our plan then?"

"Because the Conductor doesn't know I'm a Fallen Youth," said Mason, "he'll follow whatever we tell him to do."

"What's a fallen youth?"

"A Youth that for whatever reason is alive but not following orders."

"I assume that people like you aren't very common then if the

Conductor isn't asking questions?"

"It's hard to say. Some people see things, and there's always rumors. I've heard some say there's an entire prison dedicated to the Fallen Youth. And the things that go on there are not pretty."

"I think we all know prison life isn't the best," said Thomas.

"I may call it a prison, but the prisoners are meant to come out as loyal Youth. It's the things they do to get them to change that aren't pretty."

We sat there in silence as Thomas readjusted in his chair.

"Is everything you guys do despicable?" I asked.

"A loyal Youth doesn't see it that way," said Mason

"For they know not what they do," I whispered. "Let's get back to our parents, what's the plan when we get to Devil's Lake?"

"When we get there, you'll stay on the train while the three of us grab your parents and get out."

"I'm not just going to sit here while you save my parents! I'm sorry, but we would risk our lives long after you guys would give up. They're our parents not yours."

"You think you can save anyone in that condition," laughed Cody.

"Cody." Mason held his hand up. "You aren't trained, you're injured and would just slow us down."

"So then train us these next few days before we arrive."

"One day," Mason started counting his fingers, "that's not enough time for even subpar training. I understand you want to save your parents, Calvin. But you'd be putting yourself, your parents, and us in needless danger."

"I'm saving my parents," my voice started rising.

"You know full well you wouldn't be of any help," Mason pointed at me. "You wouldn't even know where they are without us."

"I never said I'm not grateful for your help. I just want to save them."

"No, Calvin, end of discussion."

"We're coming with you when we get to Devil's Lake."

"You're going to get yourself killed, Calvin," said Mason, lowering his voice, "end of discussion." He walked out of the room with Cody at his heels.

Ash watched the door until it closed. Discontent written all over her face. "I understand Mason's point, Calvin."

"Your face says otherwise."

Ash hesitated a moment. "But if I was in your shoes, I would want to save my parents. I wouldn't miss that opportunity." She looked at the door and back at me. "Let me see what I can do," a grin spread across her face as she left the room.

Thomas and I didn't say a word for a long time, the only noise a light rumble of the train on the tracks and the rain on the windows. I turned to him and finally asked, "Do you think I'd just get myself killed?"

Thomas readjusted in his chair again, taking a moment before replying. "The danger doesn't matter with family. You go and save them. I would do the same thing you're doing, Calvin." Thomas leaned forward and grabbed my arm. "And I'll be right beside you as I save my parents, too." We both smiled.

"Thank you," I said.

"Of course." Thomas squeezed my arm before letting go. "It doesn't mean I'm not scared out of my mind."

"Let's pray that fear doesn't affect us."

"Yeah…" Thomas leaned back in his chair. "Devil's Lake. That's a fitting name."

I laughed. "Yeah, I guess it is."

Ash walked into the Tac car finding Cody, still wearing his helmet, standing over the console, pressing buttons while Mason watched the monitors behind him.

"He'll still insist on coming no matter what we say," said Ash, looking at Mason.

"I know." Mason headed to the kitchen as he began brewing another pot of coffee. "But he'll slow us down. They all will. That shouldn't have to be said."

"It's his parents though, Mason. If you had the opportunity to save them, wouldn't you take it? No matter what the odds or chances of survival were?"

Mason closed the lid and started brewing the coffee. "No one in his condition is fit to go on this mission, Ash. Why are you advocating for him."

"Because he doesn't fully trust us yet."

"You don't say." Mason leaned back against the counter with his arms crossed.

"It's not just because of his file. I can see he's still testing if he can trust us."

"We rescued him from the school, freed him from the Youth at the safe house, and gave him a lifesaving blood transfusion. What more does he need to know he can trust us."

"Letting him go to save his parents would be a first. Think about it this way. What if, when we find their parents, they don't want to come with us. What if the recruits being there will help us actually rescue them?"

"They're being broken out of prison. Who in their right mind would stay?"

"Because the chances of staying alive could be higher than going with three Youth they don't know."

"It's not happening." Mason grabbed a black coffee cup and poured himself some coffee. He blew on the liquid as it steamed over his face and took a sip, putting his other hand in his pocket as he walked up next to Ash.

"Emotions and feeling can't be present on the battlefield. Fact and reason are the only things that survive. You know I'm right."

Ash breathed out, "yeah…"

"End of discussion then." Mason walked over to the tables, leaning against one as he watched the monitors above Cody.

Ash assumed the same pose as Mason, crossing her arms instead. "How many cups are you on?" she asked.

"This is number two."

"I just finished my fourth."

"You really should get some sleep, Ash, especially after your fight."

"That's a luxury none of us can afford right now."

"The emergency escape tram could work with our numbers," said Cody. "And as far as the blueprints show, there's no security devices of any kind."

"And from what I can remember being there, I can confirm that," said Mason.

Cody stood up and crossed his arms as he stepped back to examine all the monitors. "You do know we have a bet going how long you'll keep that helmet on?" asked Mason.

Cody kept examining the monitors.

Mason looked back at the monitor which showed the path their train was taking and a countdown to their destination.

"What are we going to do about our stops we miss?" asked Ash

"What's your concern?" asked Mason.

"They already know by now where we're headed. It's likely they'll try to stop us there. Plus, the passengers will start getting angry that we don't let them off."

"It's possible. We'll deal with that if it comes to it."

"Edward is chasing us, Mason, not Johan or the Youth."

Mason took another sip of his coffee "We'll be fine. But you need to get some sleep."

"I need to make sure—"

"Calvin will be fine. Let him sleep some more. Hopefully, he'll sleep right through our mission."

"You'd like that, wouldn't you."

Mason eyed Ash. "I'm ordering you to get some sleep, soldier."

Ash had a cold look on her face as she slowly stood up. "Yes, sir," she said, walking out of the room.

As the door shut behind her, Mason asked Cody. "You ready for this?"

"I'm always ready, Mason. You should know that by now."

"Just wanted to ask."

Cody turned around and headed toward the kitchen. Mason watched him before turning back to the monitors and took a sip of his coffee. "The countdown begins," mumbled Mason as he headed over to help Cody as they started making food.

Megan walked out of the bathroom, with her hands in her pockets, back to her bunk. She put her hand on the ladder rung to start climbing but paused with only one foot on the rungs.

"You alright?" whispered Thomas from the bed behind her.

She turned her head to the side, and after a moment, replied, "How long do you think he'll be out for?" She woke up with that question and couldn't go back to sleep, hoping a trip to the restroom to splash some water on her face would help her get the question out of her head.

Thomas sat up on his elbow. "He had woken up for a little bit but fell back asleep."

"How do you know that?"

"I couldn't fall asleep, so I sat with him."

"So, he's ok then?"

"Yeah, he didn't even seem phased."

Megan turned her head away from Thomas and grinned as she climbed the ladder to her bunk. She didn't bother getting under the covers or even taking her shoes off. She still wore her combat suit as she laid on her back with her hands laced together over her stomach. She tried closing her eyes, but her mind wouldn't stop racing. They were on their way to rescue their parents. That was the last thing Mason had told her before she fell into bed. She didn't know how long it would be until everyone got to rescue their parents, that is if they weren't already dead.

Before that thought could fester, the door to Megan's left opened. Light poured into the room, and as quickly as it came, it vanished, darkness consuming the room once again. The only light coming from the moon through the cracks in the blinds. Megan strained to hear what was happening. She could barely hear footsteps making their way to a bunk before sheets rustled. It sounded like someone had crawled into bed.

Megan took a deep breath and exhaled quietly, closing her eyes for a couple of seconds before opening them again. There was too much clouding her mind: will Calvin be coming with us; will he stay behind on the train; will Mom want me to go save the others parents; will Mom hate seeing Dad again; what if Dad's dead; what if none of our parents are alive; how will the others react; what if I don't get enough sleep to focus; what if I mess up because I didn't get enough sleep; what if I die?

At that, Megan shoved her pillow over her face as she started hyperventilating. She balled up the pillow in her fists as she rocked side to side. When she finally had to take a breath, she turned over to lay on her stomach, pulling the pillow over the back of her head. She then started sobbing into her sheets, unheard by anyone else in the room. And after what felt like an eternity to Megan, she finally cried herself to sleep.

Edward woke up inside one of the Youth vans. He sat up from a stretcher placed in the middle of the floor. His helmet and suit were piled on the bench next to him, leaving him in his undersuit. It took a moment to get his bearings when he realized someone was talking to him.

"General? General, can you hear me?"

"Yes," Edward replied, rubbing a hand against his chest.

"You've been shot, sir, but your armor saved you."

"Where was I shot?"

"In the chest. Right where your hand is."

Edward looked down, feeling a dull ache across his chest. "Status report?" he asked, looking over at the Youth sitting next to him.

"The Fallen Youth got away on the train, sir, do you remember the train?"

Edward would have tried searching his memory for the train if he wasn't so outraged. "What do you mean they got away?"

"You were attempting to overtake the train when you were shot out of it, sir. We have no one on board."

"Are we going after them?" Edward yelled.

"We have squads going to all the stations which the train will pass through. You're at the original station as Cory works with the train station on coordinating our recapture of the Fallen Youth."

"Take me to Cory." Edward swung his legs over the stretcher, getting light headed.

"Hold on, sir," the Youth steadied Edward. "You need to take it slow."

"Subject oh-oh-one is still out there. I can't go back to Johan without him."

"I understand that, sir—"

"Then get me some water and take me to Cory."

The back doors of the van opened, rain rushing in as Cory stepped inside with two Youth before closing the door. They pulled their poncho hoods off and took a seat around Edward.

"It's good to see you up, sir," said Cory, "are you able to take a call?"

"From who?"

"Johan, sir."

Edward stared at the radio in Cory's hand a moment before asking, "What's he want?"

"He still wants to talk to you, and he won't take no as an answer."

Edward hesitated a moment before putting his hand out, Cory handing him the radio. "This is Edward," he said ready for this conversation to be over.

"Stand down immediately, Edward," said Johan.

"We're still in pursuit though, sir. We nearly have them."

"You just lost them, Edward!" Johan yelled. "You will stand down now or face court-martial."

"They were my responsibility, and I'm getting them back, sir."

"If you refuse to comply, then you will be relieved of duty."

Edward sat stone faced, glancing at everyone in the van. "I'll bring them back, sir." Edward shut off the radio, handing it back to Cory.

There was an uneasy silence before Cory said, "We're with you, sir." The other Youth nodded in agreement.

A small grin spread across Edward's face. "Where are they expected to head to?"

"Devil's Lake, sir," said Cory. "That's where their parents are being held."

Edward looked behind him at his suit wadded on the bench. "I need a new suit," he said, getting up. "Prepare to move out, we have some Fallen Youth to catch."

Sydney waved the card key over the door pad, opening sliding doors to her massive room. A giant couch sat in front of a massive TV with cabinets full of movies and games. On the opposite side of the room was a floor-to-ceiling window spanning the entire wall. A glass door sat to one side that lead out to a patio overlooking the ocean.

"It smells like cookies," said Sydney's mom.

"Thought you guys would like a snack," said a girl, walking around the corner.

"Who are you?" Sydney's dad asked.

"I'm Grace." She shook hands with everyone as she held a plate of cookies in the other.

"How'd you get in the room?" Sydney's dad asked.

"Have they not told you. I'm your personal chef. From seven a.m. to ten p.m. you can call me, and I'll prepare whatever you request. Come on, Sydney, you must be tired." Grace handed the plate of cookies to Sydney and guided her over to the couch.

"I'm not too bad," replied Sydney.

"Trust me, you will be soon enough. Enjoy this time while you can."

Sydney sat on the couch as her parents flanked her.

"I'll be right back with some drinks," said Grace, taking off to the grand kitchen behind the couch. She grabbed one of the many glass cups from the cupboard and filled it at the filtered tap faucet. She put the three cups on a serving tray and sat it on the coffee table in front of the couch.

"Is there anything else I can get you guys?"

"I'm good, thank you," said Sydney's dad.

"Yes, thank you," replied Sydney's mom.

"Thank you," said Sydney covering her mouth through a mouthful of cookies.

"I'll be back at eleven thirty to prepare lunch," said Grace. "If you need anything before then, use the speaker next to the fridge to call me. It goes to my radio, so I'll get back with you immediately." She pulled her radio from the back of her belt and showed them before leaving.

About halfway to the door, Grace stopped and turned around. "I almost forgot. There're some presents in your bedrooms."

"Presents!" said Sydney, setting the cookies down and getting up.

"Shouldn't you—" Sydney's dad reached out to stop her.

"She'll be fine, honey." Sydney's mom put her hand out to stop her husband. "Come on." She held her hand out, and her husband took it. They walked behind their daughter as she made her way to her room.

Sliding the door open, Sydney gasped, her entire room was covered with gift bags and boxes, some on the bed and the rest on the floor. Every bag, tissue paper, and box were colored yellow.

"What in the world," said Sydney's dad as he walked in the room. "There must be over a hundred boxes in here."

Sydney grabbed a bag and yanked the tissue paper out, revealing a sunflower blouse. "I love it." She sat down to start opening everything.

"Let's see what's in our room," said Sydney's mom, dragging her husband out of the room. When the two opened their door, finding their room covered in presents, they looked at each other and smiled.

Sydney's mom sat cross-legged on her daughter's bed while her dad sat in the chair next to her bed. The two watched their daughter as she looked at herself in a leaning mirror taller than her. She spun around, and the orange and yellow sundress flew up and back down.

"How many more bags do you have sweetie?" asked Sydney's mom.

"I just have one box left. It was the biggest one, so I left it for last. What do you think?" Sydney looked down at her dress.

"As beautiful as the other ones, Syd," said Sydney's dad.

"You look gorgeous, sweetie," said Sydney's mom.

Sydney smiled as she entered the walk-in closet and closed the door.

"Why'd you have to say it like that." Sydney's mom gave her husband a stink eye.

"Like what?" He raised his shoulders.

"You know what you said." The two sat in an awkward silence.

"Is this the right thing to do?" Sydney's dad broke the silence.

"We're helping our daughter. Yes, it's the right thing to do... It's not every day we get an 'all our problems are solved' ticket."

"I'm talking about trusting these people. Syd said they did some terrible stuff to those other kids. I'm not sure if I trust them."

The doorbell rang, and Sydney's dad whipped his head toward the door. "We aren't expecting guests."

"Well, this is our first day. I'm sure people will be around throughout the next couple of days. Sydney," she yelled to her daughter, "Someone's at the door. We'll be right back."

"Alright," she yelled back.

Both parents got up and headed to the door. Sydney's dad opened the door, finding a boy wearing the formal Youth suit. He took his hat off and said, "Good afternoon. I'm looking for Sydney."

"Who are you," said Sydney's dad, sternly.

His wife put a hand on his chest. "She's changing right now."

"No worries. Why don't I introduce myself. May I come inside?"

"Of course." Sydney's mom backed up and let the boy through. He walked across the living room and put his hat under his left arm. "My name is General Blake," he said, shaking hands. "I'm in charge of this Complex."

"And how old are you?" asked Sydney's dad.

"Age is irrelevant to the YOUTH, sir."

"Why do you say that?" asked Sydney's mom.

"Because you are the parent of a Youth, I am unable to disclose that information to you. But if age is of concern to you, let me assure you that everyone in this Complex has been properly trained to serve you and your daughter's needs, as well as fulfill their missions when away."

An awkward silence followed until Sydney came out in the same formal Youth suit as General Blake.

"There she is," said Blake, walking over and shaking Sydney's hand. "I'm General Blake. It's nice to finally meet you, Sydney."

"It's nice to meet you, too. Can I just say that I love this suit."

"I'm glad you like it. I came down here to steal you for a while. I have a few papers I need you to sign."

"Of course. Do I need anything?"

"No, just follow me." Blake left the room, and Sydney waved to her parents as she followed him.

"See you later," she said to her parents.

"Bye, sweetie," said Sydney's mom.

Sydney's dad watched his daughter leave with an apprehensive expression before he and his wife began bickering about them trusting their daughter to these kids.

Blake opened a door to a small featureless gray room, a steel table in the center with a chair on either side and a single light above the table. On the table was a stack of papers and a pen. Blake closed the door and pulled out Sydney's seat before sitting across from her.

"Before we can do any more with you, you'll need to sign these papers." Blake handed Sydney the stack of papers. "This is the entire contract. By signing this, you pledge that you will complete the training to become a Youth. However, in your condition, it will take longer than normal."

"Of course," said Sydney, flipping through the papers, signing page after page. "What is this parent section?" she asked, pointing to a page with the title *Parent Contract*.

"By signing, you agree that the YOUTH will take care of your parents when you are at base and when you are out on a mission. In the event that you are to die, for whatever reason, your parents will continue to live at the Complex and be taken care of by us till they die."

"Why can't they leave?"

"When you sign up to be a Youth, you sign you and your family up for life."

Sydney nodded, flipping through more pages. "Anything else I should know?"

"By signing, you sign your life and the lives of your parents over to the cause of the YOUTH."

Sydney got to the end of the papers and looked at the two dotted lines. "What's the difference between the YOUTH and Youth?" she asked, pointing to the two spellings.

"On the first line, YOUTH is the company in which we operate under, YOUTH corp. Youth, on the second line, is the branch of the company in which you're signing up for. The YOUTH corp. has many different divisions and branches under them. Everything ranging from finance, insurance, and even agriculture. The Youth branch was initially created to help solve the foster care and orphan problems throughout the world. The Youth program and initiatives have grown since their inception, which is where you come in. Does that make sense?"

"I think so." Sydney signed the first line when Blake interrupted her.

"Before you sign that, I should mention that if you do, you will be required at the end of your training to go on two missions. In these two missions, we will have a target for you to kill. We'll make sure you can kill them, but you have to in order to be sworn in as a Youth."

Sydney's hand hesitated over the line for a long time. She stared at the line as her hand started to shake slightly. Finally, she asked, "And if I don't do it?"

"Why would you not. As a Youth, that's your job. To save the world from those that would obstruct peace and freedom. As a Youth, you need to be ready for any situation. Oh, one last note; by signing, you agree that this contract can change at any time without your consent, and you agree to all the changes."

Sydney still hesitated, and after a long while, finally signed the paper, sliding it slowly across the table and wiping sweat from her brow.

"Congratulations, Sydney." Blake stacked the papers and shook Sydney's hand. "You've taken your first step to becoming a Youth."

Megan took a deep breath as she woke up and started crying softly, her pillow still over her head. She dreamed about everyone finding their parents, but how she was the only one not happy to see hers. Everyone was upset with her and called her names. She scrambled off to the cell her dad was in. But as she approached the cell, her dad asked, "Why are you saving me?" Megan couldn't reply but tried to open the cell door. When she couldn't get it open, her dad started laughing at her Then everyone joined in. No matter what she did, she couldn't get the door open. Then she woke up.

After a minute, she stopped crying and slowly pulled the pillow off her head. Looking around the room, the lights were out and everyone was still asleep. She slowly got up, not having to get out of the sheets that were still tucked into the bed. She hopped down quietly from the top bunk with her boots and combat suit still on. Slowly pulling the bed drawers out, she rummaged around for some clothes, finding only one-piece undersuits. She grabbed one in her size and headed for the restroom.

After taking a thirty-minute shower, she got dressed, standing in front of the mirror with her suit done up to her waist, the rest hanging off revealing the formfitting undersuit. She looked at herself in the mirror and thought she looked like the race car drivers she saw growing up before they started a race. All she needed was a pair of sunglasses and a helmet. *Why am I doing this?* Megan leaned over the sink with her hands on the side of it. Why was she wanting to save her father that left her mom? She didn't need to be doing this. She already had her mom; she could go off with her and forget all this stuff about the Youth. She wouldn't have to worry about being... *Don't go there Megan, don't go there.* She splashed some water on her face before raking her hands through her hair, making it frizzy. She frowned at herself in the mirror. Looking through the cabinets under the sink, she found a hair tie and put her hair in a pony tail.

You're only doing this to stay with Calvin.

No, I'm not!

You know you're only staying to see Calvin.

No! I'm not!

Just admit it already.

Megan stormed out of the bathroom, forgetting everyone was asleep, then quietly made her way out of the bunk car. *Just distract yourself with something else.*

As Megan entered the Tac car, Mason looked over from the monitor wall. "I'm surprised to see you up?"

"Couldn't sleep," replied Megan, as she scanned the room, stopping at the kitchen.

"There's some food in the top cabinets," said Mason, following her gaze.

Without a word, she walked over and opened the cabinet closest to her. Inside were shelves chalked full of MRE's. There were four rows of MRE's per shelf and three shelves in the cabinet. Each row had ten of the same MRE. She looked through and found one she liked, Menu 8: Meatballs in Marinara Sauce. Pulling one out, she closed the cabinet and sat on the bench seat across from the monitors and started eating.

As she nibbled on a stale piece of bread, Mason pressed a couple of buttons on the console below the monitors. One of the monitors above the console changed.

"What are you looking at?" asked Megan.

"Nothing you need to be concerned about right now," replied Mason, without turning around.

"When will I need to be concerned about it?"

"I'll tell all of you at once."

Megan took another bite of her bread when Cody walked into the room through the bunk car, still wearing his combat armor and helmet.

"I hope you're still not mad at me?" asked Mason, following Cody with his head.

Cody glanced at Megan before grabbing an MRE and left.

"Cody," mumbled Mason.

"What's he upset about?" asked Megan.

"Too much, Megan, too much."

Megan debated responding but didn't have the energy. She tore open her packet of spaghetti and meatballs, eating it cold.

Mason pressed a couple buttons, and two columns of monitors changed to a map showing a path of the train. A small beeping sound accompanied a flashing dot that represented the current location of the train. Mason pulled a sliding lever to turn down the volume as Ash walked into the car wearing her undersuit. She rubbed her eyes and stretched, making her way to the coffee machine.

Megan finished chewing and asked Ash, "How's Calvin?"

"He'll make it, he just needs to rest now."

"Will he be able to save our parents with us?"

"No," said Mason. "You're all being bunked."

"What's being bunked?" asked Megan.

"Not able to go on a mission for any reason that isn't disciplinary. Did you not tell her?" Ash asked, looking at Mason.

"I was counting on them all staying asleep so I wouldn't have to tell them."

"I thought we agreed we weren't going to hide information from them," said Ash, crossing her arms.

"If they're captured, it's better if they don't know everything. But I'm not going to completely keep them out of the loop."

"I thought we were doing this because we wanted to get away from the Youth, not bring their ideals along with us."

"Not all their ideals are bad."

"And you tell me this now!" yelled Ash as she threw her hands in the air before turning around and pacing with her hands on her hips. "What else haven't you told me?"

"You need to go cool off," said Mason, pointing to the door Ash came through. "You need more sleep"

"Cool off?"

"Leave, Ash."

"Not until you tell me anything else you're hiding from me," said Ash, crossing her arms.

Megan quietly gathered her food and tiptoed to the door. When it opened, the sound caused both Mason and Ash to look toward the door. When the argument stopped, Megan stopped mid-step and slowly turned around. She stumbled over her words before finally stopping and walked through the door.

Ash turned around only to be greeted to Mason saying, "no," as he turned to look at the monitors. Ash slowly shook her head and turned around.

"Great, now I can't trust you either," she said, putting her hands in her suit's pockets, leaving from the same door she entered.

As soon as the door closed, Mason put his hands on top of the console and leaned over, slowly shaking his head. "I could say the same thing about you," mumbled Mason.

At some point while I was talking to Thomas, I had fallen asleep. But I didn't stay asleep long for two reasons. 1. my bed was horrible. It was a hospital bed, they're meant to keep you alive, not make you comfortable. 2. I couldn't stop imagining Edward doing horrible things to my parents. I don't want to even begin to name some of the things I thought of. I guess I should add a third reason, too. I was on a train. A train by itself I probably would have been able to sleep. But add everything else to it, and it made for a body that said you won't be sleeping today. At least the rain beating against the car was relaxing.

So instead, I was looking around the room, hoping there was something interesting to look at. And as you would expect for a hospital on wheels, it wasn't much different. The one cool thing was the automatic blinds. A button to the side of the window, nearly out of reach for me, took them up or took them down, and I was having fun pressing that button, watching the light change in the room as the blinds opened and closed.

Before I went to press it again, the door slid open, and in stepped Ash. She was wearing an undersuit, and her hair done up in a pony tail. "Hi," I said, a little hoarse.

"Having fun there?" she asked with a grin.

"Trying to."

"Looks like you didn't sleep well," said Ash, looking at the monitors next to my bed.

"How can you tell?"

"If you're in this bed, you're not sleeping well. I've seen it too many times. But hey, I have good news for you."

"What is that?"

"All your levels are back to where we want them. Blood, water, everything you lost over the last few days. Which means you don't need these tubes anymore."

"I like the sound of that." I gave Ash a tired grin as she started taking out all the tubes hooked to my arms. When she took out the last tube, I asked, "Are we almost there?" I sat up before Ash grabbed my shoulder, stopping me.

Ash looked away from me and exhaled before turning back. "You're not going with us, none of you are. It's Mason's call."

"I'm going to save my parents," I said, trying and failing to move Ash's arm off me.

"He won't budge, Calvin. I tried fighting for you… I knew you'd want to be there to save your parents."

That was all I wanted to do. Save my parents and get away from the Youth. Get as far away from them as I could. And now three strangers, strangers who time and again saved mine and my friends' lives, were going to save my parents. Would they even care as much about them as I did? "Is there anything we can do?" I asked.

Ash shook her head. I looked out the window across from me, feeling utterly defeated.

"Don't worry, Calvin. I'll make sure we get your parents out. I want them saved as much as you do."

"Why is that?"

Ash hesitated before replying, "That's a story for another time."

The door opened again, and Megan walked through, stopping and staring at Ash before looking at me. She looked confused and embarrassed as Ash took her hand off my shoulder.

"Hey, Megan," I said, "thought you'd be asleep?"

"That didn't work out," she said, trying to play with her bracelet before realizing it wasn't there. "How are you holding up?" she asked, trying not to look embarrassed and rubbing the back of her head.

I debated commenting on her embarrassment but decided against it. "I'm as well as anyone could be in my situation."

"I'll leave you two alone," said Ash, breaking an awkward silence.

As soon as Ash left and the door had closed, Megan asked, "Is Ash treating you well?"

"Yes, she is. She's re-re-really good at her job."

"Yes, she is. It's nice to see you not so pale."

"What are you talking about," I said, holding my arms up and looking at them. "I was already pale before."

There's a difference between almost dead pale and this is the color of your skin pale.

"Was I that bad?"

"Yeah..." Megan looked away, trying to fidget with her bracelet, which she again found not to be there.

"You can sit down," I said, pointing to the chair next to my bed, hoping to alleviate any embarrassment from her.

"Oh, yeah. Thanks." She sat down and brushed a loose strand of hair behind an ear.

She continued looking at the floor, and when she didn't say anything, I asked, "What's wrong, Megan?"

She clutched her wrist when she didn't find the bracelet again and finally said, "I want to go home, Calvin."

The answer hung between us for a while. The muffled sound of the train eventually drained from my ears.

"Me, too," I finally said.

"Then why don't we?" cried Megan as she looked up at me. "Look what Edward has already done to you." She pointed her hand toward me. "Do you want to risk him or the Youth doing that again? Doing that to the rest of us?"

"If that's what it takes to save my parents. To save all our parents," I said, without hesitation.

"Who says I want to go traipsing back into danger?"

"No-no-no one said you had to, Megan." We just stared at each other for a moment. "You're risking your life going in to save your parents. That's not something everyone can do."

"Oh, but you can?" Megan stood up, crossing her arms as she walked away from me, staring out the window opposite my bed.

"What's really wrong, Megan?" I asked. She didn't answer right away.

93

But she dragged her hands through her hair before holding the back of her head.

"I don't know, Calvin," she said just above a whisper. "How should I know. In a matter of one month, I've been to a school that did horrible things to us, manipulated us, then nearly died because I rebelled with you against the school. And now, we're running from this crazy school that's hunting us down to do who knows what to us!" she screamed, throwing her hands out at her side. Her chest heaved, and she put her hands on her hips as she caught her breath.

"Only a few hours ago I saw you nearly dead, Calvin." She started to tear up. "I can't stand to go through that again."

She was doing her best to hold back the tears, so I waved her over to me. She hesitated at first, but when I beckoned again, she slowly walked over, hugging herself. When she reached me, I put out my arms to hug her. She sat down on my bed to the right of me as we embraced, tucking her head into my left shoulder as she couldn't hold back the tears any longer.

I just hugged her and rubbed her back. Neither of us said anything, not that Megan could say anything. I just held her as we swayed back and forth with the rocking of the train.

I took for granted how I was handling the situation at hand. However, I didn't have to experience nearly dying (a weird thing to say but I think you get my point), but what we've been through would be a lot for most people. I'm sure a lot of people would have given up back at the school.

When Megan stopped crying, she laid on me a little while longer before sitting up, wiping her eyes, and sniffling.

"I'm sorry," she said. "I made a mess."

"You are not a mess, Megan." I said, tucking some loose hair behind her left ear. She looked ashamed and hung her head, turning it away from me.

"I'm sorry you have to see me like this," she mumbled.

"Don't apologize. Look at me." She slowly looked up at me. I wiped a stray tear from her cheek. "Unfortunately, there are some times in life where a mess has to be made before things get better."

Megan looked out the window behind me. "I wish it weren't like that."

"An unfortunate reality we have to live with. But not one I let bring me down."

"I wish I was as smart as you." Megan looked at me.

"My parents are the ones who are smart. I was just stupid enough that they were forced to share their wisdom with me." Megan chuckled and it made me smile.

The door to the left of us opened, and Megan's mom walked in. She froze as soon as she saw us. "Everything alright, Megan?"

She turned around to look at her mother. "I'm fine, what are you doing up?" She ran an arm over her runny nose and sniffled.

"I noticed you weren't in your bed, so I came looking for you." She looked over at me. "She didn't wake you, did she?"

"Mom!"

"She's fine," I said, holding a hand up. "I wasn't able to go to sleep. I-I enjoyed the company." I grinned at Megan.

"What happened to your shirt?" Ms. Nall asked, pointing at my shoulder.

"Just a little wet is all," I said, "it will dry."

Ms. Nall hesitated a moment before asking, "Do you care if I sit down?" She motioned to the chair next to my bed.

"Of course, please." I beckoned to the chair as Megan scooted away from me a bit.

"I just wanted to say how thankful I am," said Ms. Nall, "for your bravery and courage to come and save us back at the school. Not everyone I know would do that. Heck, I probably couldn't have done what you did."

"Thank you for the kindness. But I must say, I didn't really save you. I more fell through a chandelier."

"Don't sell yourself short. You saved us. Were it not for you, we'd probably all be dead."

Megan looked down and played with her nails. I sat with Ms. Nall's words for a moment, having difficulty processing them. I fell through a window; I didn't save anybody.

"Hey," said Ms. Nall. I looked up at her. "You're overthinking this. You saved us, Calvin. Don't let anyone tell you any differently."

"Thank you," I finally said with a grin.

"You're welcome." Ms. Nall patted me on the arm and stood up. "You get some rest, you deserve it. Come on, Megan."

I opened my mouth, and Ms. Nall gave me a look that stopped my rebuttal. She smiled and walked out through the same door she had entered. Megan gave a small wave and a grin before following her mom out. And before I knew it, I was fast asleep. I guess I did need the rest.

20

"Run the light," said Edward from the passenger seat of the van. Cory flew through the intersection, nearly hitting oncoming traffic. Another Youth, the rest of Edward's squad, sat strapped in the back. Cory weaved through traffic making his way to the next station the Renegades' train would pass, near the western border of Kentucky.

Police lights caught Edward's eye in his rearview mirror. "I'll take care of that," said the Youth in the back, beginning to unstrap himself.

"Hold." Edward put a hand out as he watched his statscreen. "We're almost there."

Cory went as fast as he possibly could, cutting off a car as he made his way to the front entrance of the station. At the ticket terminal, Cory slammed on the brakes, the tires squealing as everyone in the van slammed forward. Edward jumped out before the van had come to a complete stop, throwing his poncho hood on, and sprinting to the ticket booth. The rest of his squad stalled the police as they pulled behind the van, explaining to them the situation. The lady at the counter quickly produced a silver ticker, sliding it to Edward, who swiped it and ran off, waving his ticket to bypass all the lines.

The train had just pulled up to the station as Edward made it to the platform. The train flew by at full speed and, a moment later, was gone. Edward was frozen, watching the train as it sped away. Clenching his fist, the thoughts of a plan started formulating in his mind. By the time it was complete, Cory ran up next to him.

"Police are taken care of, sir, they're ready to assist however they can."

"No need." Edward let the fist fall from his fingers. "Find a rendezvous and call everyone back. We'll travel together and head toward Complex 4."

"Why Complex 4, sir?"

"Because that's where their parents are." Edward spun on his heal and walked back to the van.

"Are you positive, sir? Without any access to the Youth network—"

"Johan can rebuke all the access he wants, but he can't turn off an internal combustion engine. That's all we need to get to Complex 4 in time."

"Sir?"

"Cory, think, you're smarter than this. They're traveling north. They could have reversed at any point, but they continue to go north. After where they just came from, it's logical to think they want their parents back. The Fallen Youth that are with them will be able to access the prison records and see that I sent the parents to Complex 4 before we began pursuit of their children. And even if they aren't, they have to stop at some point. The more stations they pass, the higher chance every further station becomes one they'll stop. And by that point, hopefully, we've pulled ahead of them and can capture them at the Devil's Lake station."

"Yes, sir," said Cory, embarrassed, "sorry, sir."

"Be glad that mistake didn't cost you your life, Cory." Edward walked up to the van and waved over the police officer talking to the other Youth.

"How can we assist you, sir?" the police officer asked, looking slightly embarrassed at the realization these were Youth.

"I need an escort out as far as your enforcement border allows. We need to get to North Dakota as quick as possible."

"A helicopter would be much quicker, sir. And working with the other states—"

"No air travel." Edward cut off the officer. "I wouldn't put it past Johan to shoot us down." He looked toward Cory for confirmation.

"I agree, sir."

"Right then. An escort as far as you can go north. That should shave off enough time for us to catch up to them. Let's move out."

The Youth and police peeled out of the station, the police sirens blaring as the roads cleared and the pack sped out of the city. Edward was confident that subject oh-oh-one would be in his hands very soon, it was just a matter of time.

The rain had finally stopped as I woke up, this time feeling much more rested, but still sore. These medical beds needed to be redesigned. But I was at least thankful I was alive to gripe about the comfort of my stay. It was still dark when I woke up, the moon shining brightly into the car. It wasn't long before Ash came in and checked me over, wearing her combat suit and not her undersuit like the last time she visited. She looked over my stomach stitches she said she did while I was unconscious in the van. I was glad I had been stitched because that meant no one was going to pour any more of the miracle powder in it again. It made me tense up just thinking about it.

"You alright?" Ash asked with concern all over her face.

"Yeah," I said, calming back down. "I'm just glad that-that no one's going to use any more of the miracle powder on me."

All concern left Ash's face. "Yes, I'm sure you're glad about that. That's not the prettiest stuff."

"Ash, come on, you have to help us." Dakota stormed into the room with Thomas, Megan, and her mom right behind. Everyone but Megan's mom had their combat suit on.

"I already told you there's nothing I can do. It's safer for you here anyway."

"You can't take on that whole base with just the three of you!" protested Dakota. "At least let me tag along. I have—"

"No!" yelled Mason, storming into the room.

"I think your answer switch is broken," said Dakota, turning around. "It's stuck on no."

Mason swung at Dakota, who backed away and managed to throw a punch himself before Mason slugged him in stomach.

"Mason!" yelled Ash, taking a step and stopping when Mason pulled his sidearm out on her. Cody rushed behind Mason as Dakota got up, blocking a punch and taking him down. Cody wretched one of Dakota's arms behind his back and shoved him toward one of the medical beds, handcuffing one of his hands to the foot of the bed.

"You can't do this!" yelled Dakota, lashing out at Cody.

"For the last time, none of you are coming with us." Mason still held his sidearm toward Ash.

"Get that out of my face," whispered Ash with an anger and confidence I wouldn't have guessed she was capable of.

After a moment, Mason dropped the sidearm, putting it back in his thigh holster. "Let's go." He turned around, and Ash quickly dug through her combat suit while asking, "How do you expect them not to come after us, Mason?" By the time she finished, she had placed two things in my hands, flipping them over so the objects were covered.

"Out, now." He turned around in the door and waited for Ash, who with heavy steps complied. "This is for your own good," said Mason as the door closed. A second later, the sound of locks engaging came from the door.

Megan's mom was the first to try the door. "Hey!" she banged on the door. "You can't lock us in here."

"They didn't just do that?" asked Megan, stunned.

Dakota pulled and pushed in every way possible to get out of the handcuffs. After pulling on the door with Megan, Thomas came over and tried to get Dakota out of the cuffs.

I turned my hand over and found a set of keys and what looked like a key card. There were two small keys on a chain that looked the same color as the handcuffs. "Try these," I said, throwing the keys to Thomas.

"Where'd you get these?" he asked.

"Ash gave them to me. I think this is also the key to-to the door." I held up the key card.

"Well, let's get out of here," said Dakota, standing up and rubbing his wrist.

"Hold on," I said. "If we open the door now, they'll just take the card and lock us back in here. We need to wait till they're off the train." Just then, buildings appeared that blocked the moonlight into the car. "How close are we to the station," I asked, pointing to a window.

Dakota and Thomas both jumped up on a seat to see out the windows. "We're just pulling in," said Thomas.

"Wait until you see them leave, and then we'll open the door."

"What are we going to do once we open the door?" asked Megan's mom.

"Get out of this room first off," I said, taking the covers off me.

"You aren't going after them," said Megan's mom.

"And why is that?" I asked, staring her down.

"We're not risking our lives." She grabbed her daughter, pulling her to her side.

"Mom, if Calvin's going, then I'm going."

"No, you are not. I will not see you run off just to waste your life for them."

"What do you mean waste our lives?" asked Thomas, slowly standing up.

Megan's mom looked at all of us., "None of you would understand."

"Try me," I said.

Megan's mom hesitated before saying, "I'm not going back for my ex-husband. Or for any of your parents. I'm not wasting my life with these Youth just to die to save people I don't know."

Her response was a shock to me. "What's wrong with you. How-how can you say that? He may be your ex-husband, but he's a human being. Our parents are human beings. You don't want to save them?"

"Not if it costs me my life."

"The Youth could be killing them right now!" I yelled. "We don't know what they may be doing to them. If-if it's anything like they did to us, it's atrocious." I glanced at the rest of the group, seeing Thomas appear distant in thought. "I'm not going to sit by while the Youth chase us and hurt our parents. I'm going to save our parents, and no one is going to stop me. I don't care if I lose my life."

"Then you go do that," said Megan's mom.

Megan seemed frozen until that moment when she pulled away from her mother. Leaving her mom's side and walking to the other side of my bed to stand next to me. "I'm going with Calvin." She looked around at everyone else. "I'm going with my friends."

"No you're not." Megan's mom started walking around my bed when Thomas blocked her path. "You can't do this."

"Do what?" asked Thomas.

"You can't kill my daughter," she said as only a mother could.

Megan grabbed my arm and clutched it tightly. "Let me assure you," I told her mom, "that I have no intention on dying myself. I will do everything in my power, along with everyone else, to ensure we all come back from this. I can't guarantee that will happen, but that's how I'm going."

"None of that will matter when you're all dead. Now give me my daughter." She tried shoving Thomas aside when Dakota came up and grabbed both her arms. "Let me go!" she screamed.

Megan ground her fingernails into my arm, and I gently eased her hand off me. "Can you see if they've left, Thomas?"

He got back up on the chair to look out the window. "I think I see them?"

"What do you see?" I asked.

"I see three people in ponchos like ours walking out together."

"That has to be them." I looked over at Megan's mom as she tried to squirm out of Dakota's grasp. "Handcuff her to the bed, but make sure she can grab the key."

"You wouldn't." Megan's mom resisted even more, but Dakota was able to cuff her to the bed, throwing the key on the floor in front of her just out of reach. "You can't do this!"

"You're not going to prevent us from getting out of here. We're saving our parents and your ex-husband, whether you want us to or not. Let's go."

Mason, Cody, and Ash walked into the armory car, filling their suits with as many weapons as they thought they'd need. Throwing ponchos on to hide their weapons and putting their helmets on, they exited the Tac car, heading into the passenger cars. It was chaos as angry passengers were relieved the train had finally stopped. The Fallen Youth easily blended into the crowds that formed near the doors, throwing their hoods on to ensure the cameras at the station couldn't pick them up.

With cheers and sighs of relief, the doors were opened. Passengers flooded out, breathing in fresh air, running about, and yelling at the door attendants. In the complete chaos that erupted, the Fallen Youth easily slipped through the crowd and around the building. In the employee parking lot, two Youth vans sat ready. Mason pulled out his universal key and opened the first one they came to. They fired up the engine and rolled out onto the road, heading toward the Youth base, Complex 4. After they were out of the city, Ash said, "That was too easy."

"We're not being followed, though," said Mason, glancing in the rearview mirror. "Let's take the advantage while we have it."

Ash used her thermal visor to scan their surroundings for any potential Youth tracking them. After finding nothing, she turned the thermal visor off and looked back toward the town, silently apologizing to Calvin he couldn't come, and promising to bring his parents back to him.

23

"Are we really not going to listen to them?" asked Dakota, sliding the key card over the door terminal as the locks disengaged.

"What do you think," I said, hobbling toward the door after everyone helped me out of bed.

"Haha," said Dakota all excited and followed me out the door. I glanced back and saw Megan's mom was finally able to grab the key.

"Megan, wait!" she screamed, trying to unlock the cuffs.

"Hold on, Calvin," said Megan as I walked through the door to the bunk room.

"Walk and talk!" I yelled back.

"Are you sure you can do this, Calvin? You can barely walk."

"They're my parents. It doesn't matter what condition I'm in. I'm going to save them. And all due respect to Mason and them, but I'm not letting them save my parents without me."

"Especially when you get to play with all of these." Dakota walked into the next car, the armory, turning into a kid in a candy shop. "Now, which one do I choose?"

"The one that won't get us all killed, please," called Thomas from behind me.

"You're no fun.," Dakota picked up and brandished the biggest gun he could find, flashing a smug grin toward Thomas.

"Hey, focus," I said, looking around the armory. "We need to stay focused so we can catch up to them." I went through the isles until I found the cage holding the Youth combat suits and helmets.

"What's your plan, Calvin?" asked Megan, walking up to me as I opened the cage. Clearly, her fear of dying had been replaced by wanting to know how we were going to accomplish this rescue mission.

"Get some gear and-and follow them to the base. Then insist on going in with them."

"Do not listen to him, Megan!" shouted her mom from the other car.

"Ignore her, how are we going to get there?" Megan crossed her arms.

"Youth!" yelled Thomas.

Megan and I both looked out the aisle to find a Youth throwing something through the door of the medical car, rolling between Megan's mom's legs.

"Grenade!" I yelled. Immediately, Megan darted behind me to the end of the aisle as I followed her, putting my body in front of hers as a large pop sounded. I turned around to a huge cloud of smoke in front of us.

It didn't take long to realize it was pepper spray when Megan and I both started coughing and our eyes burned. I searched through my watery eyes for a weapon when a deafening bang exploded. I covered my ears as they rang, and more bangs filled the car.

In a matter of moments, two Youth were in front of us, guns raised. They shoved Megan and I to the floor. I screamed as my stomach hit the floor, and they handcuffed us behind our backs, taking us into the Tac car.

They shoved us on our knees in the middle of the room; my pain meds clearly having worn off and fire ripping through my stomach. I grimaced and fell to my side.

"Get up," said a Youth.

"I can't." I managed through gritted teeth. Someone pulled me up by my collar, choking me as I came up before grabbing me by the hair to keep me upright.

My eyes couldn't do anything but blink as the pepper spray burned all over my face. I could make out over Megan and mines coughing the protests of Dakota in the next car. I could barely see him and Thomas get dragged into the room when I was sprayed in the face with water. I coughed it out of my mouth but instantly felt relief. More water hit my face, and the burning started to leave my face.

"This is not—" started Dakota before I heard the wind get knocked out of him.

"Quiet," said a Youth.

I could see again, as the water dripped off my glasses and face, only to be welcomed by four Youth surrounding us. Everyone else was like me on the ground, handcuffed behind their backs, Dakota still struggled against his captors when one of them punched him in the face.

"Stop, Dakota!" yelled Thomas.

"I am not—"

"We can't fight back now," Thomas cut Dakota off. "Look at us."

Dakota looked around and slowly came to the same conclusion the rest of us had, the Youth had captured us, again. Fear was written all over Megan's face.

"Megan—"

"Quiet!" yelled the Youth, holding my hair and yanking it up.

I winced and turned toward the footsteps coming into the car from the passenger's car door.

"Subject oh-oh-one," said Edward.

24

Edward walked toward us with a gas mask on, and I realized the rest of the Youth wore one, too. I locked eyes with Edward as he stopped in front of me. We stared at each other a moment before he said, "I'm glad you're back."

I didn't reply. I didn't really know what to say.

"I can't believe I've made you speechless already subject oh-oh-one."

"Calvin or Fritz is much quicker to say," I said.

"It's demoralizing, isn't it? Being called a number instead of a name."

"It's more demoralizing that I got away from you for so long," I said with a smile.

Edward slapped me, and Megan let out a gasp. "How's the air?" Edward asked one of the Youth while staring at me.

To my left I could see one of the Youth look at a small handheld device. "All clear," he said. All the Youth removed their gas masks, inserting them into a bag on their belt.

Edward squatted down in front of me and spoke in a hushed tone, "Like I said, one day you'll worship me." He looked down the row of us on the floor, and I followed his gaze. "As will the rest of your little friends." A devilish grin escaped Edward as a Youth walked up next to him. Edward stood and took the helmet the Youth held out to him, putting it on and disappearing inside.

"Let go of me!"

"Mom?" cried Megan as her mom was dragged through the door. "Mom!" Megan shot up but was quickly intercepted by a Youth.

"Get your hands off her!" yelled Mrs. Nall as she tried pulling free of her captors.

"Somebody put a bag on them," said Edward nonchalantly. The women's cries and pleas filled the car before abruptly being cut off by the still bags placed over their heads.

Mrs. Nall was dragged out of the car while Megan was thrown back in line next to me.

I debated saying something about Mason saving us but held my tongue as I didn't want to give them up if Edward didn't know about them.

"I want these cars swept, and all the passengers questioned," said Edward. "Nobody leaves this station. Bring them with me." He pointed to us. We were picked up and escorted off the back of the train.

For their pleasure the Youth made us all jump. I jumped down, immediately crumpling to the ground with a scream, while Megan was pushed out and caught by a Youth below. Thomas and Dakota were able to jump down alright.

They took us off the tracks, through the train station, and to a group of identical vans parked out front, shoving us into the prison van which was most likely the one we were in a few days before. This time, instead of our hands being strapped above our heads, they kept us handcuffed behind our backs, our hands wedged awkwardly between our backs and the wall. As I was strapped in, my stomach strap was cinched extra tight. The Youth had his helmet on, but I knew as he stood up he was smiling watching me in so much pain.

When everyone was strapped in, the Youth hopped out, closing the doors, and leaving us in darkness.

"Hang in there, Calvin," said Thomas.

I took a few breaths before saying, "I don't know how much more of this my body can take."

A foreboding silence filled the van. I closed my eyes, and my mind went to so many places. On the overwhelming pain, on being back in Edwards's hands, and Mason being our only hope to get our parents. Then the engine started, shaking the car and freeing me of my overwhelming thoughts.

"Where do you think we're going?" asked Thomas.

"Not the Carnival," said Dakota.

"Wherever it is," I said, "it can't be good."

25

Mason checked the rearview mirror, looking again for anyone following him, and shut off the car lights, flipping his thermal visor on to see instead. Cody and Ash did the same, seeing the world in hues of blue and red.

The whole ride from the train station had been silent, Ash still upset about Mason forcing everyone to stay on the train, even if it did make sense. She wanted Calvin and the other recruits to be able to rescue their parents themselves, if not at least wait in the van instead of the train. It may have been stupid of her to think that with their lack of training the recruits would be any help, but if she had the opportunity to save her parents, she would go in a heartbeat, no matter if she lacked the skills to do so.

Mason pulled off the road, the jolt from asphalt to dirt knocking Ash out of her thoughts. They headed toward a barn in the middle of a field. And two miles beyond that was the Youth base, Complex 4, lit up as far as the eye could see.

"I'm not seeing anyone on Thermals," said Mason, looking toward the barn.

"Me, neither," said Ash.

The barn was cover for the emergency escape tunnel attached to the

Complex. Two rail cars, holding up to thirty people, ran from the base to the barn. Mason, Cody, and Ash would have to walk the track to ensure no alarms were tripped by calling the cars to them.

Mason pulled up to the left of the barn, putting the car right next to the wall.

"Gear check and mic-drop," said Mason, looking over his belt and checking his guns were loaded.

"Good to go," said Ash after tapping her mic-drop button on her helmet

"Ready," said Mason, looking at Cody who nodded his head and opened his door. Everyone followed, poised for battle as they made their way to the sliding door of the barn. Mason grabbed the handle while Cody and Ash prepared to enter.

Mason dropped his rifle, letting the sling catch it, counting down from three on his fingers before sliding the door open. Cody led with Ash on his heels, sweeping the room for any Youth. Mason came in a moment later, and in less than a minute, Ash called, "Clear!"

Everyone lowered their rifles, taking in their surroundings. It looked like a regular barn to the common eye. Hay, equipment, vehicles, anything a farmer would need. But an open space against the back wall caught Mason's eye. "There's the entrance," he said, pointing to it.

"I agree," said Ash, "now how do we open it."

Without a word, Cody went to the wall beside the open space toward some light switches. He took out a multi-tool and began to take off the casing of the left most switch. Pulling it off, he found a button inside. Pushing it released a groan as the floor in the open space started rising. Dirt and hay fell off the sides of the hatch as it rose, revealing a concrete ramp below. The hatch stopped just before hitting the loft above as more dirt and hay fell off the hatch onto the clean ramp.

Suddenly, the lights in the barn flared to life. Everyone's helmet beeped twice to let them know there was enough light to see without the thermal visor.

Before Mason could ask Cody why he turned the lights on, everyone's visor lit up with several heat signatures, all appearing at the bottom of the ramp.

"Fall back!" yelled Mason as he fired down the ramp, Cody and Ash following as shots were returned. Everyone bolted to the sides of the ramp, looking for any cover they could find. Cody and Ash got behind a tool shelf while Mason found a post holding up the loft to hide behind.

"How did they know we were coming?" asked Ash.

Mason turned off his thermal visor, the yellow lights of the barn blinding him a moment as his eyes adjusted, before throwing a frag grenade down the ramp, counting at least six Youth before ducking back into cover.

"Survive this and we can figure out," barked Mason.

"Even if we take them out, do we still want to continue this mission knowing it's compromised?" asked Ash, firing as the scattered Youth tried scrambling up, taking down two before returning to cover.

Mason and Cody both stepped out from cover and fired when a Youth threw a grenade, landing right between them.

"Grenade!" yelled Mason, bolting away as Cody and Ash dived into the pile of hay behind them, disappearing inside. The grenade exploded, sending shrapnel all over the room, one piece hitting Mason in the calf.

He cried out and stumbled to the ground, skidding across the ground and sliding headfirst into the wall. "So much for wanting us alive," he muttered, trying to get up, only to get up on one knee and find three gun barrels pointed at him.

"Drop it!" yelled one of the Youth surrounding Mason. He slowly laid his gun on the ground. "Where are the others?" asked the same Youth.

From the pile of hay, two gun barrels slowly extended out. In a blur of an instant, Cody and Ash, from the cover of the hay, took down all four Youth in the barn, none of them having any time to react.

Mason picked up his gun and stood, hobbling to the nearest post when the pain was worse than he expected.

Cody brushed the hay off himself while Ash ran toward Mason, hay flying off behind her. Before she reached Mason, he had pulled out the piece of shrapnel. "I've got it," he said as Ash knelt to examine his leg, her med kit already in hand. Without a word, she pulled out supplies and started patching Mason up.

One of the Youth lying next to Mason moaned and started rolling over. Mason kicked him in the side with his good leg before Cody walked over, kicking the Youth across the helmet, and slamming the butt of his rifle into the back of his helmet. The Youth lay there unmoving.

"I'm surprised you didn't kill him," said Mason.

"Waste of ammo," said Cody, examining the rest of the Youth. All of them were unconscious, catching the bullets in their armor. Very few Youth could remain conscious immediately after taking a shot to any armor they wore.

"Done," said Ash, closing her med kit and shoving it back in her backpack.

"Thanks." Mason tested his leg and walked toward the ramp.

Ash threw her bag on as she stood up when Cody shut the barn lights off. Immediately, she spotted lights through the cracks in the wood-paneled walls, lots of them, coming the same direction they just had. "I think we have company." Ash walked over to the door they had entered, stepping outside to peer around the corner of the barn. A second after she saw a line of vans coming down the road, all their lights turned off. "At least four vans coming down the road." Ash turned and ran back inside as Cody ran past her to the van.

"Where are you going?" asked Ash.

Cody never got to reply as an explosion burst through the wall opposite Ash. Fire engulfed the wall and sent splintering wood flying everywhere.

Mason was thrown down the ramp while Ash was blasted, slamming into the barn door behind her. The majority of the blast was caught inside the barn, but Cody still ducked behind the van, his suit's cooling unit kicking in from the blast of heat that escaped through the open barn door.

Cody crawled along the length of the van, sticking his head out and finding multiple vans, using the thermal visor, coming their way. He darted around the van and into the barn, flames starting to spread up and around the walls. Behind him, Ash was starting to stand up, and he pulled her the rest of the way.

"Thanks," she said out of breath.

The sound of strained wood filled the room before a sharp crack erupted. A post holding the loft broke under its own weight, sending one side of the loft crashing to the ground. Hitting the door to the underground ramp, the already damaged piston holding the door snapped, the other piston buckled and broke a moment later, sending the door slamming down to the ground, trapping Mason inside.

Bullets started ripping through the barn, forcing Cody and Ash to the ground and crawling to the nearest point of cover. A rafter burned through and fell, dropping right in the middle of the floor. Ash and Cody retreated under the still supported half of the loft, hiding behind a stack of tires.

"We have to get out of here before this place collapses on us," said

Ash as bullets started flying overhead, dropping splintered wood on their heads. Cody raised his rifle to the side of the tire and fired through the barn walls. Breaking a hole through the wood and seeing the Youth's red figures through the thermal visor. As he continued firing, the wall continued to heat up as the fire spread, making it harder and harder to pick out the Youth through the holes. Ash followed, doing her best despite the headache and pain across her back.

Another beam burned through enough and buckled, slamming down into the loft as it collapsed. Cody dived on top of Ash as wood and supplies crashed down on them.

"They've stopped returning fire," called a Youth, slowly standing to one knee. The other Youth, all prone on the ground, did the same.

"Cease fire on the barn," called Edward, "let it burn."

The Youth all stood up and continued watching the spectacle. Edward turned around and went to the prison van, pulling the doors open, and hopping inside.

"Where are you taking us?" asked Megan. Edward passed without even glancing at her, pulling Calvin's restraints off, and dragging him outside.

Calvin groaned and yelled as Edward intentionally pulled Calvin in such a way that would hurt him.

"So much for saving your parents," said Edward, pointing Calvin toward the fire. "And the next time you see those friends of yours, I don't think you'll recognize them."

"You're letting them burn in there?" Calvin asked, walking toward the fire intent to help, despite the pain and exhaustion present in his body, until Edward tightened his grip, yanking Calvin back.

"A fitting death for their crimes."

Calvin was in shock, watching the death of the only people who would help him save his parents, the first death he ever witnessed, and he couldn't do anything to help. His parents wouldn't be rescued, and he was back in Edward's grasp again. Before those thoughts overtook him, Edward yelled, "What are they doing here?"

Across the field, fire trucks drove toward the burning barn, their lights dull compared to the blazing fire. "Somebody hail them," demanded Edward.

After a minute, a Youth replied, "They're not answering our hails, sir."

"I thought we had control of that department?"

No one dared reply to Edward in his heated state. Letting him come up with an idea was a far smarter idea. Edward bit his lip, thinking through the few ideas he had at his disposal. With so many fire engines and such a small fire comparatively, there would be no convincing way to kill the firefighters and get away with saying they all died in the fire

"Code Blur, Code Blur!" yelled Edward. The Youth started running toward the fire as Edward threw Calvin on his knees, slamming the butt of his rifle into the back of Calvin's head, knocking him out.

Video and Audio Transcript Report

Complex: 3
Camera: GS-1
Room: Guard station 1 security feed
Date of Transcript: ▓▓▓▓▓▓▓▓
Time of Transcript: ▓▓▓▓▓▓▓▓

Transcript

Van Y749 pulls up to the gate. YT156 rolls down the driver window as YT497 exits the guard booth and approaches the van.

YT497: State your business?

YT156: Delivering Prisoner one-seven-five-four-nine.

YT497 looks at his statscreen, accessing the arrival schedule to confirm the prisoner delivery.

YT497: SC-Card?

YT156 hands YT497 his security clearance card (SC-Card), who inserts the card into a portable card reader (PCR).

YT497: What do you think they'll do to her?

YT156 Whatever it is it won't be enough. Not after what they've done to us.

The PCR light turns green and clicks as it pops the card out halfway. YT497 pulls the card the rest of the way out and hands it back to YT156, before motioning with his hand to the control booth to open the gate.

YT497: If you get the opportunity, make her regret what she did.

YT156 nods his head as YT497 slaps the hood of the van, driving through the now open gate.

End Transcript

———

Video and Audio Transcript Report

Complex: 3
Camera: GB-6
Room: Garage bay
Date of Transcript:
Time of Transcript:

Transcript

Van Y749 pulls in through the already open door of bay 6, stopping the van just beyond the threshold of the overhead door. YT212 leads a group of Youth, YT247, YT419, YT428, and YT496, who approach the back of the van and open the double doors. A moment later the Youth bring out Prisoner 17549, Audrey Nall, mother of Megan Nall, recruit 2. With a still bag over their head, the Youth guide the prisoner out of the van, one Youth holding each of their arms that are handcuffed behind their back. YT212 leads the group to the middle of three doors spread out across the length of the back wall of the garage, holding the door open as everyone passes through.

End Transcript

Video and Audio Transcript Report

Complex: 3
Camera: PPR-2
Room: Prisoner Processing Room
Date of Transcript:
Time of Transcript:

Transcript

Prisoner 17549 is escorted to a chair in front of the fingerprint table. YT247 and YT496 hold each of the prisoner's arms while YT212 removes their handcuffs. Each Youth transfers the prisoner's fingerprints onto the corresponding document. The prisoner's hands shake during the print transfer. Once all their prints are transferred, YT212 puts the handcuffs back on the prisoner before pulling them up from the chair. The prisoner is led to the photo booth, stood against the wall, and their handcuffs attached to the wall. Everyone backs away as YT212 removes their still bag.
YT419: Smile for the camera.
YT419 watches the preview monitor and presses

the shutter button, a flash activates, and the shutter captures multiple photos before the prisoner closes their eyes and looks away. The last photo taken shows up on the preview monitor [Refer to photo bundle 4298673].

YT419: That's a keeper!

All the Youth behind him laugh as YT212 quickly puts the still bag over the prisoner's head, silencing their protests, and escorts them out of the room.

End Transcript

Video and Audio Transcript Report

Complex: 3
Camera: P-2
Room: Prison Entrance
Date of Transcript: ████████████
Time of Transcript: ████████████

Transcript

YT212 leads the escort for Prisoner 17549. The escort stops a few paces from the entrance as YT212 approaches the guard booth. YT438 and YT461 are on duty in the booth. YT438 opens the pass-through door on the counter as YT212 pulls out his SC-Card, sliding it through the door. YT438 inserts the SC-Card into the card reader on the terminal in front of him before looking back up at YT212

YT438: And who are we moving today?

YT212 looks down at his statscreen.

YT212: Prisoner one-seven-five-four-nine.

YT438 nods as a confirmation beep sounds, and

the light turns green on the card reader, popping the card out halfway. YT438 grabs the card and returns it to YT212, who puts the card back in his belt. YT461 slides down the terminal and hits the open door button. The first door of the two-door security checkpoint system opens. YT212, Prisoner 17549, and YT247 enter. The three stand single file, each of the Youth with a hand on the prisoner as the door closes behind them. A moment after the locking mechanism engages, a red light turns on above the exit door and the x-ray bar glides across the wall. A readout on the terminal in front of YT461 shows the three figures as the scan progresses to completion. The x-ray bar completes its scan and quickly slides back to its starting position. No alarm is triggered, and after a visual inspection, YT461 approves the scan. The light above the second door turns green as the door unlocks and opens. The three exit the checkpoint and await the rest of the escort. After four minutes and twenty-seven seconds, all of the escort is through the checkpoint. They proceed into the prison with YT212 leading the way.

End Transcript

———

Video and Audio Transcript Report

Complex: 3
Camera: PS-5
Room: Prison Security Feed; Cells C21-C30
Date of Transcript: ███████████
Time of Transcript: ███████████

Transcript

YT212 leads the escort of prisoner 17549 down the hall, stopping at cell C27. After 2.3 seconds, YT212 opens cell C27. YT212 pulls the cell open and grabs the prisoner by the arm, dragging them inside. YT247 follows behind and spins the prisoner around several times before YT212 removes the prisoner's handcuffs. The two Youth exit the cell and lock it as the prisoner stumbles around before falling. The entire escort laughs as they walk away from the cell. On their way out, YT212 stops in front of cell C30, which holds prisoner 17482, their head bowed and hands clasped together.

YT212: Your prayers won't work in here.

Prisoner 17482: You underestimate—

YT419: You underestimate us!

YT212 puts a hand up to stop YT419 as he pushes his way through to the front of the group.

YT212: Your prayers are nothing against the Youth.

Prisoner 17482: You're wrong.

YT212: We will see. Especially when we kill your son in front of you.

The entire escort laughs and walks away as the prisoner sits with their mouth agape.

End Transcript

Edward stood next to Calvin's hospital bed, staring down at him with his arms crossed and his helmet on. "I do hope I have the pleasure of making you suffer when Johan decides to have you killed."

"Edward, do you copy," said Cory through Edward's helmet radio.

"Copy, go ahead."

"Johan just pulled up."

"Perfect. Prepare our troops for his arrival."

"Right away, sir."

Edward spun around, dropping his hands to his side as he exited Calvin's room. The Youth standing in the doorway saluted his general. Edward returned the salute as he made his way down the hall to the entrance of the ICU wing.

He stopped a few paces from the double doors as his Youth started pouring through the automatic door, all of them coming from the kitchenette just outside the door. They formed two lines against the hallway's walls and stood at attention; twelve in all wearing their full combat suits. Cory slid up next to Edward, standing at his right.

"Whatever happens, sir, I stand with you," came Cory through Edward's helmet.

"You're a good solider, Cory," said Edward before biting his lip. *If you punish me for finishing the mission...*

Edward waited for what felt like an eternity, biting his lip raw, when the double doors finally opened. As General Johan walked in, everyone saluted him. He strode through the doors with his hands clasped in the small of his back. Following him were eight Youth from his Personal Defense Garrison. All of them indistinguishable from regular Youth except for a small circle patch on the left shoulder. A red YOUTH logo surrounded by a half ring of golden leaves on the bottom, and nine stars surrounding the top half of the logo.

As Johan approached Edward, the two saluted each other. "Welcome, sir," replied Edward as Johan stopped in front of him.

"Take me to see them," Johan said more excited than Edward was thinking he would.

Edward nodded and spun around, stopping first at Calvin's room. Johan's Garrison stayed outside the room while Johan followed Edward and Cory inside. "Alone and sedated just as you asked, sir," said Edward, a hint of nervousness coming through. The three of them surrounded the bed, no one saying a word. Edward was glad for his helmet as he started biting his lip again.

After what felt like an eternity to Edward, Johan finally looked back at him saying, "I'm thoroughly impressed, Edward. I'd like to see the others."

Edward led everyone out of the room, going throughout the ICU wing showing all seven Renegades to Johan. As they came out of the last room, Johan asked, "And was Megan's mother taken to Complex 3 as instructed?"

"Yes, sir," replied Edward.

"Good. I appreciate you following orders this time." And there was the knife in the side. He may be acting proud, but Edward knew he was furious. It had always been hard to discern his attitude while growing up. It wasn't until he blew up that you knew he was angry. Until then, he put on the best poker face in Edward's opinion, something he could learn from.

Yet surprisingly, he let his true emotion slip through his words, or was that intentional?

"Cory," said Johan, "return to your duties. Follow me, Edward." Cory turned his helmeted head to Edward, who followed behind Johan and glanced back at Cory.

Johan's Garrison assumed their escort positions, four in front of Johan, four behind Edward. They moved as a well-oiled machine into their positions, very precise, exiting the ICU wing.

Two of Edward's Youth, who stood guard at the three elevator terminals, prepared one as soon as they saw Johan's Garrison approaching. By the time the group arrived, the far-left elevator opened, and everyone filed in. The Garrison filled the perimeter while Johan and Edward occupied the center. The Garrison member closest to the button terminal produced a key from a compartment on his belt. He used it to open the access panel, revealing wires and switches, but also revealing an additional button labeled B for basement. The Garrison member pressed it, and they began their descent.

The ride down was completely silent. Nothing but the groans of the elevator. It wasn't until it shook as they arrived at the basement that Edward realized he had bit his lip the whole way down, blood running down his chin.

The Garrison exited the same as they entered, heading left out of the elevator and coming to a couple of pallets of paper stacked taller than Johan. The paper created a square of four pallets by four pallets with one entrance on the front, wide enough only for one person.

Everyone filed in. The anticipation building for Edward as he walked inside. He knew a number of things that could happen in here. He had witnessed, and even partook in, similar scenarios. How odd it was to now be on the receiving end.

Edward stood in the center of the room, facing the wall with the entrance as two Garrison Youth stood back-to-back at the entrance, one facing in and one facing out. Without a word from Johan, the Garrison Youth relieved Edward of all his weapons: gun, knives, grenades, and shurikens, all laid or thrown in the corner of the makeshift room. They grabbed him, kicking the back of his knees, making him fall to his knees. His helmet was ripped off and thrown aside, revealing Edward's matted hair and bloody chin.

Johan stood facing away from Edward, his hands clasped together in the small of his back. "My orders were simple," he said just above a whisper. "And yet you manage to not only disregard orders," Johan's voice started rising and he turned around to look at Edward, "you manage to leave a trail of destruction in your wake that I have to clean up!" Johan screamed and started becoming very animated.

"I have to pay to keep the journalist's quiet, pay to have the evidence destroyed. I've had to order more hits in the last week than I have in the last five years. All because you wanted to be a hero.' Johan jabbed a finger toward Edward. "Those troops should be out there ensuring the rest of our plan is successful. But instead, I'm having to pull active Youth from the field. Youth we've spent hundreds of resources on to ensure they got where they are. Some of them won't be able to return because they'll be cleaning up what you call completing the mission!"

"I did complete it though."

"You threw them in a hospital because you were too afraid to have those first responders die in that barn fire. You took the easy route out. And now we're stuck here because we can't just take these recruits out of the hospital. People will start asking questions, I'll have to order more hits. Which is more money, money we don't have, Edward! What do you not understand about this."

"I thought we had plans in place if things like this happened."

"We do, but not to the extent that you did. That's why I told you to stop. You not only endangered the Youth, our cause, or mission, but you needlessly put your troops' lives at risk."

"No one died—"

Johan backhanded Edward across the face before squatting down in front of him, both of them locking eyes. Barely whispering, Johan said, "The next time this happens, you'll go straight to Misfit Island." The two locked eyes a moment longer before Johan stood up and exited the makeshift room. As he made his way back to the elevator, Johan could hear Edward's screams, until they were abruptly cut off by the closing of the elevator door.

Part 2

29

Paige laid in her bed on top of her sheets, staring at the ceiling, her right leg bent and pulled up toward her body. She laid there in her undersuit. She hadn't moved for the last hour, dreading having to be geared up and in the TAC room to get her mission brief in thirty minutes.

They're only letting me go on this mission because of how long Edward and I worked together. What if I never get promoted. What if I stay a private forever. I probably have too much red ink on my file they won't let me be promoted.

The same thoughts had permeated her mind and would not leave, keeping her in a complete state of fear. Unable to move, unable to do anything.

Then she finally sat up, hugging her one leg that was up, she pulled it against her chest, resting her chin on her knee.

What's happened to me?

She let that question float around for a while. And as she thought, she realized she had been tracing the perimeter of a wound on her left forearm left by the Interrogators. She pulled her arm up to examine it. The finger wide gap, even with stitches, would leave a scar. She traced her fingers around the wound a few more times before sliding her legs over the edge of the bed. Her hands rested on the edge of the bed as she leaned forward with her head hung low and her eyes closed.

This isn't who you are. You're Paige. One of the deadliest Youth, and you're mad that you're a private again? Once you show them how loyal you are, they'll have no choice but to promote you once they see you back in action.

Paige got up and opened the closet to the left of her bed. On a hanger was her black Youth combat suit. As she pulled off the suit, it revealed a photo attached to the middle of the hanger. The photo was of Paige and Edward on their first date, a secret date.

In the Youth handbook, it's expressly forbidden that two Youth partake in a romantic relationship. *That didn't stop us though.* Edward and Paige had snuck out into the barracks. Using crates as a makeshift table and chairs, the two had had dinner together. Even with most of the other Youth knowing and keeping watch for them, they only had about two hours together.

Before they left, Edward used his combat helmet and took a photo of the two. Edward had modified his helmet so he could take it off the YOUTH Network but not have the helmet appear missing. And any video or pictures taken while offline were stored locally in the helmet on some added memory. After the date, Edward printed out their photo and gave it to Paige. On the back of the photo, Edward wrote, "First date!" and the date below it, nearly six months ago.

How could someone who loves me punch me and get me in a session with the Interrogators? Paige held her suit up and saw the same scar on her left forearm again. She looked up the rest of her arm and saw the beginning of another wound sticking out from the edge of her shirt sleeve.

She threw her suit on her bed, part of it hanging over the edge, as she rolled up her shirt sleeve. Looking at the mirror that stretched the entire height of the back of the closet door, she examined the wound. Then she looked at her face. This was the first time she had looked at herself since her interrogation, and she wished she hadn't. She looked ragged, defeated, like she could barely carry her own weight.

Her shirt was tight enough that she could see little bumps all over her body. She lightly touched one before taking her shirt off, balling it all in her right hand. When she saw herself, she almost gasped. She slowly let go of her shirt, and it fell in a puddle next to her feet. There were more stitches, cuts, and bruises, than there was clear skin. And as Paige touched her hand to one of the stitches, she was immediately back in the interrogation room. She could remember every detail vividly, almost like she was living it again.

Every wound she touched took her right back to the moment she got it. She remembered it all. The stench of the room from her blood, sweat, and vomit, combined with the almost sterile smell that the Interrogators had, specifically their gloves. She remembered being strung up by her hands from the ceiling like a punching bag, her bare toes barely touching the cold concrete. All manner of unspeakable horror befell her before she laid helplessly on the ground in the pile of her blood and vomit.

And yet, she survived. Barely it felt like, but she was standing upright. Then she recalled the fight with Edward. In less than five seconds, he had taken her down. All because she had suggested a change in the plan. Then the image of Edward punching her before the masquerade flashed across her mind.

Paige balled her hands up and punched the mirror, making a web of cracks all the way from the impact to the very edges. But the glass was so strong, it didn't shatter, leaving Paige with a distorted, shattered image of herself.

<u>Video and Audio Transcript Report</u>

Complex: N/A
Location: ███████████ North Dakota Hospital
Camera: 2001
Room: ICU 2001
Date of Transcript: ███████████
Time of Transcript: ███████████

<u>Transcript</u>

[Note: This Transcript has been partially redacted for level 3 access]

subject 001 starts to regain consciousness after being sedated for the previous 28 days. The subject's heart rate increases and a beeping comes from the heart rate monitor. Nurse ██████ turns around from the sink and walks over to subject 001, pressing a button on their heart monitor to stop the beeping.

YT302: Let's get you ready, shall we. You have an important meeting here soon.

The nurse walks over to the counter and presses the 1 button on the comm unit against the wall.

YT98: [Through comm speaker] The General isn't available right now. Would you like to leave a message?

YT302: Tell him subject oh-oh-one has regained consciousness.

6 minutes and 24 seconds elapse before General Johan enters the room. He stops in the doorway as he stares at subject 001.

Gen. Johan: Can he hear me?

YT302: You should be asking whether he'll remember your conversation.

Gen. Johan puts his hands behind his back and walks up to subject 001.

Gen. Johan: You've caused far more trouble than I thought you could. If you were on my side, I would have already congratulated you for your work. How unfortunate it is that we don't see eye to eye.

Gen. Johan glides his right hand over the handle of his pistol, holstered against the back of his belt. He holds it there for several moments, his gaze never leaving subject 001.

YT302: Would you like me to leave, sir?

Gen. Johan holds his sidearm a moment more before releasing it and dropping his hand to clasp the other behind his back.

Gen. Johan: That won't be necessary.

Gen. Johan looks at YT302.

Gen. Johan: Ensure he's fully awake in two days. We want to put on a good show for the police.

YT302: Yes, sir.

Gen. Johan exits the room, clenching his fists behind his back.

End Transcript

Johan sat at the desk in his temporary office at the North Dakota Youth Complex, Complex 4, going over expense reports from all the damage caused by Edward in his manic chase of Calvin and the recruits. The amount of hits alone spanned two pages front and back, putting a serious dent in the Youth budget. As the line items continued, Johan's hate for Edward grew more and more, while his self-hate grew just as much, for giving so much power to Edward so quickly, wishing he had slowly worked Edward up, despite the ability he showed.

Three light dings came from the console on Johan's desk. Still looking at the report, Johan pressed the talk button and said, "Go ahead."

"The police deputy is on the line," said his secretary, "he says it's urgent."

"Put him through." Johan picked up the handset, finding a gravely male voice on the other end.

"We have a problem, sir."

"What now?" Johan closed his eyes and leaned back in his chair.

"We have some nameless on their way to the hospital." A nameless is the code name for someone who has never been introduced to the Youth, and therefore, are not loyal to the Youth.

136

"You told me that wouldn't be a problem?" Johan clenched his free hand.

"The orders came from above me, sir. I tried arguing, but they wouldn't listen."

Johan silently rocked his chair for a moment. "How many?"

"Three."

Johan let out a sigh. "How long until you get here?"

"We leave first thing in the morning."

"Alright, that should give us enough time to put on a good enough show for you."

"Are you sure? I can always—"

"Let's not be rash," said Johan, cutting off the police chief. "We can still control the situation. Let's not needlessly eliminate assets that could be ours one day. How much longer until you become Chief?"

"Just under a year, sir."

"Ok." Johan rocked his chair again. "I'd like a list of the nameless officers with names, badge numbers, pictures, and whatever records you have of their training and evaluations before they arrive."

"I'll have them to you in the next hour."

"Hard copies on this one. I don't want any money going to cover ups right now."

"Of course, I'll get that to you early tomorrow morning."

"Make it so." Johan hung the phone up, slamming it down harder than he wanted.

He sat back in his chair a moment, gathering his thoughts on everything that needed to be done now, before pressing the intercom button to his secretary, "Gather all the ICU leads in fifteen minutes."

<u>Video and Audio Transcript Report</u>

Complex: N/A
Location: ███████████ North Dakota Hospital
Camera: 2000-98
Room: ICU Entrance
Date of Transcript: ███████████
Time of Transcript: ███████████

<u>Transcript</u>

The double door entrance to the ICU opens as Nurse ██████, YT302, walks in with four police officers from the  Police Department.

YT302: And if there's anything else you need, grab any of the nurses and they'll find me.

Police Chief █████: Thank you, nurse.

YT302 walks behind the central counter while the officers head off to interview the patients in the ICU and the hospital staff [for individual interviews with the patients and staff reference transcripts #489753-489787]

201 minutes and 58 seconds elapse when the interviews are concluded. The police officers gather at the entrance to the ICU as YT302 approaches. Police Chief ██████ hands YT302 a business card from his vest pocket.

Police Chief ██████: Here's my number in case you need it. And your staff rotation is this Thursday, correct?

YT302: Correct.

Police Chief ██████: Alright. We'll be back around the same time as today to get the rest of your staff's interviews. Thank you for your cooperation today.

YT302: Of course. We're happy to help the ██████ Police Department.

Police Chief ██████: We appreciate it. Have a good day.

YT302: Have a good day, officers.

YT302 smiles and waves. The officers return the gesture with waves and head nods as they exit the ICU wing.

<u>End Transcript</u>

Johan picked up the phone in his office desk with the police deputy on the line.

"Did I give you enough time?" asked the Deputy.

"Just enough, yes."

"Good. We've been debriefing on the interviews, and none of the officers have noted anything strange or out of the ordinary."

"Let's keep it that way. Are you willing to do what's necessary if they start asking too many questions?"

The deputy hesitated a moment before replying, "Yes, sir."

"Keep up that attitude, and you'll be Chief before you know it."

"Thank you, sir, I won't let you down."

"Yes, I'd hate to lose such a loyal YOUTH." Johan hung the phone up, leaned back, and started rocking his chair with his eyes closed, relieved something finally went right. And it was only a matter of time before all the setbacks Edward had caused would be remedied.

I woke up after what felt like an endless dream. I was walking in a serene valley with a beautiful lake. I slowly made my way around the perimeter, throwing rocks every now and then from a stack in my hand. Every time I'd throw a rock, my gaze would always gravitate to the ripples the rock made. And the longer the dream went on, the bigger the rocks got. They started out as tiny pebbles and grew to about the size of my hands by the time I woke up. But I always had rocks in my hand... no matter how many I threw.

When the fog finally left my eyes, I realized I was in a medical room of some sort in another uncomfortable hospital bed. I tried to scratch my face, but my hands wouldn't move. I sat up to find my hands tied down to the bed and pulling against them, they wouldn't budge. I started freaking out and pulled harder against the straps. Frantically looking around to find something to help, I froze as I looked through the glass door. A Youth stood just outside. All he did was stare at me.

Then a nurse rushed into the room. "Were you ever going to tell me he woke up?" she asked flustered, stepping over beside my bed, pressing various buttons, and looking at the machines next to me. I didn't take my eyes off the Youth until the nurse stepped in between us. "He's not going to hurt you, I promise," she said.

"The last I remember—"

"I won't let them hurt you," the nurse interrupted me. She seemed genuine in her words. "Now, let's get these off you," she said, starting to undo the straps around my hands. As I watched her, I'd steal glances at the Youth, who was still eyeing me, at least with his helmet he was.

When the nurse got the straps undone, I rubbed my wrists, they were red and the skin raw.

"I'm sorry about that," the nurse said, looking at my wrists.

"Why-why is that?" I asked.

Another Youth approached my door and started conversing with the Youth already there. The nurse stepped around the bed so her back was facing the two Youth. She messed with the tubes hooked into my arms as she whispered, "I was against them."

"Why is that?" I whispered back.

"You're not a criminal, but you're being held as one."

"A criminal? What—"

"Quiet," she hissed.

"You told him he was a criminal?" said one of the Youth as he opened the door and both walked through.

The nurse pulled the last tube out of me as she said, "He wanted to know why he was restrained to the bed."

"You were told not to tell any of them," said the same Youth as before.

"And you really believe he would have liked not knowing why he was restrained," said the nurse, turning to the Youth on her right. "Especially when he probably doesn't remember what happened."

Now that I thought of it, I couldn't remember how I got there. But those thoughts were interrupted by the nurse and the Youth arguing.

"You need to follow orders. We don't want another recruitment disaster," said the Youth now staring down at the nurse.

"Don't give her a second chance," said the other Youth, looking down at my arms. "You were told not to remove their restraints." The Youth grabbed the nurse's arm.

"I have a patient to attend to," said the nurse, managing to break free from the Youth's grasp, before both Youth grabbed her arms. "Let me go!" she screamed.

"Hey!" I yelled grabbing for one of the Youth. They swatted my hand away, and one of them let go of the nurse, pulling out their pistol from their thigh holster and pointing it at me.

"Stand down!" the Youth yelled. I slowly raised my hands, realizing it was hard for me to do so, as the nurse screamed being dragged out of the room by the other Youth. Her cries slowly dwindled until they were abruptly cut off.

The Youth holding his gun at me holstered it, walked out of the room and slammed the door closed. He took up the same position outside my door as when I first woke up.

I realized my hands were still in the air, and I dropped them, falling like bricks against the bed. I took a couple giant breaths, feeling like I had just run a marathon as my throat started to become dry. I found a small table next to my bed that had a cup with a straw. My arms felt like they had no strength as I stretched over to grab the cup. I took a sip out of the straw, finding warm water. It was actually nice having something warm on a dry throat.

But I set the cup down in my lap feeling exhausted. I took another sip, this time finishing the cup, and set it back on the table. And before I knew it, I was fast asleep.

The Youth threw the nurse from Calvin's ICU room into the empty storage closet just outside the ICU wing. This was the only room on the floor without a camera that the Youth could monitor. It was a private bathroom that had been converted without Johan's approval. The Youth used it for all manner of heinous acts. Most recently, it had been used for interrogating Youth thought to be Renegades.

After the Renegades broke out Calvin and the other recruits from Complex Red 2, a massive investigation was conducted across the entire YOUTH organization, not just the defense branch of the Youth, looking for anyone with even a hint of unloyalty in any of their ranks.

The nurse covered her nose as she spun around to face the Youth just as he slammed the door shut and locked it. The closet smelled of bile and blood. Stains of various colors covered the walls and floor.

"I'm not a Fallen Youth!" screamed the nurse. The Youth didn't even look at her, instead, contacting the Interrogators through his statscreen. Every facility where Youth were stationed long term had Interrogators on staff. Two could be called up at a moment's notice.

"The Interrogators will find the truth," said the Youth.

The nurse charged the Youth. The two sparred a few moments, the nurse putting up a good fight, before the Youth was able to kick the nurse's leg. As she fell, the Youth grabbed one of her arms, wretched it behind her back, pulled her to her feet, and slammed her into the back wall. A crack tore through the air as the nurse's nose broke against the wall. She cried out, her free hand flailing around trying to get the Youth off her, who held her against the wall. The Youth grabbed her free arm and pinned it to the wall.

"If you aren't a Fallen Youth, why'd you try escaping?" asked the Youth.

"Because," said the nurse strained, "you're being ridiculous." She tried everything she could to escape the Youth's grasp, but she was unsuccessful by the time the door opened and the Interrogators, one boy and girl, walked in. Their clean white clothes in stark contrast to their surroundings. The boy carried a clean silver briefcase, which he held up and removed a pair of handcuffs from inside. He handed them to his partner, who with the Youth's help, was able to put them on the nurse behind her back. The boy set the briefcase on the ground, pulling out two pairs of white medical gloves, handing one to his partner. They both put them on as the boy pulled out a small pin hook from the briefcase. Along the wall were various points to attach items from the Interrogator's arsenal. The Interrogator found a hole about waist height to attach the pin, sliding it in, and twisting until it locked in place. The nurse was shoved over, and the chain of her handcuffs locked into the hook.

She yanked against the hook before stopping, realizing she wasn't going anywhere. "You're making a mistake!" she yelled.

The Youth turned around without a reply and walked out of the room. As he closed the door, he cut off any more of the nurse's cries for help. And as the Interrogators began their work, no one heard the nurse's screams through the soundproof walls.

<u>Video and Audio Transcript Report</u>

Complex: N/A
Location: ███████████████ North Dakota Hospital
Camera: 2000-486
Room: Temporary Office for JYT1 [Part of Johan's Garrison]
Date of Transcript: ████████████
Time of Transcript: ████████████

<u>Transcript</u>

The Interrogator male, YTI047, places a folder on JYT1's desk. The Interrogator female, YTI048, stands just behind her partner.

YTI047: The nurse is a fallen youth, sir. She fell shortly after the Mainframe Compromise, as suspected. She does not claim to know any other fallen youth in this facility, but with further sessions, we expect to yield who else she may know.

JYT1 flips through the folder.

JYT1: What tipped you off to her allegiance?

YTI047: YT267 reports when subject oh-oh-one had regained consciousness, they asked why they were restrained to the bed. Fallen youth 2654 replied that the subject was a prisoner and proceeded to remove their restraints.

JYT1: [To himself] After I directly told them not to answer that way, especially to him.

JYT1 closes the folder.

JYT1: Nice work you two. Get cleaned up.

JYT1 points at the Interrogators' bloodied and dirtied clothes.

JYT1: I'll have a van prepared to take the fallen youth back to Complex 4 for further interrogation. I want you to remain here, though. Understood?

YTI047 & YTI048: Yes, sir.

JYT1: Dismissed.

Both Interrogators stand at attention before turning on their heels and exiting the room.

End Transcript

Video and Audio Transcript Report

Complex: N/A
Location: ████████████ North Dakota Hospital
Camera: 2000-76
Room: 2nd floor elevator terminals
Date of Transcript: ████████████
Time of Transcript: ████████████

Transcript

The elevator security team, made up of Viper Squad, Ember Squad, and Silver Squad, patrol the elevator terminal and the surrounding hallway.

[YT327 is located in the security room of the ████████████ North Dakota Hospital along with YT334.]

YT327: Attention elevator security, we've lost the security feed in elevator one. What are you seeing down there?

YT389: We have movement on elevator one. I don't see us expecting anyone at this time.

YT334: No, we are not expecting anyone at this time. Treat them as hostiles.

YT389: Copy that. Defensive positions!

The elevator security team spread out across the hall. They wait 4.59 seconds before elevator 1 arrives, the light above the door blinking in confirmation. Before the doors open, YT389 yells out:

YT389: Halt! Exit the elevator with your hands above your head!

The elevator doors open as smoke spills out from inside. A thick cloud flows into the hallway.

YT378: Thermals!

All the elevator security team activate their thermal visors.

YT378: I'm not seeing—

Multiple explosions and flashes of light come from inside the elevator.

YT389: Return fire!

The team fires into the elevator for 1.87 seconds before stopping.

YT389 slowly approaches the elevator with his rifle raised.

YT389: Security, lock down this floor.

YT327: Already on it.

YT389 enters the elevator, disappearing into the smoke.

YT389: It's clear. Security, do we have video of anyone entering or exiting the elevator.

YT334: Someone wearing a black hoodie with a black baseball cap, navy jeans, black shoes, and black gloves. Unable to identify sex or skin color at this time.

YT327: Hostile filled the cabin with smoke as soon as the doors closed, halting the movement of the elevator until our cameras couldn't see.

    YT389: The emergency exit! Pry the other door open, and see if they're in the elevator shaft.

    The elevator security team goes to the other two elevator doors and force them open.

    YT378 leans out into the elevator shaft. Looking around, he finally points up the shaft.

    YT378: The door is open on the next floor. Should we pursue?

    YT389: I want one squad to remain here—

    YT373: Viper squad will stay here.

    YT389: Everyone else move!

    The rest of the security team climbs the inside of the elevator shaft in pursuit of the hostile.

End Transcript

The black clad figure sprinted across the third floor, pulling out a small device from their pocket. They pressed a button, and all the security cameras went down. They ran two more steps before spinning around and running back in the direction they came. As they passed the elevator, they pulled a pepper spray grenade from their coat pocket and dropped it in front of the open elevator door, just as one of the Youth started climbing up.

The grenade went off as the black clad figure rounded the corner, and the Youth yelled for everyone to get down. A white plume of smoke began to fill the hallway and creep down the elevator shaft.

"Hold your breath," said the same Youth as he pulled himself up and through the smoke. It wasn't long before the smoke got to the Youth as they passed through it or it reached them in the shaft. Everyone hacking and coughing, their eyes stinging so much they could barely keep them open to see.

The black clad figure pulled the fire alarm, opening all the public doors requiring a key or code. She ran through the door to the wing of the hospital situated above the ICU. Everything was chaos as nurses, patients, and family members scrambled around. Some screaming, some crying, and others in shock.

"I'm sorry," mumbled the figure under her breath. She ran into someone, nearly falling, as she made her way to room 3010. The room was empty and the lights out. She closed and locked the door, the only light coming through the window on the opposite side of the room. Keeping the lights off, she carefully made her way through the room, feeling around the bed until she found the rope. Earlier that day, she had gotten weights from the physical therapy wing of the hospital and loaded as many as she could onto the bed, covering them with a blanket. Along with locking the wheels of the bed, it wasn't going anywhere anytime soon.

Checking the rope was securely tightened on the bed leg one last time, the black clad woman pulled out a small explosive, a little bigger than the size of a quarter, from her zippered pant pocket. One side had adhesive that she stuck to the window. On the other side of the explosive was a single button. She pressed it twice, turning the button red, and ran to duck behind the bed, covering her ears.

The explosion was only a sharp pop, but it shattered all the glass, sending it everywhere. As soon as it had all fallen, the black clad woman grabbed the rope and a blanket. The window was too small to walk through, so she laid the blanket over the window sill. She carefully climbed out, not wanting to put too much weight on any glass under the blanket, and hopped out with the rope

She repelled down the side of the building, her hands the only thing keeping her from the three-story drop. She made her way to the window below, stopping just above it and jumped, letting the rope glide through her gloved hands. As she fell, she tightened her grip again on the rope, swinging back toward the wall and landing against it on her feet. Now she was under the window, taking what rope was left, and tying it around her waist. With her hand free, she took out another small explosive, pressing it twice, and setting it on the window. She threw her head down, and shattered glass rained over her, the hat brim and hood keeping it out of her face.

She shook herself to get any glass off and pulled a pepper spray gun from the back of her belt. Ensuring it was loaded, she used her free hand and pulled herself up toward the window. Inside, the Youth wasn't posted at the door, but another ran past the door in the hallway. The black clad woman ducked down below the window, only to pop her head up and see the Youth entering the room.

She got three shots off, creating a cloud of smoke just in front of the door. The Youth didn't have time to dodge and walked right through the cloud. He waved the cloud away and tried shooting the woman but missed from his watering eyes. The woman risked the opportunity and fired toward the Youth, hitting three shots across his chest. A cloud of smoke enveloped him as the woman climbed through the window.

The Youth backed up as he waved away the smoke, barely able to see now. In one swift motion, the woman climbed inside the window, ran around the smoke, grabbed the Youth's rifle, and kicked him between the legs. The rifle went off once, only hitting the wall, before the woman pulled it out of the Youth's grasp as he fell to the floor. Some of the smoke got to the woman as her eyes started stinging, and she swung the butt of the rifle into the Youth's helmet, swinging a second and a third time before the Youth was on the floor, unmoving.

"Who are you?" asked Calvin, pulling against his restraints.

"I'm here to break you out," said the woman.

"Are you here to break my friends out, too?" I asked the girl as she came over and undid my restraints.

"I'm breaking all of you out."

"Are you one of the..." I hesitated not knowing if she would know what I was about to call her. "Are you one of the Renegades."

"A what?"

"A Renegade. It's what I call the Youth who don't follow Youth anymore."

"Oh, you mean a Fallen Youth." She hesitated a moment before replying, "Yes. It doesn't matter now if they know that."

"A Fallen Youth. Why is that?" I asked, as the girl undid the last restraint.

"I escape with you, or the Youth potentially kill me for breaking you out if I'm caught."

"We'll make sure you escape with us," I said, hopping out of bed, glad for the physical therapy I was told I did, but still couldn't remember any of it. I was also glad I was given a set of clothes to wear instead of the smock, even if they were just PJ's. I pulled on the slippers next to the bed and asked the girl, "Wha-what's your name?"

"Memory. Here, take this." She pulled out a gun from the back of her belt, handing it to me. I carefully took it, pulling out the mag, and finding pepper spray balls inside.

"Don't trust me with real bullets?" I asked, putting the mag back in and stretching my legs, chastising myself for when I floundered the pepper spray gun back at the school and hoping I could actually operate the gun in the heat of the moment.

"I've never seen you shoot before so forgive me if I'm hesitant." Memory took the belt, thigh holster, and rifle from the Youth on the floor.

"What's the plan?" I asked as she headed to the door. I jumped back as bullets tore through the room. Memory cried out and slammed against the wall of the door. She fired off a few shots and threw a grenade. I covered my ears the moment before the bang. Memory popped here head out, shooting a few, and ducked back inside.

"You're shot!" I said, pointing at her bleeding arm.

"It just grazed me. I'm fine."

We heard someone yell, and Memory glanced outside. "Follow me," she said, leaving the room. I stuck my head out of the door to see the commotion, finding Mason on top of a Youth as they fought on the floor; the Youth's gun across the floor from them.

"Stand down!" yelled Memory, pointing her rifle at the Youth.

The Youth managed to flip Mason off him, pinning him down with one hand, and bringing the other hand up to punch him. Memory shot the Youth's arm as it came up, and he fell off Mason, clutching his arm.

Mason scrambled up, grabbing the Youth's rifle, smashing the butt across his helmet three times, bits and pieces scattered as it broke and the Youth slumped to the floor.

"Get everyone into that room." Memory pointed to a room diagonal from mine.

"Where is everyone?" I asked.

"In these rooms." She pointed to the rooms on the outside of the hallway starting with mine and ending with the one she just told us to gather everyone in.

"Here," said Mason, taking a knife off the Youth he just knocked out, handing it to me, handle first.

"Thanks." I headed toward the room next to mine. I burst through the door and found Thomas strapped to the bed.

"Calvin!" he yelled as I started cutting his restraints.

"Thomas, are you ok?" I asked.

"Yeah, I'm good. What's going on?"

"We're getting out of here."

"How did you escape?"

"One of the Fallen Youth helped us." I cut the last restraint, pulling Thomas out of bed. "Nice PJ's," I said, and we both laughed before hugging.

"Can you walk?" I asked, holding his arm.

"Give me a second." Thomas stretched his legs before taking a step. "I think I'm good."

I let go of his arm and watched him take a step before going to the door, checking both ways for any Youth, and heading to the next room.

Inside, Megan was trying to pull herself out of her restraints. "Calvin!" she screamed the second we came in the door. "What's going on out there? They aren't going to kill us, are they?"

"We're not going to let that happen," I said, cutting her restraints off. Megan started crying, and her body relaxed as she stopped trying to escape.

"Now's not the time to cry, Megan." I handed Thomas my knife, who was on the opposite side of the bed, and cut the rest of Megan's restraints.

As soon as Thomas finished, Megan pulled me into a hug as she cried into my shoulder. Gunfire came from outside the room, and Megan bolted up to see where it was coming from, still holding onto me. I turned my head and saw Memory run down the hall away from the room we were to meet at.

"Hey," I said, turning back around to look at Megan. I wiped some of her tears away and said, "We're not out of this yet, come on."

As I helped Megan out of bed, footsteps came running up and stopped behind me. "Get her up, they're almost here," said Mason.

"Can you walk?" I asked Megan just before a bullet hit the door, shattering the glass. I whipped around to find Mason squatted down firing back toward where the shot came from. Megan covered her ears as she dropped to the ground.

After a few shots, Mason stood up and waved us through the door. "Move, move, move!"

I pulled Megan up and ran through the door, Thomas right on our heels. Glancing down the hall where Mason was shooting, Youth lay scattered near a set of double doors. I quickly turned away and headed toward our meeting room.

Inside it was just another room like ours. The window, however, looked out on the roof of the first story. A moment later, Mason ran in followed by Cody, Dakota, Ash, and Memory.

Mason noticed me looking through the glass wall by the door. "They're not dead, Calvin," he said. "Remember, bullet proof armor?"

He slapped me on the arm as Memory said, "Stand back," pushing her way through us to get in front of the exterior window before shooting it. I covered my ears as the shot rang out and the glass shattered. "Ash, follow the wall around the building. You'll find a pack with our rendezvous location."

Ash started making her way to the window, grabbing a blanket on the way.

"Wait!" cried Megan, "where's my mom?" She frantically looked around.

"They didn't bring her here," said Memory. "Now get—"

Mason fired out the door and stepped back into the room. "Get going," he yelled. Cody helped Ash place the blanket on the windowsill.

Megan cried out again, "But she—"

"She's not here," said Cody, grabbing Megan's arm and pulled her toward the window.

"No! Let go of me." Megan tried to escape Cody's grasp as he climbed through the window after Ash. "Calvin!" she looked back at me.

"If she's not here, she's not here," I said, walking up to Megan and nudging her forward.

"But, Calvin—"

"We don't have time."

Mason started firing again and yelled, "Pull her through, Cody."

Cody pulled Megan who resisted before I pushed her, forcing her to climb through. Mason and Memory were both firing out the door now.

"Thomas!" I yelled at him and motioned to the window. Dakota was right behind him, and they both climbed out.

"You're not going to make it," said Memory.

"We can make it!" cried Mason.

"You won't make it off the roof, now go!" Memory ran out across the hall into the central area of the ICU wing, crouching behind a counter.

Bullets started flying toward us, breaking the glass wall as Mason and I dropped to the floor, stumbling up and running toward the window. Mason dove through and didn't touch any of the edges. As cool as it was,

I had to stop myself from trying the same, instead, climbing through the window, taking off after Mason across the roof.

"Stay as close to the wall as you can," said Mason as we sprinted after everyone. When we turned the corner, the rest of the group had stopped behind an HVAC unit, at least what I thought was one. Cody was digging through a bag on the ground and pulled out a rifle.

"Get down!" yelled Cody, looking at us as he fired back toward our escape window. Mason and I slid to a stop behind a different HVAC unit as bullets ripped across the roof. I looked down at Cody, who had his gun pointed up in the air, completely away from the window. It wasn't until he pulled the trigger and there wasn't a bang that I realized it must have been a pepper spray rifle.

"I can't reach inside, Mason!" yelled Cody, "you have to take them out."

Mason raised his rifle and leaned out from behind our cover. I covered my ears as Mason fired and quickly ducked back, bullets spraying the ground around us.

"Switch spots," said Mason. I scooted over, and he fired again, this time getting off far more shots before having to duck back.

"One left!" called Cody.

"Switch again," said Mason.

After four more shots, Cody yelled, "You're clear!"

Mason bolted up and sprinted toward the rest of the group. I chased after him, my body was already aching. I gasped down air as I sprinted toward the edge of the roof. Everyone was going down an emergency escape ladder. Mason disappeared just as I arrived at the ladder. I spun around and climbed down, the cage surrounding the ladder gave me extra reassurance as I descended to the parking lot below.

Mason was waiting for me when I made it to the bottom. "Follow everyone to the red semi," he said, pointing to the bright red semi with a green trailer on the far edge of the parking lot, way too far away.

"Oh boy," I said, taking a breath, my body ached even more than before. I took off following Thomas, who ran from car to car crouching behind each one. We played this game about halfway through the parking lot before a cloud of white smoke exploded on the car next to me. Then another, and another on the opposite side of me.

"Run," screamed Mason, "get out of their firing range!" He came out of nowhere behind me, picking me up by my arm as I was still crouched behind a car, pulling me after him until he let go, and I ran on my own.

Clouds of smoke popped up everywhere around us, we weaved through the cars trying to make it harder for them to hit us. That was until a cloud burst off a car in front of Mason, and he ran right through it. I halted to a stop and went around the car as Mason kept charging forward. I heard him yell, and when I caught up to him, he was wiping his eyes.

"Are you ok, Mason?" I asked.

"I'm fine," he replied before running into a mirror of a car.

"Here, follow me," I said, grabbing his arm and leading him through the cars.

A few rows of cars later their shots stopped reaching us, so we stopped weaving around the cars and headed straight for the semi.

The cars thinned out the further we ran, and as we approached the semi, everyone started going up a platform on the back of the trailer.

"Run, Calvin!" yelled Thomas.

"The cloud's going to get you!" screamed Dakota. I looked behind me to find a massive white cloud moving with the wind, directly toward me. It was all the pepper spray the Youth had shot at us.

"You gotta run, Mason," I said, running as fast as my aching body would let me.

"I can't see!" yelled Mason.

"Just run!" I didn't look back at the cloud to see how close it was, Thomas's face was all I needed to know it was on our heels.

The ramp to the trailer lifted all the way up, and Cody pulled the rolling door up. Everyone was gathered on the edge of the platform, hands out ready to pull us up.

"I can see now!" yelled Mason, shaking my arm away. We sprinted side by side, giving it everything we had. Mason pulled ahead of me slightly, making it to the platform first. He jumped, Dakota and Thomas pulling him up. I was just behind him. Trying to be like Mason, I jumped, slamming into the platform, and knocking the wind out of me. I should have jumped more up instead of forward. Either way, Cody and Ash pulled me up, dragging me inside the trailer as Dakota pulled the door down. Before it closed, I could see the cloud of pepper spray barreling toward us, reaching us just as the door slammed shut, and the trailer descended into darkness.

"Where's the light?" asked Dakota.

"Hold on," said Ash, "nobody move." Ash gently set me down as I panted, unable to move. Laying on the floor of the trailer, I could feel the vibrations from Ash's footsteps.

"I think some of it got in," said Dakota before coughing. A moment later, bright white lights turned on above me. I put my hand up to cover my eyes as they adjusted to the light.

"Away from the door," said Ash. Before I could catch my breath and sit up, I was dragged further inside the trailer. Dakota kept coughing, and when I could finally sit up, I saw a faint haze near the trailer door.

As I took a look around the trailer, I found I was sitting right next to a go-kart.

"Awesome!" said Dakota, having stopped coughing and eyeing the same go-kart I was.

"Everyone eat one of these, quick," said Ash. I spun around as Ash threw something at me. I caught it and found what looked like a small granola bar. In very basic red text on top of the wrapper was printed POWER BAR, and below that in smaller text was printed WARNING: ONLY CONSUME ONE BAR EVERY SIX HOURS.

160

I ripped the packaging off and took a bite. It tasted like those bland cereals. There was no flavor at all, and it left a chalky after-taste.

"This tastes horrible," said Dakota.

"Just eat it," said Ash.

"I can force feed him if we need to," said Thomas, grinning at Dakota.

"That's disgusting," said Dakota, taking the rest of the bar and shoving it in his mouth.

"Grab your vest when you're done," said Ash, pulling a black bullet proof vest from a crate.

"Need some help," said Thomas, walking over and offering his hand. He pulled me to my feet, and we grabbed a vest, quickly throwing it on.

"Cover your ears," said Ash. I spun around to find her leaning over one of the go-kart engines. Thomas and I covered our ears as the engines roared to life, echoing throughout the trailer. Our fingers didn't do much to stop the noise as Cody started another go-kart, and Mason started the last two. Megan stood there in shock, her uneaten power bar still clutched between her fingers.

"Megan," I said, walking up and shaking her slightly.

She blinked and looked up at me. "Yeah," she said weakly.

"We're not out of this yet, come on," She nodded and followed me.

Four karts were lined up single file in the trailer. Each kart was a two-seater, the seats facing back-to-back. With the engine between them. In front of the back seat was what looked like a long barreled gun sticking straight up.

"Calvin, you'll be my gunner," yelled Ash over the engines, pointing to the back of the third kart. "Thomas, you'll be Dakota's gunner." She pointed to the second cart. Mason looked at Ash like he was unhappy about the decision but didn't rebuttal and took the first kart, pulling Megan into the gunner seat of his kart while Cody took the last cart all by himself.

"How do we operate this gun?" asked Thomas, hesitantly.

"Pull it down, rack the slide, and pull the trigger," said Ash, making her way to the door.

"Do we have to kill them?" Thomas asked me.

"I don't think you can." I pointed to the line of ammo coming from the gun. "It's pepper spray balls."

"That makes me feel better," said Thomas, relaxing a bit and heading to his seat. I got in my seat as Ash was asking for thumbs up from everyone. I put my seat belt on and pulled the gun down, locking the barrel when it was fully seated horizontal to the ground. I tried out the range of motion, turning it from side to side and even up and down slightly, realizing after the fact I had pointed it right at Cody behind me.

I turned around as Ash pointed to me with a thumbs up. I gave her one back, and she counted down on her fingers from three. On one, she leaned down and yanked the trailer door open.

Mason's tires squealed as he took off, flying out of the door and crashing to the ground. Surprisingly, his kart kept going. Ash sprinted back to our kart as Dakota took off. I could see the shock on Thomas's face as he flew forward in his seat.

Ash jumped in her seat and floored it, not even putting on her seat belt. I flew forward and braced myself against the gun. Cody followed close behind as we jumped out of the trailer, hitting the ground with a bone shattering crash.

We set off toward the back of the parking lot, heading onto a connecting side road. There were a group of Youth running toward us, a few stopping after they saw us to look back toward the hospital as a garage door opened. Inside I could make out a few motorcycles and a van.

"You see them, Calvin!" yelled Ash over the wind whipping around us.

"I see them!" I yelled back.

"Get ready to fire."

I grabbed both handles on the back of the gun, my hand over the thumb button that I assumed would activate the gun as Cody passed us and shot up to the front of our group

"What's he doing!" I yelled at Ash.

"He doesn't have a gunner!" she replied.

I watched Cody a second longer before turning back around, realizing I was the only one between us and the Youth. We took a turn, and I lost sight of them. A few moments later, five motorcycles came around the corner. I pressed the thumb button, and a stream of pepper spray balls rocketed toward the Youth. They easily dodged the first few shots until I figured out the aiming and range of the gun, then I started making shots.

At first, I only hit their bikes, which had little to no effect on any of the Youth.

"Aim for the head, Calvin!" yelled Ash as we took another turn.

I anticipated them coming around the turn and fired before they were there. I got a Youth right in the chest as he turned the corner, losing control of the bike and swerving off the road. He crashed into a chain link fence and flew over it.

"Nice shot, Calvin!" yelled Ash.

The Youth replied with returning fire. Ash swerved just in time to miss a shot, a cloud of smoke bursting on the ground beside us. More followed as Ash swerved back and forth across the road.

"Are you going to fire back?" yelled Ash.

"I can't aim when you're swerving everywhere!" I yelled back.

Clouds of smoke started bursting around the Youth as Thomas and Dakota slowed down and pulled up beside us.

"Need some help?" yelled Dakota.

Ash stopped swerving, and the Youth stopped firing, letting Thomas and I both fire back, taking down three more Youth.

With two Youth left, one of them swerved from our side of the road to the opposite side of the road, firing at something that wasn't us. I turned around to look at what the Youth was firing at when I saw a car in the opposite lane swerving toward us.

Ash yanked the wheel as we missed the car and jumped the curb, fishtailing through the grass before hitting a tree.

I blacked out for a moment on impact, and once I got my bearings back, turned around to make sure Ash was ok, only to find her not in her seat. Looking around and not seeing her, I unbuckled myself and found her behind the tree, face down on the ground.

"Ash," I yelled, running over to her, flipping her over to find her vest had taken the brunt of the impact. "Ash, Ash. Come on, wake up," I said, shaking her and brushing the dirt off her face. Her eyes fluttered open as she groaned, "Calvin?"

Something zipped past my ear. I locked up to find one of the Youth barreling toward us on his motorcycle. A cloud of smoke exploded in front of us, so I quickly dragged Ash to cover, lying her up against the tree facing away from the Youth.

I grabbed the gun in the back of the kart and went to fire at the Youth, but it wouldn't rotate far enough over. I picked up the back of the kart and rotated it so the gun could face him as smoke clouds burst all around me. It wasn't as heavy as I would have thought, but it still took everything in me to move it, especially as the shots got to me, and I started coughing. As soon as I thought the gun was in range, I dropped the kart and fired, my face now on fire.

E.E. Cooley

Multiple shots hit the Youth in the chest just before he reached us, causing him to swerve at the last moment. I dived away from the kart as the bike went the opposite way into the tree, spinning and flipping multiple times before stopping a way behind me. I cautiously sat up, not seeing the Youth near the bike. I quickly scanned the area, finding him standing up and running right toward me. But not to me, for his gun laying on the ground between us. I glanced at the gun on the kart, and it wouldn't reach the Youth. I darted up and raced the Youth to his gun.

He got to it first, but as he brought it up, I slammed my shoulder into him. We both tumbled to the ground as my shoulder exploded in pain. I shook it off, getting to my feet, and running back toward the Youth. He shot me in the shoulder, a cloud bursting all around me. I immediately started coughing, and I had to close my eyes to keep the sting at bay. I tumbled to the ground, wiping my eyes to no avail as another shot hit my chest. I got on all fours and started hacking and coughing, unable to see anything.

"You really caused us all this trouble," said the Youth, sounding slightly mechanical through his helmet speaker, "and yet here you are, wallowing on the ground after only two shots. You're pathetic."

"I'm—" I tried saying before coughing. "I'm—" I couldn't get any words out without coughing. I tried once more to the same result.

"I thought I heard you had a stutter," the Youth started chuckling. "I'd kick you, but you're not even worth that."

I was finally able to open my eyes, only to squint them as they filled with water, and looked up at the Youth.

"Is that all you got?"

A cloud exploded against the Youth's back, then another, and another. "Run, Calvin!" screamed Ash.

I crawled away as a cloud began to form around the Youth. I wiped the water from my eyes and saw Ash on the kart gun shooting the Youth over and over again. My eyes started to water again, and I couldn't see her, but I could see the big white cloud that formed around the Youth. He tried moving away, but Ash kept laying into him, and the cloud grew bigger. I crawled further away as the cloud started drifting, and I started hacking again. Eventually, the Youth was consumed by the cloud, but I could hear him coughing up a storm. He even threw his helmet out of the cloud. It rolled over near me as he walked out of the cloud blind. His hands up trying to feel his surroundings as every hole on his face had something

164

coming out of it.

I felt a tug on my arm and found Ash pulling me up. "Can you see?" she asked.

"Barely—" I coughed out.

She guided me toward the kart, at least that's what I thought until I heard running water. "Bend down," she said guiding my head. She splashed water all over my face, and immediately I felt better. As the water drained from my face and my vision returned, I found myself next to a water fountain. We were near a playground where I could see everyone running back off toward their cars. "Can you see now?" asked Ash. My vision started to get better, and I stopped coughing, but my face still burned.

"Yeah, yeah." I sputtered and coughed once more.

"Come on." Ash took off sprinting toward the kart. I followed, passing the Youth who was still blind, now crawling around on the ground.

"Put-put your seat belt on this time," I said, hopping into the kart.

"Yeah," said Ash flooring it. The gun was still facing up so I could sit down, and as I flew forward from the acceleration, my head hit the gun.

"Ow!" I yelled out, putting my hand over my head.

"You ok?" asked Ash.

"Yeah, I'm fine." I put my seat belt on and lowered the gun.

As we came to the road, Thomas and Dakota were headed toward us. They stopped on the road, and we pulled up next to them on the sidewalk.

"You guys alright?" asked Thomas.

"We're good," I said.

"That was pretty cool how you took down that Youth," said Dakota.

"Cool." I hesitated. "I don't know if-if cool's the right word."

"Don't sell yourself short," said Ash. "Has anyone seen Mason or Cody?"

"Right there," pointed Thomas down the street where we had come from. They stopped next to Dakota and Thomas's kart.

"Where have you been?" asked Ash.

"Taking care of the van full of Youth," said Mason, pointing his thumb behind himself.

"And you didn't invite me?" said Dakota, "Come on."

"I could have used you. My gunner needs some practice," he said without looking at Megan.

"Sorry," she said shrinking.

"Follow us to the safe house," said Mason, taking off down the street as we all followed.

Finally able to take a breath, I thought back to everything that had just happened in about the last half hour, though it felt longer. I never saw myself jumping out of a hospital window and climbing down their fire escape. I'm sure my dad would have loved to be with me then. We'd always talked about going on adventures. I'm sure he's jealous I got to do something cool and dangerous without him.

And then I remembered the girl who got us out. In the chaos of everything, I didn't realize she hadn't made it out with us.

"Ash!" I yelled, turning around.

"Yeah?"

"The girl that-that helped us escape, Memory, do-do you think she made it out?"

Ash was quiet a moment before replying, "I don't know."

"Does she know where we're going?"

"If she's the one that gave us the map, yes."

"What map?"

"The map from the bag on the roof, Cody has it." Ash pointed to him.

"Where are we going?"

"I'm not quite sure. It was just an address."

I slowly turned around, saying a prayer that the girl was able to escape. And if not, that she'd be able to escape. I didn't talk the rest of the ride as we rode the outskirts of whatever city we were in. The Youth never catching us the entire way.

Video and Audio Transcript Report

Complex: N/A
Location: ███████████ North Dakota Hospital
Camera: 2008
Room: ICU 2008
Date of Transcript: ███████████
Time of Transcript: ███████████

Transcript

Various Investigator Youth [IY] take pictures, lay down evidence cones, and investigate the ICU where the fallen youth escaped out the window.

IY37: [To IY36] Finding any prints?

IY36: A few so far.

IY36 pulls a print off the floor as IY37 takes a picture of a bullet next to evidence cone 3 [refer to photos in evidence file 3286].

JYT1 enters room. Everyone in the room stands at attention facing JYT1.

JYT1: At ease. What have we found?

IY36: Lethal rounds appear to have been used by the fallen youth and the Youth who were stationed here. None of the fallen youth appear to be injured based off current evidence. We've currently swept half the rooms for prints, and as soon as we're done will verify with the security footage who escaped.

JYT1: Very good—

JYT4 enters the room.

JYT4: Sir, we believe we have the Youth who assisted in the breakout.

JYT1: Back to work.

JYT1 turns, walking with JYT4 out of the room.

JYT1: Take me to them.

End Transcript

Video and Audio Transcript Report

Complex: N/A
Location:  North Dakota Hospital
Camera: 2000-98
Room: ICU Entrance
Date of Transcript:
Time of Transcript:

Transcript

YT448 kneels on the ground, handcuffed behind her back, JYT12 and JYT16 beside her and YT9 behind her. YT448 keeps her head down as JYT1 and JYT4 approach.

JYT1: [To JYT4] Where did you find her.

JYT4 motions to the Youth surrounding YT448.

JYT4: According to them, she exited the room of the escape, ████████████████████████████

JYT1 looks down at YT448.

JYT1: Where are they going?

YT448 doesn't move.

JYT1: You can join your friend with the Interrogators, or you can tell me now.

YT448: I don't know where they're going.

JYT1 kicks YT448 in the stomach. She falls forward, gasping.

JYT1: We both know that's a lie. Take her to the Interrogators.

The three Youth surrounding YT448 pick her up, dragging her out of the ICU wing.

JYT1 looks at his statscreen to view a message from Johan [Refer to statscreen file JYT1-4579087 for message].

JYT1: Johan's requested me. Find Kyle [JYT2] and tell him he's in charge till I get back.

JYT4: On it, sir.

JYT1 exits the ICU while JYT4 goes the opposite way.

End Transcript

Johan sat at his desk, reading through the After Action Report of the recruitment failure, Operation Growing Allegiance, from Edward, who sits on a couch to the side of the room near the door; wearing a prison jumpsuit while two prison guards stand next to him.

The intercom in the desk lightly dinged three times, and Johan pressed the talk button on the edge of the desk, "Yes?" he asked.

"Marcus is here to see you, sir," said Johan's secretary from the waiting room outside.

"Send him in." Johan thumbed off the intercom and closed the folder of the After Action Report.

Marcus, Johan's #1 personal Youth, designated JYT1, opened the door, saluting his general while holding his helmet in his opposite hand.

"At ease," said Johan, saluting back and walking around his desk. "As you are aware, we only retained two of our six initial recruits from Project Endeavor. After reviewing all the data available to me, I have decided that you, Edward, are unfit to make any more decisions on recruits in your current state, even as an adviser."

Edward clawed his fingers into the couch, gritting his teeth behind his lips.

"From this point forward, Marcus will take over Project Endeavor while you remain in solitary confinement for three months on the aguapan diet. Before that though, I expect you to bring Marcus up to speed with everything you've done and your shortcomings with the first group of recruits. Understood?"

"Yes, sir," said Edward, clearly holding back his anger.

"I expect a report in ten days on your progress, Marcus, understood?"

"Yes, sir."

"Dismissed." Johan walked back around his desk, sat down and continued reading the file from before while Edward and Marcus filed out of the room, Edward flanked by his escorts and hate apparent all over his body.

<u>Video and Audio Transcript Report</u>

Complex: 4
Camera: 49876
Room: 7-3
Date of Transcript:
Time of Transcript:

<u>Transcript</u>

[Note: This Transcript has had redactions removed for level 5 access]

General Edward with his escort, and General Marcus [JYT1] exit General Johan's waiting room. JYT1 walks out and to the right while Gen. Edward stops as his escort closes the door and looks at JYT1.

Gen. Edward: Being Johan's number one and

getting promoted wasn't enough for you?

JYT1 stops and turns around.

JYT1: You did this to yourself, Edward.

Gen. Edward: Even though my plans failed, I remedied the after effects.

JYT1: At too great a cost.

Gen. Edward: You would rather subject oh-oh-one and the other fallen youth still be out plotting their next move? We had them.

JYT1: We had them in a public space, Edward!

JYT1 walks toward Edward.

Gen. Edward: That we controlled.

Gen. Edward walks to meet JYT1 while his escort stays by the door watching the confrontation.

JYT1: We controlled a floor.

JYT1 stops inches from Gen. Edward.

JYT1: Don't deny we didn't have adequate control of the building.

Gen. Edward: We had enough control we could have snuck them out if need be.

JYT1: With as many witnesses in that hospital? You would have not only stalled our plan but put us in debt to ensure we were covered by pulling a stunt like that.

Gen. Edward: You only doubt my plan because one group of recruits got away.

JYT1: I know you have no self-awareness of the effects your actions have. You would have been far better to kill the nameless first responders than let them take everyone away. It would have been far less hassle to make it look like the first responders died in the line of duty then having to deal with what you got us into.

Gen. Edward: You would have had a problem ten times what you do now if I hadn't gotten us here.

JYT1: You made it ten times worse. How do you not see that?

Gen. Edward swings toward JYT1's face, who

blocks and steps back. The two move down the hallway fighting, Edward's escorts unmoving. After 22.4 seconds JYT1 lands a punch on Gen. Edward's stomach, who doubles over before narrowly dodging a knee to the head. Swinging around he tackles JYT1, pushing him against the wall before immediately being thrown off. JYT1 gets three punches in and shoves Edward to the floor. Taking a step back, JYT1 pulls out his sidearm, pointing it at Gen. Edward as he starts to get up.

JYT1: Stand down!

Gen. Edward hugs his stomach and kneels on one knee, eyeing JYT1. After 9.6 seconds Gen. Edward sits down. JYT1 holds his sidearm out for 2.6 seconds before holstering it and turning around. walking back the way he originally went.

The escorts pick Edward up under the arms, pulling him up and dragging him a few steps before he gets his feet under him and starts walking, the escorts still holding him as they head back to the prison.

<u>End Transcript</u>

I had been watching the garage door for the last twenty minutes waiting for Memory to arrive. We were inside an old warehouse that had been converted into a safe house, and a big one at that. But I didn't care about what the safehouse had, I was more concerned for Memory.

"She didn't make it, Calvin," said Mason as he passed by.

"If she's anything like you, she could have made it," I said without peeling my eyes away from the door. We were told to stay away from all the windows to prevent a street camera or patrolling Youth from seeing us, so all I could do was look at the door and pray it opened.

"I know she didn't make it, Calvin," said Mason more adamantly. "With as many Youth as we saw, even I couldn't have made it out."

"And God continues to defy the impossible and-and make it possible," I said, crossing my arms. "Look at us now."

"We made it this far without God," said Mason as I heard him walking off, "Memory is going to need a lot more than God to get her out.

I balled my fists and turned around wanting to yell at Mason. But I stopped, realizing my rebuttal would be pointless. But then I got a different idea. "We have to go back for her then."

"We need to regroup and rest, and none of us are in any condition to mount a rescue mission."

"Which is why they wouldn't expect it. While they chase—"

"Enough, Calvin!" yelled Mason, spinning around. "You're going to get yourself killed if you go back in there."

"And she isn't?"

"We'll go back for her, Calvin," said Ash walking up to us, "just not right now."

"We can't—"

"Enough!" yelled Mason. "You're too naive and innocent with thoughts of grandeur you've conjured up from all the movies and books you've seen. If you go back to save her by yourself, you're dead. There's no writer to save you and no Deus ex machina. And even if they don't immediately kill you, the Youth will make your last moments as miserable and inhumane as possible."

"Are you done yet?" Ash put her hands on her hips.

In a much quieter and more threatening voice, Mason said, "You don't leave or you risk revealing our location and getting us all killed. Do you want that on your Christian conscious?" Mason turned around and walked off.

"Let's not have this go on anymore," said Ash, stopping me as I stepped toward Mason.

"And why is that?" I asked still eyeing Mason.

"I understand, Calvin, I do." Ash stepped across my line of sight. "I want to go back for her, too, but not like this. We're not prepared for it. We'd end up right back where we were, and I know you don't want that."

I accepted her point and took a step back.

"We will go back for her, Calvin, we just want to make sure we do our best to ensure it actually happens."

"You're right." I turned around, putting my hands on my hips.

"It's noble what you want to do, Calvin." Ash put a hand on my shoulder.

"Which means squat if-if you don't actually do it."

"Not at all, because I know you'd run out that door and do everything you could to save Memory. But you also value the lives of your friends and don't want to risk their lives unnecessarily. I wish I had the same spirit as you."

"You do?" I turned around and looked Ash in the eyes.

She nodded and took her hand off my shoulder. "The Youth have brainwashed us so much that blind faith is gone from all of us. We make tactical and emotionless decisions, nothing but facts and numbers. If it doesn't pass — that's it, doesn't go."

I let her words sit in my brain for a while. I walked away from her as connections were made, raking a hand through my hair as I asked, "So how do our parents fit into your facts and numbers?"

Ash slowly took a step toward me. "The Youth killed my parents, at least that's what I've been told. I never got the opportunity you did to save them. So, if we can do that, and destroy the Youth while we're at it, that fits right in line."

"That sounds more emotional than-than it does logical."

"Their brainwashing didn't work on everyone." Ash grinned at me.

I grinned back, keeping my hands on my hips.

"Oh," concern spread across Ash's face, "Calvin, your head."

"What?" I asked, feeling around my head, finding a cut.

"I didn't realize it was that bad." Ash walked up and moved my hand as she examined it, pushing my head down to see it better. "Let's get you cleaned up."

"I'm fine, it's not even bleeding."

"We're not arguing about this either, come on." Ash grabbed my arm and led me toward a set of stairs that led to a mezzanine.

"Do I get—"

"Nope."

"Not even—"

"Nope, the nurse is in charge now."

"It's not that bad," I said, sitting down at the kitchen table.

"You have a gash the size of my thumb on your forehead," said Ash, sitting on the table top cleaning out my wound.

"My body will heal on its own."

"And I'm here to help it heal quicker." Ash grabbed something out of her bag. "This is going to sting."

"If you're using—ow!"

"I'm cleaning it with alcohol." Ash grinned.

"Not every wound needs cleaned out like this."

"Well, this is one of them that does. Do you really want a scar?"

"Who-who says I wasn't looking forward to a scar?"

Ash stopped working and put her hands on her hips. "Are you telling me you want a scar that says 'I didn't have my seat belt on and hit my head on a gun?'"

"A gun I used to save us."

Ash started laughing. "It doesn't matter if you saved us or the entire world. When people ask you how you got that scar, you can't say 'because I didn't have my seat belt on.'"

"We'll just leave that part out," I said, waving my hand dismissively.

Ash continued to laugh as she started her work again. We sat there in silence with grins on our faces until she finished.

"There we go," she said, putting her tools in her bag.

"Thank you," I said, feeling the dressing.

"You are very welcome. Oh, one more thing." Ash leaned over and kissed me on the cheek.

I sat there dumbfounded for a second before replying, "What, um, what-what was that for?"

"A thank you... for saving me."

"You are, um, very-very welcome."

Ash giggled. "Looks like I owe you one." She started peeling her gloves off, balling them up and throwing them in the trash can by the door.

"Nice shot," I said as they hit the bottom of the can.

"Thanks." Ash hopped off the table and grabbed her bag. "Will you walk with me?"

"Of course," I said as Ash offered her hand and pulled me up out of my chair.

"That seemed harder than it should have," I said, a little wobbly as I followed Ash out of the room.

"That energy bar you took is wearing off."

"How long does it last?" I glanced down at my watch, forgetting I didn't have one anymore.

"About six hours depending on your body."

"That's not very long," I said as we exited the kitchen to the right. I immediately grabbed the handrail and glanced out over the warehouse.

"You can do a lot in that time depending on how motivated you are."

"Fair point."

Ash stopped outside the door to the boys' bunk and spun around to face me. She glanced at me holding the rail before asking, "Do you need help getting to your bed?"

"You-you probably have to ask that don't you?"

"As the team medic, it *is* my duty to ensure the well-being of those I'm working with."

"Even if it's ten steps away?" I said, pointing toward the bunk room.

"Even if it's ten steps."

We grinned at each other.

"I think I'll manage, but thank you. If you hear a crash though, it's probably me, and you are more than welcome to come help."

Ash laughed, unzipping her hip pockets and putting her hands inside. "Ok then, just make sure I don't have to patch you up all over again."

"If it ends the same way this one did..."

Ash chuckled before walking back toward the kitchen. She stopped right next to me, our shoulders nearly touching as she looked up at me. "Get some rest." She hit my arm with her elbow and grinned. "You deserve it." She slowly walked off.

I stood there with the biggest grin on my face before I turned around and asked, "Wait!" Ash stopped, keeping her hands in her pockets as she spun around. "If you saved me before we got on the train and-and I saved you before we got here, wouldn't that, um, mean we're even?"

Ash pursed her lips and looked down a moment before looking back up. "It does appear you are correct. But why don't we say I still owe you one."

"And why is that?"

Ash smiled. Even dirtied and bruised, she still managed to look cute as she spun around and walked away.

I stood there grinning, again, and dumbfounded, again, for what felt like an eternity watching Ash walk back to the kitchen. When she entered, I pushed myself off the railing and made my way to the closest bed in the bunk room. Thomas and Dakota were crashed on two beds next to each other, both on the bottom bunk.

I was glad they were asleep, as I'm sure I would have been the talk of the town, or more appropriately, the talk of the bunk, with all the flirting Ash and I were doing. Something I'm sure Dakota would try to explain to Thomas.

As I fell into bed, I didn't have the energy to take my shoes off. The second my head hit the pillow, my eyes were closed. I clasped my hands together across my chest, and before I knew it, I was asleep. Before I succumbed to my tiredness though, my thoughts were on Ash. It hadn't fully set in yet that a girl was flirting with me. More importantly, that I was flirting back.

You would think that when your parents had been taken by a maniacal teenage soldier, getting them back would be at the front of your mind. I barely knew this girl, and she was already taking up more rent in my head than she needed. I didn't even know if she was a Christian. Before I knew it, I was swimming in my thoughts; from Ash, my parents, the Youth, and by some miracle, I was able to fall asleep despite the chaos in my mind.

Dakota walked up and stopped next to Thomas holding a bag of chips. All of us but Mason stood in a circle around a table in the middle of the safe house's main floor.

"We just had breakfast?" said Thomas, eyeing the bag of chips. After we had woken up and had some food, we had been instructed to wait downstairs for our orders, hopefully to find our parents again.

"That was a tiny breakfast," said Dakota.

"I got full from that meal, and that normally never happens," said Thomas.

"A tiny person getting filled by a tiny meal, what did you expect?" said Dakota through a mouthful of chips.

Everyone started laughing.

"Did you just call me tiny?"

"T-I-N-E-Y. Tiny"

"T-I-N-Y," I jumped in.

"Close enough," said Dakota.

"I am skinny," said Thomas, pointing at himself.

"Skinny, tiny, scrawny. All the same."

"A mouse in tiny. Do I look tiny to you?"

"If I squint really hard," said Dakota, squinting, "you just look like a tailless mouse."

"Sorry I'm late," said Mason, walking up to the table, throwing down a stack of manila envelopes and stopping any rebuttal from Thomas.

"What do ya got, Mason?" I asked.

"Grab a folder, we need to make this quick," he said, opening his own folder. We all grabbed one, flipping open to a skew of papers, pictures, and diagrams. "Inside you'll find Operation Turbulence. This is the first official operation for us. For those of you that have been waiting for this day, I'm glad to be sharing it with you."

"Who do you mean by us?" asked Dakota, finishing up his chips, crumpling the bag, and shoving it in his pocket. The annoyance clear on Mason's face.

"All of us opposing the YOUTH."

"That's too long of a name. Don't tell me you haven't come up with a name for yourselves?"

"We were more concerned with keeping ourselves hidden from the YOUTH," said Mason with spite. "This isn't a band."

"But you have to have a name to get behind. Every war has sides with distinct names."

"We don't have time for naming. Do you want to know the plan or not?"

"I agree with Dakota on this one," I chimed in. Everyone turned their heads toward me. "If I've pieced together everything that I know correctly, than this is far bigger than just us." I motioned to everyone around me. "We should have a name to rally behind. Every great rebellion has had some name to call everyone together. We should do the same."

"I agree," said Ash before Mason could reply. "Any ideas."

When no one replied I suggested, "What about Renegades?" There was a collective murmur of agreements.

"I haven't heard that one before," said Thomas. "I like it."

Mason sighed. "Then from this moment on we, and anyone who opposes the YOUTH, shall be known as the Renegades. Moving on." We all optimistically looked at each other as Mason continued.

"First thing, on the right you'll see pictures of your parents." I glanced down to find pictures of our parents cooped up in what looked like prison cells. Each one by themselves trapped behind a door of steel bars and surrounded by concrete walls. "These were taken off security cameras less than twenty-four hours ago from our Washington state Complex. Inmate transfer sheets indicate that they've been there the entire month we were in the hospital. Unless we want a redo of last time we tried freeing your parents, we'll need to move quickly. No doubt by now it's been discovered these photos were copied."

"What's to say they don't get moved again by the time we get there, or they've already been moved?" I asked.

"Johan has taken over command from Edward. He won't waste money moving prisoners around when he has an army at his disposal."

Before I could reply, Ash said, "He's cheap, Calvin. He won't waste money moving your parents unless the Youth there are all defeated." That was the reassurance I needed. The last thing I wanted was to be playing a game of cat and mouse finding my parents.

"Under these pictures," continued Mason, "is a blueprint of the complex. The red line is our entry path to the detention block, and the green line is our exit path." The top page showed all three levels of the complex, one being a basement. The next three pages had blown up views of each floor.

"I see we're entering through the roof," said Thomas, "but I don't see how we get up there?"

"That's where the challenge is," said Mason. "We'll be skydiving."

"No way! That's sick," said Dakota, slapping Thomas's arm.

"Yeah..." said Thomas, weakly.

"Oh, don't tell me you're afraid of jumping out of a plane?"

"As someone who hasn't done it before, I think it's alright to be a little scared."

"That didn't sound like a little."

"I'd like to see you spell little correctly?"

"Enough!" said Mason over them. "If you want to decipher this yourself, go right ahead. It won't be my fault you get killed because you don't understand the plan."

"Mason!" yelled Ash.

"Sorry," murmured Thomas.

"Don't start with me, Ash," he said without looking at her.

"Everyone calm down," I said. "Mason, is there a possibility to tell us enough of the plan to get to this plane I assume we're going to use for skydiving, and then tell us the rest of the plan on the plane?"

"That was precisely my plan. But if these two yahoos don't shut their mouths—"

"They won't interrupt again." I glanced at Thomas and Dakota. Thomas readjusted himself and flipped through his folder while Dakota stuck his tongue out at me. *Immaturity at its finest.*

"The rest of your folder," continued Mason, "has details on how to operate your combat suits. There will be a full operators manual for you on the plane. You'll also find details on how to operate your parachute. There won't be any practice runs, so it's imperative you memorize these steps or jumping out of the plane will be the last thing you do." Mason closed his folder and held it at his side. "From here, we'll head to the YOUTH airbase where we'll pick up our plane. You have thirty minutes to get suited up in the armory. Ash will help you with anything you need. Dismissed." Mason headed toward a van sitting near the garage doors.

Something about that conversation made me not trust Mason. The last mission we did Mason insisted on none of us going. Now it was like we had always been a part of the team. Something had changed, and it made we weary of him. I must have been eyeing him a while because Megan tapped my arm. "You coming?" she asked.

"Yeah." I eyed Mason once more before following Megan. "What do you think about Mason?" I asked, putting a hand in my pocket as we walked side by side to the armory.

"What do I think... what do you mean?"

"Do you trust him?" I asked. Maybe I shouldn't have been so open with such a question.

"So far. Do you not?"

"Something just is-isn't sitting right with me."

"He seems to genuinely want to help us," said Megan, tucking a stray hair behind her ear.

Before I dug my team and I in any deeper a hole of mistrust, I stopped myself, and what perfect timing it was that we arrived at the door to the armory. I let Megan go through the door first, and as I entered, I was like a kid in a candy store.

The armory was even better than I had imagined. Far cooler than what I envisioned my action figures had growing up. As I entered, on the left and back walls were lockers with a bench in front. To the right was a wall full of weapons lockers.

"So, is this ours," I asked, spinning around to look at everything, "or the Youth's?"

"Technically both," said Ash.

"How is that?" I stopped, spinning and faced Ash.

"We paid for it with mostly Youth money."

"How did you buy it without getting caught?" asked Thomas.

"We have our ways," said Ash. "But right now, let's get you suited up."

"What do we get?" asked Dakota, rubbing his hands together.

"Find your locker and you'll see."

We all made our way over to the lockers. Our names scratched on a scrap piece of paper stuck in the middle of the door. Mine was on the far end next to Thomas's. I opened the door and inside was a treasure trove.

"You'll see your suit, boots, undersuit, helmet, chest rig, and weapons inside."

"Finally, a real gun," said Dakota, immediately grabbing his sidearm and examining it.

"Those are non-lethal," said Ash, walking toward Dakota. He gave her an exaggerated frown. "It's only until you get more training," she said, patting him on the back and walking off.

"We got nearly a week of training back at the school!" cried Dakota, throwing his arm up. "How much longer—"

"You don't have enough training, Mason's orders" said Ash, pointing a finger at Dakota. "End of discussion."

I smiled, shaking my head as I turned back to look through my stuff. I pulled out my suit by the hanger. It looked exactly the same as the one I had before, minus the rips in the stomach.

"If the suits don't quite fit," said Ash, "I apologize. We didn't have time to modify them. So, they're just standard sizes."

"It's better than having no armor." I grabbed everything except my sidearm from the locker and headed toward the door.

"Where are you going," asked Ash as I passed her.

"To-to the restroom to change."

"You're not going to change in here?" she asked, looking genuinely confused.

"I didn't grow up in the military lifestyle. I like my privacy. Plus, I'm not changing in front of a girl."

"I think I'll do the same," said Thomas, following me out the door.

"I like your thinking," I told him as we walked side by side out the door toward the restroom.

"I'm surprised Mason is actually letting us help on this mission?" asked Thomas.

"I-I was wondering the same thing."

"What do you think changed?"

"It's hard to say. Maybe our insistence on saving our parents the first time made him not want to argue again."

Thomas held the door open for me, and I thanked him as we stepped inside. I grabbed a stall and changed into my suit. Thank God I could get out of these sweatpants. I had been stuck in them since our escape from the hospital, and we hadn't had any time, or given any clothes, to change. As comfy as they were, sweatpants were not meant to be worn outside the house. It made me feel weird. That's mainly because growing up, I never wore any. I just didn't like them. And whenever I saw people wearing them, they always looked like pajamas.

After I changed, I piled up my dirty hospital clothes and went to look at myself in the mirror. The suit fit like a glove. And seeing myself in it for the first time, I loved how it made me look. I felt like I was a spy who just got all his gadgets before his mission. Not to mention the suit smelled like a brand-new car.

After examining my suit some more, I hiked my foot onto the counter to tie my boot as Thomas walked out of his stall.

"These look sweet," said Thomas.

"Indeed, they do."

"I couldn't appreciate them as I frantically put it on to escape a psycho teenager."

"I don't know if psycho is the best word," I said, re-tightening my gloves. "Most teenagers are psycho to a degree."

"To the point of killing others though?"

"He's a psycho-psycho then."

"That's one way to put it." As Thomas tied his shoes, he asked, "Why do you think this is happening to us?"

I stared back at Thomas in the mirror a very long moment before answering, "I don't know."

We stood there in silence a moment before I added, "It's less about asking why and more about relying on God to get through it."

"This time seems a little different though."

"And how is that?" I asked, turning to face him.

"Did you see those pictures, Calvin!" he snapped. "Who knows what they've done to our parents, and why? Why us?"

"I don't know, Thomas, I don't know. But I saw the pictures, too. You don't think I felt that uncontrollable horror when I saw my parents? You can't give in to that fear. We have God on our side."

"And what if they die?"

I took a breath before replying, "Let's pray that doesn't happen."

Thomas turned around and put his hands on his head. "What have we gotten ourselves into, Cal?"

"This is one of those times when—"

"When it's less about asking why and more about trusting God, I know," said Thomas, spinning around. "But I'm about to go jump out of a plane and infiltrate a facility where our parents are being held," Thomas swung his arms as he spoke. "A facility filled with kids, of all people, kids our age, who locked us up in a hospital for the last month. Who have gone back and forth between wanting to brainwash us, wanting to kill us, wanting to capture us! Maybe they've had enough. Maybe they'll just kill us and be done with us. Maybe… Maybe…" Thomas started crying and put his hands back on his head. "Maybe I'm too scared to save my parents."

I quickly took a step forward and pulled Thomas in for a hug. He slowly took his hands off his head and wrapped them around me as he cried into my shoulder. "Don't you dare think you're the only one scared here. I'm just as scared as you." I started to cry, too. "And I can't bare to see my friend like this." We both stood there crying, holding each other as tightly as we could.

When we could cry no more, we pulled apart from each other.

"You look horrible," said Thomas sniffling. We laughed.

"It must have been a good cry then?"

"It was for me," said Thomas, taking his glasses off and wiping his eyes.

I copied him and asked, "Do you feel better?"

"Surprisingly… I do." Thomas smiled.

"Look at that smile." I smiled back, patting him on the shoulder.

"I didn't think my first cry would be with someone." Thomas put his glasses back on and we both laughed. "Don't tell anyone about this, would you, Calvin?"

Whenever Thomas asked me a question using my name, I knew to take him seriously.

"I wasn't planning on anyone finding out about this."

Thomas grinned. "Thanks ,Cal."

"Of course." We stood there a moment just staring at each other. "We should pray before we head out."

"I agree," said Thomas.

We threw our hands on each other's shoulders as I prayed. Prayer for our protection, for our safety, and to rescue our parents. Prayer to be brave in the face of danger, not to fear, and not to lose hope.

46

"Where have you been," asked Dakota as Thomas and I returned to the armory.

"Just chatting," I said as we made our way to our lockers. Everyone else was sitting on the bench in front of the lockers all suited up with their helmets off. I opened my locker and pulled out my pistol, locking it into my right thigh holster. Grabbing my balaclava, I shoved it into my helmet, pulling them and my chest rig out.

"Are we ready," I asked, closing my locker.

"Ready," said Ash, standing up. "Do you need help with your chest rig?"

I examined it a moment before letting her help. It was similar to a backward backpack. The straps went over your shoulder, but instead of the compartments being on your back, they were on your chest. The compartments were far smaller than a regular backpack and replaced with magazines and pepper spray ball. As well as some other compartments with items I'd have to look at later.

After Ash helped Thomas put his chest rig on, we all headed to the van. She waited by the door as we filed out, stopping me before I exited. "Can you hang back a moment, Calvin?"

"Sure." I stepped aside as Thomas walked past. Megan eyed us as she walked by but kept on walking. Once the room was empty, Ash said, "Follow me," motioning with her arm. She led me across the room to the weapon cages. Pulling a key from her belt, she unlocked one of the cages, grabbing a pistol inside, and offering it to me.

"What's this for?" I asked.

"This is for knowing how to operate a firearm," said Ash, meeting my eyes. "And because I trust you."

My eyes lingered on the gun a moment before I replied, "I appreciate your trust, Ash. But the last time I had to use a pepper spray gun, I locked up and couldn't fire it. I also now know what I'm fighting, and I-I don't think I could pull the trigger."

"We all freeze the first time we have to pull the trigger at a live target. But that's past now."

"I still don't think I could pull that trigger, Ash."

"And why is that?" she asked perturbed.

"Because they're just kids."

"And that stopped them from trying to kill us?"

"No," I said, throwing my hands up defensively, "but that doesn't give you any reason to return death with death, especially with these." I pulled my pepper spray gun from its holster.

Ash put a hand on her hip. "I thought once the bullets started flying for you all bets were off?"

"In most cases, just not this one."

Ash shoved the gun into her holster and started closing the weapon cage. "The not-killing approach isn't going to get you very far with the Youth." She locked the locker and walked past me as I grabbed her upper arm to stop her. She looked at my hand then up at me with a face that warned me about taking this any further.

"Don't think I won't shoot someone, if necessary, but only as a last resort." As we stared at each other, I could see the gears turning in Ash's head before she finally replied, "When dealing with the Youth, it should be your first and only resort."

I loosened my grip, and Ash pushed free, grabbing her helmet from the bench, and storming out the door. I stood there motionless, staring at the weapons locker a moment before exiting the room.

No one spoke a word when I got in the van and well after we had left the safe house. The second we pulled onto the main road, everyone became tense. Like a fog of war settled over everyone as we all realized what we were about to do. What was only a thirty-minute car ride felt like an eternity. We left the safe house just after the sun had set, and not long after, Mason flipped the van lights on.

We could see the lights of the airfield long before we could see the airfield itself. A mound surrounding the airfield just off the road prevented us from seeing in, though. It was just a grass mound, but it was very steep, and at least two to three times my height. You weren't getting up there without some assistance of some kind.

"Look," said Thomas, pointing down the road. We could see an entrance to the airfield. And that entrance had Youth outside it.

How are we going to get through this?

No one made a sound as we slowly pulled up to the entrance, coming to a stop in front of a set of steel doors as tall as the mounds next to it. A Youth stood with a rifle in front of the doors; they looked as if you'd need a missile to break through them, or a really strong truck to ram into them.

There was a small guard box to the right of the doors built into the mound. A small window showed two Youth standing up and exiting, one staying just inside the door, the other approaching our van.

Mason rolled his window down as the Youth approached. "Looks like a nice evening for a flight," the Youth said.

"So long as there isn't any turbulence," replied Mason.

The guard nodded. "Good to see you, sir." The two shook hands.

"That's not the code," said the Youth by the gate, raising his rifle and walking toward the van. The Youth by the booth ran out and tackled him before he could swing his rifle around in time, slamming him into the hood of the van. The Youth with the rifle took one hand off his gun as he braced himself against the van. In that moment, the Youth by our window lunged forward, grabbed the rifle, and wretched it out of his hand, breaking his wrist in the process. A loud snap filled the air as the Youth's screams were cut short as he was slammed into the hood of the van. Once, twice, and a third time, before falling limp to the ground.

"Awesome," said Dakota behind me.

The Youth, who I now knew were Renegades, drug the unconscious Youth into the booth. A moment later, the gate started to open at a crawl, slowly revealing a road that ran parallel to a line of arched hangers. One of the Renegades finally came out of the booth, running up toward Cody's window, who put it down.

"Hanger two at the far end," said the Renegade, pointing down the road. "The pilot is ready and waiting. Good luck on your mission, sir." He slapped the hood twice and walked off toward the booth.

Mason started to drive away before glancing at the booth and slammed on the brakes, sending everyone inside forward, with Thomas even hitting his head on the seat in front of him, which got a laugh out of Dakota.

"Preston!" yelled Mason.

Preston turned around just as he was entering the booth.

"Why don't you two come with us," said Mason. "You're as good as dead if they find out."

"With all due respect, sir, I don't think they'll find out. And if they do, then I'll take that risk if it means having our guys at this airfield. I'd hate to see us lose this."

Mason sighed and look down the road before turning to Preston. "You're a good soldier, Preston. Hopefully, we fight beside each other one day."

"I'm hoping for the same thing, sir. Now get out of here so you can kick these guys in the butt."

"Nobody says that anymore, Preston," said Mason.

"I do," said Thomas, holding his hand up.

"That explains a lot," said Dakota.

"And what's that supposed to mean," said Thomas, whipping his head around behind him to look at Dakota.

Cody let out an audible sigh. "We have a plane to catch, Mason."

"Yes, thank you guys." Mason floored it as debris hit the underside of the van. "Everyone get ready."

As we passed through the gate, flood lights lined the road on the left of us, each post passing in a blur as we flew down the road. The arched hangers were black with a giant white number painted above the back entrance doors. They started at twenty and descended as we went down the road.

"Move to the door," I said, pointing to it.

Thomas scooted out of his seat, and I followed. We took the second bench, behind Ash, while Megan and Dakota took the third one behind us.

"You ready?" I asked, looking at Megan. She just nodded her helmeted head.

"I took a deep breath and closed my eyes a second before shoving my helmet on."

"Everyone mic-drop," said Mason as we neared our hanger. I clicked the button on the right of my helmet, and a small beep alerted me the mic-drop had been engaged. Now we could talk freely among ourselves without our external helmet mics alerting everyone to our position.

The giant white 2 of our hanger was now in sight. Ash got out of her seat and had her hand ready on the door handle.

We pulled up to the building and screeched to a stop. Ash slid the door open and, before it was opened all the way, hopped down and started waving everyone out.

I got out last. As I was waiting, I saw Cody attach something to the center console.

"Come on, Calvin!" yelled Ash. I grabbed my chest rig straps and jumped out. Thomas was holding the door handle to the hanger with Mason opposite him, rifle ready.

"Everyone behind Thomas, let's move," said Mason. I got in line behind Megan. We were up against the wall to the left of the double doors.

Mason, Cody, and Ash were against the wall to the right of the doors, each with their rifle drawn and looked like they were ready to pounce.

"Open the door *quickly* on three, Thomas," said Mason. "Ready?"

Thomas readjusted his grip on the handle. "Ready," he said.

"On three," said Mason. "One. Two. Three!"

Thomas yanked the door open, and Mason brought his rifle up, sweeping it across the room before entering. Cody and Ash followed behind him.

Thomas started waving Dakota through the door when I stuck my hand out. "Wait!" Dakota stopped and turned around. "Wait for them to give the all clear."

"All clear," said Mason a second later.

Dakota turned around, and we followed him through the door.

"I'm last," I said, grabbing the door from Thomas.

"Thanks," he said, heading inside.

"Cut the chatter boys," said Mason. He sounded like he was right next to me as his voice came through my helmet. I had forgotten about all our mics being linked together.

I scanned the area behind me before heading inside and closed the door.

I heard the plane long before I saw it. Its roaring engines filled every corner of the hanger. My helmet automatically adjusted the noise level, so it wasn't deafening.

In the middle of the hanger was a massive plane with its back ramp folded down. The plane was completely black with four engines, two on each wing. At the top of the ramp, Mason, or who I assumed was Mason since we were all wearing the same outfit, was walking up to someone climbing down a ladder from the front of the plane.

"Looks like a nice evening for a flight," said Mason. That was the same code used when entering the airfield. The code must have been answered correctly when the boy jumped off the ladder and shook Mason's hand. He wore what looked like a pilot's jumpsuit with a different looking helmet than the rest of us. It had a much bigger visor that was pushed up and had no chin piece, leaving his whole face exposed.

Mason hit the mic-drop button on the side of his helmet. "Thanks for helping us out, Jeremy."

I couldn't hear what the Renegade said, but he got right next to Mason's ear as he yelled something to him.

"This is everyone," replied Mason. "Let's go," he said, waving us up. I climbed the ramp with Dakota in front of me and Thomas and Megan behind me. Cody and Ash were checking the hanger as we made our way up the ramp.

"Are you positive there's nothing on Thermals?" asked Ash.

"The engines are creating too much heat," said Cody. "I can't be sure."

"Then get on the plane before we find out," said Mason.

I looked behind me as Ash ran up the steps. Cody swept his rifle across the room one last time.

"Freeze!" said someone I didn't recognize over our helmet speakers. Cody froze as Youth came out from around the plane and through the entrance doors to the hanger.

Everyone else inside the plane turned around as the Youth grouped around the bottom of the ramp. One of them yanked Cody's rifle out of his hands and passed it back into the group of Youth.

"Drop your weapons, hands in the air," said a different Youth. Something clattered behind me as I whipped my head around to see Youth pouring through the side door of the plane, their rifles trained on us. I turned around and met Megan's helmeted face. I didn't have to see her face to know how she felt, how we all felt. Caught right at the finish line.

"Hands in the air or we shoot," said the first Youth. Ash slowly bent down and set her rifle on the ground. "Kick it away," the Youth ordered. She complied, kicking it with her right foot and put her hands on her helmet. Cody had his hands on his helmet, but his right hand was hovering over his statscreen on his wrist.

"Hand away from the statscreen!" yelled a Youth, walking past from behind me. His rifle raised at Cody. The second it clicked in my head, a white flash overtook my eyes as the wall exploded in front of me.

When I finally got my bearings, the world was chaos around me. The inside of the plane was bathed in a flickering orange light. I pushed myself up and found a rifle lying just beside me. A Youth on the ground near the back of the plane started to get up and walk toward the rifle. I quickly slid the gun behind me before standing up and charging at the Youth, who did the same toward me. We collided as I tried tackling him, but he grabbed me and threw me on my back, knocking the wind out of me.

I arched my back trying to look behind me. The Youth had almost made it to the rifle. I rolled onto my stomach, pulled out my gun, making sure the safety was off this time, and shot three rounds at the Youth.

A white cloud immediately engulfed him as he turned around, trying to find his attacker, only to immediately wave his hands trying to get rid of the cloud. I got on my knees as the Youth stumbled backward into the wall, his hands searching the floor for his gun. I mustered all my strength, held my breath, and ran full boar at the Youth, driving my right shoulder into his chest. The Youth slammed into the wall again as I was forced to take a breath, inhaling the outskirts of the pepper spray cloud. My eyes immediately began to water, and I started coughing. My eyes burned to the point it was too overwhelming to think about anything else. I went to rub my eyes, forgetting I had my helmet on. I threw it off and stumbled backward, kicking the rifle away trying to wipe my eyes.

I looked up a second before the Youth slammed into me. I felt all my breath leave me before I saw stars. When my vision returned, I had a massive headache, a face that felt like it was on fire, and a barrel of a rifle pointed at me.

"Stand down," said the Youth, holding the rifle, kneeling in front of me. I really had no option, that is until the Youth pointed his gun up to my left. Then someone from my right kicked the Youth in the helmet, sending his head back and landing on his back. As the Youth sat back up, the butt of a rifle swung around and hit his helmet, sending him back to the ground and staying there.

"Need a hand," said Megan, walking up from my right, sticking her hand out.

"Thanks," I said, wiping my eyes and coughing my guts out before grabbing her hand.

"Let me help," said Thomas, stepping away from the Youth he had clocked in the head with his rifle, and offered his hand to me. They both pulled me up and steadied me when I almost fell forward from their pull.

"Where are your glasses?" asked Megan looking around. I would have helped were my eyes not watering like a waterfall.

"Where's your helmet, too?" asked Thomas.

"There," said Megan. A moment later, she came back with my helmet, digging out my glasses from inside.

"Do we have any water?" asked Megan as I started a coughing fit.

"There should be some in your bag," said Mason walking up. I could feel the effects of the pepper spray wearing off when water slammed into my face. I coughed and sputtered the water out of my mouth when another wave crashed into me.

"Ok, ok," I said stepping back.

"That should help," said Mason, closing the water bottle. "Cody, check the tail." Mason started walking off behind us with the pilot not far behind.

Megan and Thomas walked up to me as I tried to wipe the water off my face.

"You alright," asked Megan.

"Yeah. What about you guys?"

"We're good," said Thomas.

"Th-thanks for saving me back there."

"Don't mention it," said Thomas.

"Calvin," said Ash walking up to us, "what happened?" She took off her backpack.

"I walked," I coughed a couple of times. "I walked through a pepper spray cloud."

"Here, dry off," said Ash, throwing me a towel. Megan stepped back as I caught the towel and wiped my face off. "Feeling better?"

"Yes," I finishing wiping my face. It still stung, but the rest of the side effects had stopped. "Thank you."

"Of course, I'll take that back."

I handed the towel back to Ash, and she started wiping her suit. The white towel came away with red stains.

"What's that?" asked Megan, pointing at the towel.

"Blood," said Ash, without looking up and continuing to wipe off the rest of her suit.

"Here's your stuff, Calvin," said Megan almost in slow motion. She handed me my helmet and glasses, walking toward the front of the plane. She nearly ran into Dakota as he walked up to both of us, both of them swerving to avoid hitting each other.

"Sorry," said Megan, without looking back or stopping.

Dakota looked at her then back at us. "What's wrong with her?" he asked, pointing a thumb behind him.

"I'm not sure," I said, eyeing Megan as she started to climb the ladder.

"Well then, are you going to use that?" asked Dakota, pointing to Thomas's rifle.

Thomas looked down and examined the rifle, turning it over once. "I take it you will?" he asked, looking up at Dakota.

"Why do you think I asked?"

"Fair point, here." Thomas handed Dakota the rifle.

"Cool." Dakota examined the rifle for himself, checking the ammo count and looking down the sights. He started to walk off but stopped, turning around to face Thomas. "Thanks," he said before walking down the ramp.

Thomas and I both looked at Dakota and then at each other.

"I didn't expect that," said Thomas.

"Neither did I."

"Alright," said Ash, throwing her bloody towel toward the tail of the plane. I followed it as it landed on the carnage that was at the base of the ramp. The explosion left a gaping hole to the outside in the wall. Youth and rubble littered the ground and the tail of the ramp. I prayed that as soon as we left, they would all get back up, but deep down I knew most of them wouldn't. It made me sick, so I looked away.

"I need your help moving the bodes and debris out of the plane," said Ash, motioning for Thomas and I to follow. I hesitated for a moment before walking with them. I was surprised that Thomas immediately followed Ash over, no hesitation whatsoever.

One by one we dragged everything off the ramp of the plane. Inside, Mason and Cody were doing the same, tossing everything out the side door.

"Thank you," said Ash when we finished. "I know that's not easy."

"Let's just be done and move on," said Thomas very monotone, glad that I wasn't the only one affected by this.

"Is the tail clean?" asked Mason, walking up to Ash.

"All clean."

"Go ahead and close the ramp. Everyone else to the cockpit."

Ash ran off to the ramp while the rest of us followed Mason up the ladder at the front of the plane. At the top was a small room that led into the cockpit. Megan had her helmet off and was sitting in a chair behind the pilot. She turned her head to look at us as we entered.

Out the windows I could see the hanger doors slowly sliding opening with giant rotating yellow lights just above them.

"Craft Y4791, cease pre-flight procedures immediately!"

"Turn that off," said Mason.

"Yes, sir," said the pilot, flipping a switch.

"Shouldn't we keep that on so we-we know what they're doing?" I asked.

"They won't give us anything," said the pilot. "They'll keep saying the same thing over and over."

Cody rushed up to the windows and leaned over the console. "Three squads moving in," he said, taking his backpack off and digging out his sauna tarp.

"What are you doing?" asked Megan.

Cody tied the tarp around his neck like a cape. "Don't wait for me," he said, exiting the cockpit.

"I'm coming with you," said Dakota.

"You're staying right here," said Mason. "Nobody else leaves."

"If he's willing to come, I'll take him," said Cody as Dakota dug out his sauna tarp.

"He hasn't had enough—" started Mason before being cut off by Cody.

"You know far too well that he's more than capable of handling himself!" yelled Cody.

"I'm trying to keep him alive so he can see his parents," said Mason.

Dakota stopped and turned around. "And who says I want to see my parents?" The two locked eyes a moment before Dakota turned to follow Cody down the ladder.

"Doors are almost open," said our pilot, breaking the silence, "everyone strap in."

I grabbed a seat against the back wall after taking a glance out the windows hoping to see Dakota and Cody but finding no one. I folded the seat down from the wall and strapped myself in as the plane shuddered forward. Thomas grabbed the seat next to me.

"Everyone keep quiet until we're airborne," said Mason.

"Copy," replied Ash.

"Hold departure! Hold departure!" screamed Cody. "Enemy has RPG's."

"RPG's?" asked Thomas.

"Rocket Propelled Grenades," replied Mason.

"I know what it means," said Thomas as the plane came to a stop, still inside the hanger.

"Cody, you need to get out of there!" yelled Mason.

When Cody didn't reply, Mason got up and looked out the window. "I can not lose you, Cody."

There was silence on the radio for what felt like an eternity when finally, Cody replied, "RPG's destroyed. You're clear for takeoff."

"Copy. Thank you, sir," said the pilot as he pushed a lever, and the plane started rolling forward again.

"Alright," said Mason. "Now get back in here."

"Not until all hostiles have been eliminated."

Mason stood up and backed away from the window. "How long until we're set on the runway for takeoff?" he asked the pilot.

"About five minutes."

"You have four minutes to be on this plane, Cody."

It seemed odd to me that Mason didn't seem concerned at all about

Dakota. Like he wasn't in as much danger as Cody was.

Mason went back to his seat and strapped in. We slowly made our way down to the end of the side road, which wasn't very far as it started just to the left of our hanger.

We slowly turned off the side road that connected all the hangers and onto the main runway. As we turned, I could see that there were double the hangers across from ours, and the runway ran the length of the hangers.

When we finally turned facing down the runway, I could just see our hanger out of the corner of the window to our right. Three groups of Youth lined the fronts of the hangers approaching our hanger. The closer I looked though, only some of the Youth were moving, others were on the ground unmoving. One Youth advanced toward the hanger when all of a sudden, they fell backward.

"Cody, we're leaving. Get on this plane now!" yelled Mason.

Two more Youth advanced at the same time toward our hanger, and one after the other, they both fell back, one twisting around and falling on their stomach.

Then Dakota and Cody both came sprinting out from the right side of our hanger. They each had their sauna tarps on, flapping like capes as they ran toward the plane.

"Takeoff," said Mason.

"What?" I screamed, "they're almost here."

"Take off now," said Mason, getting up and heading out of the cockpit. I looked out the window and saw Cody had a considerable lead on Dakota and had changed direction from running toward the front of the plane instead of the back, where the door was. I jumped out of my seat and followed Mason.

He took two steps down the ladder before sliding the rest of the way. As much as I wanted to slide down like him, I didn't know how. And it would be quite a fall if I messed up. So, I climbed down as fast as my arms and legs could take me.

At the bottom, I spun around to find the back ramp closed. and Mason opening the side door.

"Come on!" he yelled as the engines revved up to their max. The plane started rolling forward. and I nearly fell over from the lurch. I stumbled over to the side door just as Cody hopped in. and Mason helped pull him in.

The plane started gaining speed as Cody turned around to look out the door.

"He's not going to make it," said Mason. When neither of them moved. I rushed to the door. Dakota was nearly there, but with the speed of the plane. it didn't matter.

"Dakota. run!" I yelled. He threw his rifle down and started running away from the plan and pointed himself further down the runway. I knew what he was doing. but he'd get one shot at it.

The plane was gaining speed quickly. and Dakota's line wouldn't give him any room for error. I braced myself against the door frame. I held out my hand as Dakota was steps away, both of his arms pumping. Just before our paths crossed. he jumped, and that's when I saw he wouldn't make it.

I stuck my hand out as far as I could. Dakota grabbed my hand just before his body slammed into the side of the plane. His weight nearly wretched me out of the door when someone grabbed my belt. With my body half out the plane and both hands holding onto Dakota, more hands grabbed around me, keeping me from falling any further out the door. Dakota was starting to flail in the wind as he grabbed onto the arm of my suit with his free hand.

My belt slowly started tugging me back inside as the plane started lifting off. Dakota was now a flag in the wind, his legs down the length of the plane flapping about. The other hands around me grabbed onto Dakota before we were all pulled inside.

I fell in a pile of bodies well away from the door, before we started rolling. I rolled over and over, unsure which direction I was going, my hands flailing for anything to grab. They found something round, and I grasped it before I flung over onto my back and lost my grip as someone grabbed around my waist and stopped me.

"Grab, grab," said Cody. I looked up and found a slot that my hand launched to. When my hand was inside the slot Cody let go, and I grabbed the slot with my other hand, using all my strength to hang on. I felt like I was hanging off the edge of a roof. Something wasn't right. I tried looking around, but my helmet kept me from looking too far. And I was more concerned about not letting go and falling.

"Level the plane!" I heard Mason say strained.

"Hold on," said the pilot.

My arms started burning as my legs searched for something to help hold my weight. One of my feet found a hold, and I put as much weight as I could on it. But as I did, my foot slipped. Cody grabbed the back of my suit, and my feet slipped trying to find the hold again. When it found it, I froze.

It felt like more than an eternity as my muscles burned, starting to shake when the plane finally leveled out and I collapsed on my stomach, my helmeted face flat on the floor. Everyone was gasping around me as wind continued to whip around us. I slowly pushed myself up, seeing Megan close the door with who I assumed was Ash. The air sounded like it was being squeezed out from around us as the door latched shut.

"Who's hurt," said Ash, running over to us with Megan close behind.

With one hand, I took my helmet off, looked around as all of us on the floor did the same, except Cody, who used his sniper to push himself to his feet. He walked off like he wasn't even phased as I sat up on my elbows. I met Dakota's gaze. "Thanks," he said between breaths, "both of you."

"I'm not leaving you behind," said Thomas, his head popping up past Dakota.

"Neither am I," I said. Mason sat up, catching his breath. We locked eyes and I said, "He made it, Mason."

Ash went through everyone to make sure we were alright after pulling Dakota into the plane. Surprisingly, Dakota walked away with only a few bruises, mainly from crashing into the side of the plane. I was sitting on one of the fold-out seats against the wall, leaned over with my elbows on my knees examining my helmet, when Ash walked up.

"Hi," she said grinning at me.

"Hi." I looked up and set my helmet in the seat next to me.

"How are you feeling," she asked, kneeling in front of me, laying her bag next to her.

"I'm alive. About all I could ask for right now."

Ash chuckled as she pulled out some rubber gloves and pulled them on. "Does anything hurt?"

"Not really," I said, looking myself over.

"Positive?"

"Yes?"

"You were hanging out of a plane holding Dakota as the plane took off," said Ash eyeing me over. "I was expecting something to hurt."

"Now that you say that, I would be expecting myself to hurt, too."

"Hmm…" Ash started undoing the collar of my suit and started pulled the zipper down before I grabbed her hand and stopped her.

"What are you doing?" I asked, eyeing her.

"I... Well," she looked down, almost embarrassed, before looking back at me. "I wanted to check your chest and stomach. And... I didn't know if you'd let me after the whole changing thing back at the safe house."

"One," I said, still holding onto her hand, "we're not back at the safe house. Two, you're the doctor here. So, if you're concerned about me, I can make some exceptions."

"Oh, well, ok then."

When Ash didn't let go of my zipper, I said, "I can undo the zipper myself, Ash."

She looked down at the zipper before quickly letting go. "Yes, sorry."

"You're alright," I said, undoing the zipper down to my waist and pulling my arms out of the sleeves, leaving the suit to hang around my waist.

"Now, tell me if any of this hurts." Ash started pressing against my chest and stomach, and in that instant, she was back to the Ash I first met. But for a moment there, I saw the fifteen-year-old girl that she really was. The one who wasn't the warrior, who didn't know how to kill. She was fifteen-year-old Ash who was nervous around a boy she liked. It was the most human thing I had seen her do yet.

And it made me sad that, in an instant, all the splendor and childishness could be turned off, almost like she was a computer and a new program booted up, overriding the old one. She was like a switch that could be turned on and off. You want Youth Ash, on, but you turn off fifteen-year-old Ash, and vice versa. A kid shouldn't be like that, yet the Youth made her into this. And who knew if it could be reversed.

"Calvin!" said Ash like she had asked for me before.

"Yes, sorry."

Ash hesitated a moment before asking, "What were you thinking about?"

"Thinking about? Why do you ask?"

"You were staring at me."

"I-I was staring at you?"

"Yes. And what were you thinking about?"

"Well, I-I-I was thinking about you."

Ash pulled her hands away from me. "Of course you were."

"What do you mean of course I was?"

"I don't think I have to explain that."

"Are you saying I'm like all other boys."

"Not at all, Calvin."

"Then what do you mean?"

"I need to check your stitches," said Ash, pulling up my undershirt.

"Wait-wait, we were just talking about—ho! Your hands are freezing!"

"I stuck them in dry ice just for you," she said with a satisfied smile.

"What was that for?" I cried.

"I'm joking," said Ash cracking up. "I can't believe you actually believed me."

"Well, I don't know what's in your bag," I said, pointing to it.

"Did you see me put my hands in my bags?"

"Well, I-I wasn't really looking."

"Well, where were you looking?"

Before I could answer, Dakota walked by. "Looks like someone's getting special treatment," he said, stopping behind Ash.

I was already shaking my head, but before I could look up at him, Ash, without turning around, elbowed Dakota in the groin. In an instant, he was on the floor. My mouth hung open in both pain and astonishment as I watched Dakota wither on the floor. Ash just grinned, and I started laughing.

I looked down the row of seats toward the tail of the plan and found Thomas was completely hysterical.

"It's not funny," managed Dakota through gritted teeth.

"How wrong he is," I said to Ash. She just gave me a devilish grin as she continued examining my stitches. I grabbed my shirt from her and held it up.

"Does this hurt?" she asked.

"No."

"And here?"

"No."

"And here?"

"That's-that's a little tender."

"Ok," she leaned back from me. "Everything looks fine, but don't be surprised if you get some bruising later. Nothing you can't handle."

"After what I've been through, I'm not sure there's not much I couldn't handle."

Ash hesitated a moment, looking away before replying, "Why did you hesitate back when we moved the bodies off the plane?"

"You saw that?"

Ash nodded. I didn't know how to respond. It was a combination of a lot of factors. One second, they were all in front of me, ready to take me and my friends prisoners. The next second, the majority of them were most likely dead after the explosion. I know I had said I would kill, if necessary, but looking the Youth in the eye, something changed. It wasn't just about protecting my life. It was about saving these brainwashed kids from the living nightmare they were in.

"It's complicated," I finally told Ash.

"Seeing dead bodies for the first time is. I just want to make sure the next time you see them you don't freeze up again, especially in battle."

"I can't guarantee anything... but I'll do my best."

Ash took off her gloves and threw them in her bag before closing it up. "So, um, you're all good."

"Yes. Thank you," I said, nodding.

We stared at each other for a second too long, and then it became an awkward silent stare. Ash immediately stood up, grabbing her bag. "I better get going." Ash walked off back to the ladder to the cockpit, but after a few steps, she stopped and turned around. "Try to get some rest. You'll need it." She turned her head down slightly, only looking back up with her eyes and gave me a grin, before spinning around and walking off.

I grinned back at her when I saw Dakota start to stand up. "How did you manage that," he said weakly.

I looked back at Ash as she climbed the ladder, disappearing into the cockpit. "Honestly, I don't know."

"I wouldn't have done it the way you did it, so if you want me to teach you sometime, I'm more than willing to be your teacher."

I glared at him.

"What," he sounded so innocent. "I normally don't do this for free."

"Do you want Ash to come back down here."

"And do what?"

"Sounds like teach you another lesson."

"You wouldn't?"

I grabbed my helmet, "She's-she's a call away."

He quickly stood up, "Fine, you win this time, Fritz." He took off toward the back of the plane.

I looked down at Thomas who gave me the goofiest smile and thumbs up. I didn't laugh as much as I would have, because Dakota's words were stuck in my mind. Not his exactly, just what they reminded me of. How Edward always called me Fritz. A chill ran through me as I thought back to when he had us all lined up at the first safe house.

It's amazing how one word can bring back so many memories without your permission.

We were all huddled together in the cargo hold of the plane. After a quick glance through the training manual, we were as well prepared for our skydive as anyone could. It was a little more difficult than just pulling the chord. Steering was a whole 'nother beast. That was what worried me the most. All I could do now was pray I remembered everything I read and didn't freeze up.

Mason and Cody were talking on a private channel and were off near the rear of the cargo hold, while the rest of us formed a circle, conversing with each other.

"I take it you've done this before, Ash?" I asked.

"Yes, yes, I have. Many of times."

"How many?" asked Dakota.

"Too many to count."

"What was the first time like?" asked Megan.

Ash looked down to readjust the straps on her pack before answering, "I was ten. They told me how to operate the chute and threw me out the plane. Almost exactly like what we're doing to you." Everyone but Megan laughed. And then the reality of what Ash said set in

But before I could process that thought any more, our pilot came over our helmet speakers. "Fifteen minutes to drop."

We all looked back and forth between each other before Mason and Cody joined our circle. "Ready?" asked Mason to a chorus of nods. "Good. Everyone seal your suits."

I pressed the button on my statscreen Mason had directed us to earlier. I immediately felt my suit tighten, especially around my neck. I tried to readjust my suit only to be more uncomfortable.

Mason noticed me messing with my suit and said, "You'll get used to it, Calvin. Now, everyone in line."

We arranged ourselves in a single file line just before the start of the tail ramp. Cody started the line, followed by Mason, Thomas, Dakota, Megan, me, and Ash.

"We're all ready, Jeremy," said Mason.

"Depressurizing cargo hold, now," said our pilot. "Going dark." A second later, all the lights turned off. The only light came from the moon through the porthole windows that dotted the walls of the plane.

"Everyone mic-drop," said Mason. I heard the familiar ding as I pressed the mic-drop button on the right side of my helmet.

We stood there in complete silence, swaying with the movement of the plane. Each second felt longer than the next. I was going to see my parents again, that was out of the question. Would I survive the skydive, would any of us survive a skydive having not ever done one? All we had to do was follow Ash's instructions for when to pull our chutes and follow her to our landing site, the rest was up to us.

A red light lit up on the wall sucking me out of my thoughts. "Five minutes to drop," our pilot said, immediately followed by the tail ramp opening. Wind started swirling around us, threatening to knock us over at times.

"Remember to run down only after the person in front of you has jumped," said Mason.

"What if we don't?" asked Dakota.

"I don't want your chutes getting tangled with how little training you have."

Again with the training for Mason. I still couldn't get out of my mind why he had let us come on this mission. Before I could come to any conclusions, the red light turned green. Cody ran down the ramp, diving off. Mason followed suit, but Thomas was frozen.

"What's wrong?" asked Dakota.

"I don't know if I can do this," said Thomas.

"You can do it, Thomas," I reassured him.

"You have to jump now, Thomas!" yelled Ash.

"Can we—whoa!" cried Thomas as Dakota picked him up, holding him under one arm like a suitcase as he ran down the ramp. "What are you doing, Dakota? Dakota. Dakota, wait! Wait, wait—Noooo!" Thomas screamed as Dakota jumped out of the plane with him.

"Go!" said Ash, frantically

Megan took a hesitant step forward before taking another, then running down the ramp. As soon as she jumped, I sprinted down the tail and jumped. I had the biggest smile behind my helmet as the wind whipped around me. I looked around and was surrounded by a beautiful painting. Nearly invisible clouds blended with the lights of surrounding towns, some even bleeding through the thinner clouds. It was such a peaceful sight. My body relaxed as I let the wind move me how it wanted, looking side to side trying to take in as much of the stunning view as possible.

"This is awesome!" screamed Thomas.

I looked down to find Thomas spinning in circles.

"Look what you would have missed out on," said Dakota.

"Thanks, Dakota."

"Don't mention it."

The two tried to give each other a fist bump, only to find navigating while in the air far harder than they realized. One would move and the other would end up moving away or flying right past them. It was very entertaining to watch.

"Cut the chatter boys," said Ash. "Twenty-five seconds till chutes up." Chutes up was the term used for when we would open our parachutes.

I pulled my arms to my side and dove toward Megan. When I got next to her, I opened my arms, so we were right next to each other. I wanted to ask her what she was thinking. She had been quiet since we left for the airfield. But this wasn't the time to ask when everyone would hear our conversation through our radios, so I gave her a thumbs up.

She looked up and immediately returned the thumbs up, which gave me some hope that she would be alright.

"Chutes up in five." Ash started counting down.

I maneuvered away from Megan as best I could before grabbing the chute cord.

"… Two, one. Deploy, deploy, deploy!"

I yanked my cord and heard the chute deploy. A moment later, all the straps pulled against me as the chute fully opened. I grabbed the two bars that fell over my head, holding them level.

"My chute won't deploy!" cried Thomas. I looked down trying to spot him through all the opened chutes. When I finally spotted him, he was frantically pulling his release cord like a madman.

"Spread your limbs, slow your descent," said Ash far calmer than I was.

"Thomas, use your backup chute," I said, utterly helpless now that my chute was out.

Then Ash flew past me like a missile, her hands were locked to her sides and feet pointed like a divers, as she shot headfirst toward Thomas. At the last possible second, she flailed her limbs out as far as they would go, slamming into Thomas a second later. She wrapped one arm around him and the other fiddled with his pack.

What was probably less than ten seconds felt like an eternity. Everything seemed to freeze around me as I said a prayer. This is not how Thomas was going to die. This is not how any of us were going out. Yet here we were. Not knowing if I was going to lose my friend, my oldest friend, the one I grew up with. Who in a few moments would be a puddle on the ground without his chute.

No, no, no. I couldn't be thinking like this. Not now. God was going to save him. He had to, right?

The eternity ended, and I was snapped back to life as Thomas's chute flew out of his bag. Ash moved to the side of Thomas, pulled her legs up, and kicked off him. An instant later, the chute opened.

"Ha ha!" I screamed and was accompanied by even more applause. In the middle of our cheers, Ash's chute opened.

I quickly started counting the chutes to make sure we had everyone, made harder by the darkness, but I counted five chutes. "We're missing two chutes!"

"Mason and Cody will deploy theirs later than us," said Ash.

"Cut the chatter," said Mason. "Radio silence unless you need help or are moving on your objective."

"Yes, sir," replied Ash instinctively.

Not another word came from anyone as we descended through the darkness.

Cody barreled headfirst toward Complex 3, still not having deployed his parachute. He was waiting until the last possible moment so any Youth on the roof wouldn't have much time to react.

The top of Complex 3 was completely dark. But lights from the wall and fence surrounding the complex made everything else look like the middle of the day.

Cody turned on his thermal visor and was greeted to four Youth patrolling the roof. Flipping his thermal visor off to see his statscreen, Cody checked his altitude, waiting until 5,000 feet to deploy his parachute. An alarm beeped in his ear when he reached 5,000 feet. Cody turned back on this thermal visor and pulled his parachute cord.

The sound of the parachute opening would be lost to most ears, but the advanced range of hearing offered by the Youth helmets made Cody stick out like a flare in the night.

The Youth on the roof closest to Cody started scanning his surroundings. Cody immediately noticed this shift and pulled out his sidearm, the SR-10, with a silencer.

Forsaking controls of the parachute for just a moment, Cody aimed and fired, taking down the Youth, who fell just behind an HVAC intake box. The other Youth on the roof immediately scanned their surroundings as they ducked for cover.

Cody took one down before they could get to cover. Then changing his direction of descent, flying parallel to the roof instead of toward it, Cody was able to reveal the last two Youth and take them out before they even had a moment to react.

Double checking the roof was free of any more Youth, Cody holstered his sidearm and descended toward an open area on the roof without any fans or terminals to obstruct his landing. Just like the other 127 jumps he had done, Cody casually hit the roof running and quickly slowed to a complete stop, jerking his parachute down to the ground. He expertly disengaged the safety harness and dropped the parachute pack on the ground behind him.

"LZ one clear," said Cody, running over to the nearest Youth and grabbed their rifle with a sling. Then taking the extra rifle mags and adding those to his chest rig. He pulled his sidearm back out and popped in a fresh mag before reinserting it in the holster.

Cody rushed to the entrance leading downstairs, swinging the door open quickly and sweeping the landing for Youth. From this point on, his thermal visor would be limited in use. Any YOUTH building was designed with walls impervious to letting heat through. From here on out, the Renegades would have to rely more on their training and less on their technology.

With his finger on the trigger, Cody slowly made his way down two flights of stairs, checking under the staircase before approaching the first floor door. Now came the hard part, breaching a door where you had no idea what was on the other side. Cody knew exactly what the layout of the building was beyond the door. A long hallway parallel to the door running half the length of the base. A training room, barracks, and sleeping quarters on the right. A restroom, maintenance, and security room to the left. But none of that mattered if there was a squad of Youth just down the hall.

Cody could very easily bypass the lock on the door and make a quiet entry. But just in case someone was on the other side, he pulled a small directional explosive from his chest rig. It was a small rectangular box about as big as Cody's hand. On the back, he pulled off the plastic covering an adhesive strip and stuck the explosive just above the door handle, ensuring the arrow labeled 'BLAST DIRECTION' on top of the device was facing toward the door before sticking it on.

The front side had a cover that Cody flipped up to reveal a few buttons and a small screen. One button activated a countdown, below which was a dial that would set the time on the courtdown. To the left of that was a button labeled 'PAIR'. Cody pressed it, a red light above the button blinked to alert the user that the explosive was ready for pairing. On his statscreen, Cody pressed the corresponding pair button. After two more blinks, the light on the explosive turned a solid green, confirming the pair. Now as long as he was withing five miles of the explosive, he could activate it with a double click of the *Detonate* button on his statscreen.

Cody closed the lid and ran up to the next landing of the stairs, crouching down and aiming his rifle at the door. After a breath, he double clicked the detonate button.

The sound of the explosion would have made most go deaf, if not have severe hearing loss with how close Cody was to it. But thanks to his helmet, it protected his hearing, making the explosion sound more like a few balloons popping at once.

For such a small device, the explosion blew smoke and dust everywhere, slowly filling the stairway. Cody cautiously made his way to the door, finding a gaping hole a little bigger than his hand around where the explosive was. By the sound of the explosion, most would have thought the hole to be two or three times the size, but the reinforced door surrounded by half foot thick concrete walls would take a far bigger explosive to make any real dent, as they were designed to do.

But all Cody needed was to destroy the door lock. He lightly touched the edge of the door hole, ensuring it wouldn't burn him. Finding it adequate, Cody pulled the door inward with ease.

The smoke on both sides of the door was starting to dissipate. Hiding in the smoke, Cody turned his thermal visor on to check the hallway for Youth. When none appeared, he sprinted to the left of the door, stopping at the third door near the end of the hallway. As he ran, an alarm started blaring, deafening to anyone without hearing protection.

"LZ two clear," said Mason over the radio.

Cody didn't have much time. Before approaching the door, he dropped his rifle, letting it hang by the sling, and pulled out another directional explosive. Immediately pairing it as he stopped and secured it to the door in the same manner as before. He took two steps to the right of the door, turned his back, and detonated the explosive.

The door swung inward as Cody threw a shrapnel grenade followed by a smoke grenade. He turned on his thermal visor and hoisted his rifle up, entering the room and incapacitating the two Youth inside, taking their weapons away from them. These were technicians, so they weren't wearing the same armor and helmet as Cody, but wore all black, consisting of boots, pants, a long sleeve shirt with a bullet proof vest underneath, and a thigh holster for a sidearm. Each one had shrapnel lodged in various places across their body.

Cody turned off his mic-drop and held his rifle up to one of the Youth's chests. "Disable the alarm," he said. When the Youth didn't reply, Cody smacked him in the nose with butt of his rifle, the breaking of his nose unable to be heard over the alarm. The Youth lay on the ground moaning and holding his nose as Cody yanked the other Youth up by the collar, forcing him over to the wall of monitors. The Youth hobbled over, barely able to stand on his own.

Cody knew how to disable the alarm, he just needed the right code or the other Complexes would be notified. Fighter jets would be there withing the hour, and reinforcements would parachute down in less than two. Making any escape nearly impossible.

"What's the password," said Cody, sticking his rifle into the Youth's back.

Without his helmet, the Youth's response would have been drowned out by the alarm. But instead, it sounded crystal clear. The Youth knew this, so he didn't yell when he replied, "I'm just like him."

Cody immediately slammed the Youth headfirst into the console, who slumped to the floor.

Cody slid under the console and ripped an access panel off. He dug around cutting, stripping, and doing all sorts to the wires until the alarm turned off. He bolted back up to a countdown message that read 'ENTER PASSWORD' with a one minute countdown. Cody would get two chances to enter the correct password, a ten-digit number. He tried the password that was good back when he helped Calvin and the other recruits escape. An error message popped up on the monitor above him. This wasn't good. He tried another password, this time instead of an error he got a message that read 'REINFORCEMENTS INBOUND. T-35:47' and the message started counting down. No time to worry about that now.

Cody slid over to another monitor and started hitting buttons. The monitors all changed to the security camera feeds. He isolated all the feeds to the prison, searching for the recruits' parents.

216

"Targets located in cells C23 through C30. I repeat, targets found in cells C23 though C30. That's c as in car; c as in car."

"Copy that, Cody," said Ash, "making our way to the elevators now."

"Also be advised," said Cody, "we have a situation flux, I repeat, a situation flux."

52

"I thought you said that wasn't going to happen," said Mason, wrapping a bandage around his left calf. He stood on the stairway landing between the first and second floor, already having planted a directional explosive, the DE-2 on the door to the first floor, just like Cody had done.

"Stick to the plan, and it won't be a problem," said Cody.

Mason tied the bandage and cut off the excess before blowing the DE-2.

Ash landed with ease onto the roof, quickly and expertly disengaging her parachute pack and shoving it off.

"I'm not gonna make it!" yelled Thomas.

Having barely turned around, Ash found Thomas coming in too high over her head. She jumped up and grabbed his foot, being pulled his direction but landing back on the roof. Ash's feet skidded across the roof as the two slowed down, but not fast enough. She used one hand to brace herself as she smashed into the waist high concrete wall surrounding the edge of the roof. She nearly lost her grip on Thomas, having to use both hands to keep a hold of him. With both feet, she pushed off the wall and pulled Thomas to the ground. They both collapsed on top of each other as the parachute slowly descended and covered them.

Ash immediately threw the parachute off her and bolted up, digging through the rest of the parachute to find Thomas. "You alright?" she asked uncovering him.

"Great," he said, catching his breath and giving a thumbs up.

"What are you two doing?" asked Dakota, as he landed next to them, running a short distance before stopping. He put his fists on his hips in a power pose with a huge grin on his face behind his helmet.

"Pull it down," said Ash, clearly annoyed. She jumped up and pulled down Dakota's parachute.

By the time everyone's packs had been taken off and the parachutes moved, Megan floated down, but off course.

"To your left," said Ash motioning with her hands. Megan readjusted, and too much.

"Back the other way," said Dakota.

They played this game all the way until Megan's feet hit the roof, tumbling down immediately after. Ash helped Megan up while Thomas and Dakota pulled the parachute down.

"Anything hurt?" asked Ash.

"Nothing too bad," replied Megan. She stood up and brushed herself off.

"I was worried there for a second," said Thomas.

"Only Calvin left," said Dakota looking up at him.

"Nice job, Calvin," said Ash, "just a little to your right."

Calvin was nearly to the roof as he adjusted his descent.

"Too much!" cried Ash. But it was too late.

"No, no, no—" yelled Thomas as Calvin slammed into an HVAC box, sticking to the side as his parachute pulled him into it.

Everyone sprinted over to where Calvin had hit. But just as they arrived, the parachute pulled Calvin backward, toward the edge of the roof. Dakota jumped out, grabbing Calvin's ankle as he was pulled over the edge. Dakota started going with him when Thomas grabbed Dakota's belt. A second later, Megan grabbed onto his belt as well, but even with both of them, they were having little affect, threatening to pull all of them over the edge.

Ash stopped and dug out three shurikens from her belt, launching them toward Calvin's parachute. All three connected with wires and sliced them like butter. But one wire remained, the parachute dangled and continued to pull Calvin. Ash judged the distance from the wall too far for her to reach with a knife and pulled out another shuriken.

"What are you doing?" cried Thomas, "Help us!"

"Hold him tight," Ash took a breath as she lined up her shot, throwing the shuriken as soon as she finished exhaling. Ash had done this throw a million times. All the Youth had. But time always froze for Ash as the shuriken was about to hit its target, this time was no different.

The shuriken finally connected with the rope, slicing through and dropping Calvin, who slammed into the wall.

The last thing I remembered was deploying our chutes as we jumped from the airplane. The next thing I knew I had a massive headache, and it felt like all the blood was in my head. Then I realized I was upside down, my arms dangling above my head.

"Whoa!" I frantically grasped at whatever was nearest me as I tried to look up, finding a Youth holding me, or was it a Renegade?

"Hold on, Calvin," said Dakota through my helmet as I was pulled up. Then another Youth, or a Renegade (we really needed something to distinguish us from the Youth) reached out to me.

"Take my hand, Calvin," said Ash.

I reached up my left hand as she grabbed it with both of her hands, yanking me up and over the wall. I tumbled to the ground next to Dakota. Ash was immediately over top of me, examining for anything she could fix, with Megan close behind her on the opposite side of me.

"Are you alright?" asked Megan, looking me up and down.

I didn't have to answer when Ash asked, "Where does your head hurt?"

It was making my head hurt just being bombarded with questions. "Does everywhere help you out?" I asked looking at Ash.

"Turn your head," said Ash, moving my head away from her. "Does the back of your head hurt any more than the rest?"

My head started to clear up, probably from all the blood leaving my head. "Now that you say it, it does."

"Megan, hold his head while I take his helmet off." Ash started removing my helmet as Megan cradled my head. Ash unplugged the wires before fully removing my helmet, then pulled my balaclava down around my neck. When Ash was done, Megan gently laid my head on the roof.

A second later, Ash grabbed my head and picked it back up, before Megan took over for her. Ash looked at me as she took her gloves off, almost like she was talking to me, but she wasn't saying anything. Then she pressed the mic-drop button on her helmet. "Can you hear me now, Calvin."

"Yeah," I said.

"Ok, I'm going to examine the back of your head for any injuries. Tell me if anything hurts." As she felt around the back of my head, Dakota and Thomas walked up, leaning over me at my feet.

"Well, well, well," said Dakota. "How'd you manage to pull this off, Calvin? You have not just one, but two women taking care of you, and you don't even have a girlfriend."

"I bet that's more than you've had," said Thomas.

"Then you would have lost that bet," said Dakota, looking over at Thomas, more than likely glaring at him.

"He would have won actually," said Ash, without looking up at him.

"Excuse me," said Dakota, standing up and crossing his arms.

"You're not bleeding," said Ash, completely ignoring Dakota and pulled her gloves back on. "Your helmet took most of the impact." She showed me the spiderwebbing cracks that covered the back of my helmet, barely visible in the darkness of the roof. "Worst case, you get a concussion, best case, you have a really bad headache."

"Well, I'm glad to hear that," I said, slowly sitting up.

"Are you lightheaded?" asked Ash, putting her hand on my back.

"No. Could you help me up just in case?"

"Of course." Ash stood up with Megan and the two pulled me up.

After a moment, I got my balance. Megan let go of me, but Ash kept a hand on my arm.

"Take a few steps for me," said Ash.

"I'm fine. Let's go—"

"Just take a few steps with me, please."

222

"I'm fine, look." I walked a few steps toward the door that led to the roof, stopping halfway. "Is the doctor convinced."

"Yes." Ash let go of my arm. "Thank you. Let's grab you a new helmet."

"From where?" I asked, looking around as Ash walked over to one of the Youth that had been guarding the roof. "Oh no, I'm not taking one of those."

"You need a helmet, Calvin."

"Not if it's off a dead body."

"This is war, Calvin." Ash handed me the helmet. I stared at it, not wanting to take it. But I knew my helmet saved my life before, and it could very easily save me again. I slowly reached out and took the helmet.

"Come on," said Ash, taking off toward the door. I pulled my balaclava back on, connecting the wires coming out of it to my helmet and shoved it on. The cool air from the fan inside was almost too cold, but I knew as soon as I started moving, I'd be glad for it.

"Come on, Calvin," said Megan through my helmet. I clicked the mic-drop button and made my way to the door, clicking it once more before hearing the familiar ding sound, letting me know the external mic was off.

Thomas held the door open for us as we made our way down the stairs. Ash had picked up a rifle and was checking her surroundings as she led the group down the stairs.

Thomas closed the door and fell in behind me. I pulled out my sidearm, ready for anything that might meet us in the staircase.

As I turned the corner of the landing, I found a hole where part of the wall should have been. The door was opened inward with the handle completely missing. A light veil of smoke still hung in the air as Ash checked the hallway before stepping outside and motioning us to the left.

"Stop before the turn in the hallway," said Ash. Before we made it to the turn, there was an open door with a little smoke wisping out of it. Dakota was the first to stop, the rest of us crowded around the door. Inside was a wall of monitors, all of them displaying what appeared to be security camera feeds. There were Youth inside who had clearly lost a fight, but still appeared to be breathing, at least I thought so.

"Get to the turn," said Ash, pushing us past the door. "Dakota, take the back of the line."

Everyone filed past Dakota with Ash taking the lead. I took one more glance inside the security room and found on a monitor a Youth inside that looked like they were in an armory. They were tying wires together that were attached to small boxes.

Dakota scooted past me and picked up a rifle from a rack on the wall. "Dakota," I said, stepping forward when a buzz sounded behind me and something sprayed my back. I ran inside and turned around to find the concrete wall broken, clearly where a bullet had hit it. A moment later, bullets lit up the corridor.

"Behind the wall, behind the wall," I heard Ash scream. Dakota stuck his head out the window and fired his own rifle down the hallway at our attackers. I brought my sidearm up, ready to fire when the bullets stopped or Dakota ducked back inside.

"What's going on down there, Ash?" asked Mason.

"We have a squad in the east corridor approaching us. Most likely from the east barracks."

"I agree," said Mason.

I glanced back at the monitors and found the Youth who was in the armory. This time I saw the boxes in front of him read C-4. "Hey, I've got someone on the security cameras that looks like they're about to detonate a huge pile of C4."

There was a moment of complete silence on the line before Mason replied, "Ash, get him away from the console."

"I can't right now," said Ash.

"Then find a way—"

"Hold on," I said, "wh-what are you not telling me?"

"We're gonna die," said Megan.

"No, you're not," said Mason. "Ash, get him away from the console now!"

"No," I said firmly. "What's going on Mason? Don't hide anything from me."

Dakota came back inside and grabbed another rifle from against the wall, glanced at the monitors, and stopped in his tracks. "No way. There *is* someone about to detonate a bunch of C-4."

"Just tell them, Mason," said Ash.

"Tell us what?" asked Thomas.

"No," said Mason, getting more frustrated.

"Tell us what?" I asked again.

"Shut it, Calvin."

"He's blowing up the complex, Calvin," said Ash.

Again, there was complete silence on the line.

"With us in it?" I asked, gripping the edge of the console.

"No, you idiot!" cried Mason. "Once we're out of the complex."

I breathed a sigh of relief, I didn't realize I was holding in, my grip loosened on the console. And then it hit me, everybody was going to die in this base... everybody.

"You'll regret this, Ash," said Mason coldly.

"Yeah, well get over it," said Ash.

"Why does she look familiar?" asked Dakota, looking at one of the monitors.

I glanced over at the monitor, finding a girl huddled behind a bed with what appeared to be her parents. "It's Sydney!" I yelled. "We have to get her out of here before this place explodes."

"Hallway clear," yelled Ash.

"Try to find a way to contact her," I said, barely hearing Ash. Dakota and I both immediately spotted a microphone sticking out of the console. I adjusted it and saw the sea of buttons with no idea which one to press.

"How do you work this?" asked Dakota, leaning over my shoulder.

I found the on/off button next to the base of the mic, the button lit up red after I hit it. Below it were buttons going in sequential order starting with 101.

I looked up at Sydney's camera and saw it labeled 202. I found the 202 button and clicked it as it turned red as well. Then Ash, Thomas, and Megan came charging into the room.

"Sydney," I said into the mic, "Sydney can you hear me?" She didn't respond.

"Your mic-drop is on, Calvin," said Ash.

I pressed the mic-drop button and the off beep sounded. "Sydney. Sydney, can you hear me?"

Sydney and her parents looked up and around the ceiling.

"Calvin?" said Sydney, slowly standing up.

"Sydney, I don't have time to explain. But someone is trying to blow up this base. You need to get out of here."

"Sydney, do you know this person?" asked Sydney's dad.

"Of course I do, This is Calvin, the one from the school."

"And why should we believe him after what he did?" asked Sydney's mom.

"What I did," I asked. "I was saving everyone from the Youth?"

"Calvin, we need to go," said Ash.

"Hold on a minute." I put my hand up. "Sydney, just listen, there—there's a bomb about to destroy this building. You need to evacuate everyone before it blows."

"How long until the bomb goes off?" asked Sydney's dad.

I hesitated before answering, "It goes off once we leave. But this was *not* a part of my plan. I'm only here to save my parents. And… Sydney," I looked over at Ash, "we can rescue you, too."

I looked back at the monitor. Sydney rubbed the back of her neck and looked at the ground. "I'm not leaving, Calvin."

Not leaving? It took everything not to just scream at her. What was keeping her here. Was she oblivious to what the Youth had done to us? "Why?" I finally asked.

"Calvin," said Ash leaning next to me, "we don't have time for this."

"We can't just leave her!" I burst out.

"She's made up her mind, Calvin."

"I think the Youth are doing-dooing something to make her stay. They've probably threatened her parents or—"

"Calvin. That's not the voice of someone being threatened. That's the voice of someone who willingly chose to stay."

I looked up at Sydney, trying to find something, anything that would prove my point. But there was nothing. There had never been anything. And some place deep inside of me, I knew Ash was right, but didn't want to admit it.

"You can't save everyone, Calvin," said Ash, grabbing my right arm. "Let's—" Ash glanced behind me.

"What?" I asked, turning around.

"There's an evacuate button." Ash sped past me to the end of the console. She lifted a clear box over a small red button, slamming it with her palm. A message popped up on the screen above the button saying 'EVACUATE. PLEASE PRESS AGAIN TO ACTIVATE EVACUATION.' She pressed it again, and all the screens on the wall started flashing red with 'EVACUATE' on the center screen. Spinning red lights turned on in the corners of the room, accompanied by an alarm and a female voice that came over the speakers saying, "Evacuate, evacuate. This is not a drill," on repeat.

I was glad my helmet reduced the noise because it would have been overwhelming having the blaring alarm and the evacuate message playing constantly.

"We have to go, Calvin," said Ash. I glanced back at the flashing screen. In between the flashes, I saw Sydney and her parents frantically grabbing things from around the room.

"I understand wanting to save everyone, Calvin," said Ash walking up to me. "Unfortunately, you can't." I didn't want to turn away from the screen. I felt like I was giving up on Sydney. But I turned toward Ash, flanked by everyone else. We were here to save our parents, I couldn't forget about that.

"Ok," I said, feeling defeated.

Ash grabbed my arm, pulling me toward the door. "Let's go," she said tenderly, pressing my mic-drop button and letting go of my arm, checking the hallway before motioning us through to the right. "We need to hurry before they wake back up."

"Wake back up?" I asked.

"Their armor," said Ash, pointing to her chest. "It only knocks you out if you get hit in the armor."

I was the last one out of the security room and glanced down the hall behind Ash. Some of the Youth were starting to stir. I was glad to see that. But for others, they weren't so fortunate.

"Stop before the turn," said Ash, pulling away. I turned around and jogged with Ash as we caught up with everyone. The same spinning red lights in the security room lined the walls of the hallway, basking everything in red.

Dakota was first to the turn, followed by Thomas, Megan, and me. Ash came to the turn and peeked her head around the corner, immediately greeted by bullets whizzing by, chipping the concrete wall behind her.

"Want to help me out, Dakota?" asked Ash.

"With pleasure."

"Wait until this detonates and fire." Ash dug out a grenade from her belt, pulled out the pin, and chucked it down the hall. Ash ducked behind the wall and readied her rifle. A moment later, the grenade exploded with a bang that echoed down the hall.

Ash and Dakota sprang around the corner and fired off some shots, a few seconds later, Ash shouted, "All clear."

I glanced behind me just to check on the Youth, and one of them started to sit up. I pulled out my gun and fired, missing the first two shots, and the third slamming into the Youth's stomach. A white cloud of smoke exploded in his lap. The Youth started waving their arms frantically trying to fan away the cloud, only to fall on their back and start crawling away from the cloud.

"Come on," said Ash, grabbing my arm and pulling me around the corner. She let go, and we started running down the hall. "You need to reload."

I glanced down at my gun and saw the slide was locked back. I pulled a fresh mag from my belt and exchanged it.

We hopped over four Youth on the ground, all which appeared to be alive, which was a relief.

We stopped again at the next turn in the hall, another right, when we heard gunfire just beyond.

"Mason," called Ash. "We're entering the west corridor. Are we clear to proceed?"

The gunfire stopped. "You're clear," said Cody.

Ash jogged to the front of the line and peeked her head out, then stepped fully into the hallway and waved everyone through.

As I came around the corner, Cody came around the next corner running toward us, hopping over a pile of Youth on the ground.

"How's the elevator coming?" asked Cody.

"I could use your help," replied Mason.

Cody beat us to the set of elevators. Before we got to the elevator, Ash ran inside a room. Inside I saw it, the pile of C-4. I couldn't focus on what Ash was doing when I was looking at a giant pile of death and destruction. Ash came back out of the room, blocking my vision of the C-4, and breaking me out of my trance. But the more I looked, the worse it got. There were grenades, dynamite, and all other manner of explosives I wasn't familiar with stacked together.

Ash stopped in front of me holding a bunch of backpacks. "Everyone take one," she said, distributing them to us. Ash closed the door behind her and threw her backpack on. I slowly did the same and followed everyone to the elevators.

When we arrived, there was a crate in the middle of the elevator. Both Cody and Mason were messing with wires coming from an access panel behind the floor buttons.

"What are we doing," asked Thomas.

"Hold on," said Ash.

Cody and Mason started throwing the wires back inside the wall and reattached the access panel. Then Cody slid the lid off the crate, revealing a pile of grenades. "Start pulling the pins out of the smoke grenades," said Cody, "and throw them back inside the crate."

We all started pulling the pins out. I had to show Megan what to do, but in less than a minute, the crate was finished.

"Outside, quick," said Ash. The smoke was billowing out of the crate as Cody leaned inside the elevator from outside and closed the door. As the doors were closing, I noticed a second set of elevator doors on the opposite side. A double sided elevator, don't see those often.

"To the stairs," said Ash, moving us toward the door just to the right of the elevators. Mason held the door for us, Ash being the last one through. "Make sure to weld the door shut," said Ash as she passed Mason.

As we descended the stairs, with Cody leading, Ash suddenly cried out. I spun around, Ash's rifle clattering to the ground and found Mason slam Ash into the wall, holding her by her neck. He lifted her up against the wall, her feet coming off the ground. She desperately clawed her hands at Mason's arm, her feet scraping against the wall trying to find something to stand on.

It all happened so quickly I just froze. My body didn't move. I couldn't see or hear anything except Ash's gasps. I wanted to move, but it was like someone else was controlling my body.

"Drop her!" screamed Cody, but I couldn't look to see where he was.

Ash started digging around in her belt with one hand when Mason used his free hand and pulled out his sidearm, pointing it at Ash's stomach.

"Drop her, Mason!" yelled Cody.

"I told you you'd regret it," said Mason. "This whole mission is now in jeopardy because of you. That is unless you're still a Youth?" Mason dug his gun into Ash's stomach.

"Are you crazy," yelled Dakota.

"Drop her or I shoot you, Mason!" yelled Cody.

Ash's breaths were starting to come fewer and farther between. Mason was going to kill her.

"Not until-Ahh!" Mason cried out as Cody shot him in the leg and immediately buckled. In that instant, I was free. The fear and overwhelm left me, and I sprinted up the stairs, tackling Mason. He let go of Ash as we collided on the ground. In an instant, Mason's elbow connected with my helmet and his other hand punched me twice in the gut. I lost my grip on him, and he shoved me away.

As I rolled onto my back, Cody had climbed up on the railing surrounding the landing. He jumped off and landed on top of Mason. Past them, Ash was on all fours, coughing between gasps of air. Everyone else started making their way up the stairs to help Ash.

"She could still be a Youth," said Mason, trying to shove Cody off him.

"That's insane," said Cody.

"And how do you know?"

"Because I know her better than you do."

"She left you and you think you know her?" said Mason laughing. The two wrestled some more, everyone staying out of it. Then Cody was able to flip Mason onto his stomach, twisting his arms behind his back. Cody took one arm and twisted it far more than necessary, threatening to break it as Mason cried out.

"Now, you're insane," said Mason.

"Cody," I yelled, "don't break his arm."

"Listen to him, Cody," said Mason.

"You're pathetic," said Cody, twisting Mason's arm even harder.

"Cody, stop," said Ash over Mason's screams with what little strength she had regained. A second later, Cody released the tension on Mason's arm, pulling out a plastic tie from his belt, binding Mason's hands together.

"You alright?" asked Thomas, walking over and kneeling next to me.

"I'm good," I said, "can you help me up?" Thomas offered his hand and pulled me up.

Cody pulled Mason to his feet while Dakota and Megan helped Ash stand up.

"We need to move," said Cody, pulling Mason to his feet and shoving him toward the stairs.

"Will you make it down the stairs," I asked Ash, walking up to her.

"I'm fine." Ash let go of Dakota's arm, bent down to pick up her rifle, and started walking down the stairs no problem. She was definitely a trooper. I didn't think I'd be able to walk off nearly being strangled.

We started descending the stairs, and Cody opened the door to the basement, without having to blow the lock, and looked back and forth inside before closing it.

"Why-why didn't we need to blow the door?" I asked.

"The evacuation," said Ash, "disengages all electronic locks except for the prison."

"Why is that?" I asked, making it to the last stair.

"To ensure everyone can get out, even without their badge." That gave me hope that the Youth would actually listen to the evacuation order and escape before the explosion. But who was I to say they weren't being issued orders to ignore the evacuation.

"Wait here," said Ash, heading to the door.

"Make sure he doesn't escape," said Cody, looking at Dakota before shoving Mason to the floor in the corner of the stairwell.

"He won't," said Dakota, walking past Cody and raising his rifle at Mason.

Ash clicked a button on her helmet before opening the door, stepping into the basement greeted by a wall of smoke. Those had to be our smoke grenades from the elevator. If those were, that was an ingenious idea. Send smoke billowing from the elevator on the floor you were about to enter to blind the enemy.

Cody followed behind Ash as some smoke drifted into the stairwell. The door closed, and the rest of us stood in silence, Thomas anxiously glancing up the stairs.

"She's already betrayed us," said Mason.

"How has she betrayed us?" asked Dakota.

"You weren't supposed to know the plan. Now if you get caught—"

"We aren't going to get caught," said Dakota taking a step toward Mason. "That is unless *you* get us caught?"

"Which plan?" I asked. "The one to save our parents, or the one to blow up the base with all you Youth in it?"

"There was only ever one plan, Calvin," said Mason. "It's always been to blow up the complex. We would save your parents if it was no risk to us."

"No risk," I said my voice rising.

"Half of the people in this room don't want to save their parents, Calvin." Mason looked around at everyone, and I followed his gaze.

"Do you want to save your parents?" I asked Thomas.

"Of course I do," said Thomas.

I looked over at Dakota. "Do you want to save your parents."

After a moment, Dakota replied, "I was more in it for the adventure."

"But do you want to save your parents?"

The door at the top of the stairs burst open and echoed down to us.

Footsteps doing the same, it sounded like there were loads of Youth coming down.

"They're coming down the stairs," said Dakota pulling Mason up.

"Hang on," said Ash, "I'll meet you back there."

I grabbed the door and yanked it open as bullets started raining down around Meagan. She ducked out of the way and ran through the door, followed by Thomas, Dakota with Mason, and me. I slammed the door shut as I walked into the cloud of smoke. I couldn't see anyone or anything around me.

"How do we get through this?" asked Thomas, speaking my thoughts.

"On the left side of your helmet is a button," said Ash, "just like the mic-drop. Press that." I did as she said, and my whole vision lit up different shades of blue. As I moved my head, I found the outline of two people in orange. This was like a thermal camera, picking up heat signatures and showing them back in shades of blue and orange. Even with the smoke, I could see the outlines of the cold concrete walls around me, lit up in blue.

"Whoa," said Dakota, just as mystified as I was.

"That's your thermal visor," said Ash. "Let's you see heat signatures." I started following Dakota and Mason when the door behind us slammed open. I spun around and saw multiple heat signatures at the door, so I immediately bolted down the hall.

The Youth must have been turning on their thermal visors because I was positive they would have been shooting at us already.

I followed everyone as we came down a hallway that took a left. I passed Cody and Mason when a figure started running toward us. "Who is that?" I asked.

"Probably me," said Ash. "You can turn your visor off. The smoke is starting to dissipate." I turned off the thermal visor and found Ash running toward us. The smoke now just a light haze in front of us, and thicker behind us. "Follow Cody. Stay against the wall," she said pointing to him, kneeling against the wall with his rifle pointed down the hallway.

I immediately hugged the wall, putting my back to it as I progressed forward. The hallway was lined with doors on either side for a way, ending with a single door next to a window.

"Get against the wall, you idiot," said Mason, "unless *you* want to put a giant target on our heads."

I turned my head and saw Dakota pulling Mason toward the wall. Further behind, Ash's muzzle flashes lit up the smoke as she fired at the incoming Youth from the stairwell.

"Ash, something is wrong here. Get back," said Cody

"Why," asked Ash.

"There should be guards at the prison entrance and there's none."

"What? Where are they?"

As I walked past a door, it opened behind me. I barely managed to turn around and see a syringe in the Youth's hand coming toward me. I swatted it away as the Youth changed tactics and shoved me against the hallway wall.

I heard a bang as the Youth went limp against me, falling to the ground. Down the hall, Cody's barrel was pointed to me.

"Get down, get down," said Ash, running down the hall toward us. "In a room, any room."

"Ash?" asked Cody clearly concerned. But she couldn't answer when bullets started flying down the hall. I dived into the open door the Youth had just come out of. I stood up, looking back out in the hallway when I had a feeling to look back in the room. I turned around finding two more Youth running up toward me. I pulled out my gun and sprayed them both, white clouds of pepper spray engulfing them. Immediately, they were coughing and stumbling. I emptied my mag into them, replaced it with a fresh one, and carefully sneaked past the pepper spray cloud. I checked the L shaped room and found no one else wanting to kill me. But I did find someone strapped to a table around the corner. I looked back at the Youth I had just shot and figured they'd be out of it for a while. That's when I noticed they were wearing medical smocks, one of them an operating gown.

I looked around in the room to find various medical equipment scattered about. Scanners, vials, smocks, gloves; it looked like an operating room. I slowly made my way over to the person on the table. They were wearing a Youth undersuit, strapped down by thick leather straps across their legs and stomach. With individual straps on their ankles and wrists. Then I saw their face.

"Eve?" I asked, running up to her side, remembering to turn my mic drop off.

She slowly turned her head toward me. "Calvin?" she asked weakly, "what are you doing here?"

"Well, I was here to save my parents, but now we're adding you to the list. That is if you are Eve?"

"Yes, I'm surprised you recognized me?" Last time I saw her was when we danced together at the masquerade. That felt like a lifetime ago.

"Calvin, what's going on in there?" asked Ash.

"Ash," I said, looking toward the door, "I found Eve."

"Hold on," said Ash.

"Ash is here?" asked Eve.

"Yeah," I said, looking back down at her, "and Cody and—" I noticed her arms and stopped mid-sentence. Eve's arms were covered in green lines. And not lines colored on her skin, this looked like it was inside of her. "What did they do to you?" I asked, lightly tracing the green lines.

"I'm not too sure. They've been injecting me with stuff. Now all my veins are turning green." There was a small table next to Eve's head with vials of green liquid. I picked one up, the label reading INHM-35 with a list of ingredients I couldn't read underneath it.

I immediately set the vial down and started unstrapping Eve. "I'm getting you out of here," I said.

"No, you need to go."

"I'm not leaving you behind."

"I think I'm dying, Calvin."

I froze a moment, before taking the straps off again. "We can save you," I said as gunfire sounded outside.

"Sounds like you need to leave."

"I am not leaving you behind!" I yelled. "I don't care if you're already dead. You're coming with us." I undid the last strap and started sitting Eve up. "Do you think you can walk."

"I'll get you killed if you take me out there." Eve's eyes looked weak, far weaker than any eyes I'd seen before. "It hurts just to hold my head up, Calvin."

The green vials next to the table caught my eye. I grabbed one, shoving it in a zippered pocket on my pants, before grabbing Eve under her legs and under her back. As I picked up her clearly malnourished body, her body was like a rag doll. One arm was on her lap while the other hung down. She barely had any strength left as she nestled her head against my chest.

As I came around the corner, the Youth I had shot earlier started to get their bearings. They were coming toward me when Ash wacked both of them on the head with one swipe of the butt of her rifle. The Youth both toppled to the ground.

"Wow," I said, frozen with Eve in my hands.

"Eve!" said Ash, running up. She took her gloved hand and moved some of Eve's greasy hair out of her face. "Oh, Eve, what have they done to you?" Ash saw Eve's dangling arm and picked it up, examining the green lines before her head darted around the room. She gently let Eve's arm down and ran around the room, grabbing various items.

"What are you getting," I asked as she tore off her backpack and ripped it open.

"Anything that can help her," said Ash, shoving papers, vials, and anything else she could get her hands on. She grabbed so many of the green vials, all of them clinking against each other. She went behind the table where Eve had been and pulled out a rolling board that was hidden in the dark. On it were various charts with dots and comments written on it. Ash pulled the papers off and folded them into her bag. She put her bag on the table, doing a last check before closing it and putting it back on.

"Let's go." I followed Ash out to the door where we stopped. She checked the hallway both ways before stepping out. We headed down to the single door at the end of the hall, where everyone else already was. Cody was climbing through the window next to the door that had been busted out, glass scattered all over the ground.

As Ash and I approached the group, a click came from the doors. Thomas pulled it open, holding it as we all passed through into a short hallway that had a window looking into the room Cody had crawled into. Dakota opened a second door that led us into the prison. I had to squeeze through with Eve, careful not to bang her against the walls.

Once inside, it was about as drab and hopeless a place as you could get. There was minimal lighting, and none of the rotating red lights from the evacuation command. All the walls were concrete, it reminded me of an old war bunker.

Cody exited the room he had broken into through a door next to the one we came out of. Now that I got to look at it more, it looked like a checkpoint set up. You would enter into the hallway, and the people in the room could verify your info, keeping you from entering the prison and locking you in the hallway if something didn't check out.

"Ash," said Cody, "take them to their parents cells. C23 through C30. I'm going to weld these doors shut."

"Hold on," said Dakota, barging past Cody and into the checkpoint room.

E.E. Cooley

"What are you doing?" asked Cody.

Dakota lifted a lid to a crate attached to the wall. Above the crate was a rack of rifles with corresponding mags. "Grabbing these," said Dakota, taking off his backpack, pulling small boxes out from the crate and setting them in his backpack.

"What are those?" I asked.

"Explosives," replied Cody. "Used to bring down this ceiling and block the prisoners in, if necessary," Cody pointed to the ceiling above us.

Dakota put the last explosive in his bag and zipped it up. Before he left, he grabbed two rifles from the rack and strapped them to the side of his backpack. "Never know when we might need these," said Dakota, grabbing a couple of mags from the rack and shoving them in his pockets. He threw his backpack on as he ran out the door.

Cody shoved it closed and pulled out a small handheld device from his belt. It looked like a small RC car controller. "Everyone look away," said Cody, pressing something on the side of his helmet. Before I looked away, he activated the device. It created a very bright light that made me see spots. But it was a portable welding device, or something that super heated the metals together. Whatever it was, it was cool.

"Let's go find your parents," said Ash, pulling out a flashlight from her belt and attaching it to her rifle on the side of the barrel. We followed her down the hallway that led to a branch going both left and right. The light from Cody's welder flickered, making our shadows grow and shrink as we made our way down the hallway.

When we came to the branch, we took a left. Both ways were nearly completely dark, the only light coming from very dim lights in the center of the ceiling. Ash carefully checked a branching hallway that took a left, before clearing it and moving past it. Down that turn were prison cells on both sides of the hallway, steel bar doors by the looks of it. Those felt out of place next to all the tech of the rest of the complex.

When we came to the next turn, the hallway stopped, forcing us to turn left down another hall. The cells on the right side of the hall were solid steel doors. No windows or anything, just a small square cut at the bottom of the door. It looked like it could be a door for food to be passed to the prisoner. The left side of the hall had the steel bar doors as before. Ash used her flashlight to search the cells on the left of the hallway. Immediately, the person inside shielded their eyes with their hand.

"Dad?" asked Thomas.

"Your mic-drop is on," said Ash.

We all clicked our mic-drops off. "Dad," asked Thomas again.

"Thomas?" said his dad hoarsely. I immediately recognized his voice. Thomas bolted over to the cell and threw his arms through the bars. Thomas's dad struggled to get up but managed to stand and hug his son.

"Thomas, is that you?" said a female voice. Ash shined her flashlight to the next cell. A woman crawled over to the cell door, leaned against it, and stuck one hand out while she covered her eyes with the other hand.

"Mom!" Thomas ran over to his mother, kneeling and hugging her through the bars. I had the biggest smile as I watched the reunion. Then I started hearing voices further down the hallway.

"What's going on?"

"Who's there?"

"Are we free?"

"Thomas, is Calvin with you?" It was my dad. If Ash had a light, I should have one, too. I gently set Eve on the ground and searched my belt, finding a small pouch. I undid the cover and found the flashlight. I turned it on and ran down the hallway, shining the light in all the cells as I went. Near the end of the hallway, I found him. "Calvin," asked my dad, holding a hand over his eyes. He was standing up in his cell.

"Dad!" I screamed, running over to the cell, throwing my arms inside as we hugged."

"Oh, Calvin," said Dad, "I'm so glad you're ok."

"I'm glad to see you're ok, too." We nearly began crying when a gunshot echoed from down the hallway, a flash of light illuminating the hall for a millisecond. I looked up to two more gunshots before one of the cell doors opened.

"Everyone go find your parents," said Ash. "I'll unlock the doors."

Everyone started moving down the hall looking through the cells. I looked back at Dad when I heard another voice from the next cell. "Calvin," said my mom.

"Go see your mother," said my dad, patting me on the shoulder before I could reply. I ran to the next cell and found my mom standing up. We hugged through the bars.

"Oh Calvin, you're alive." She kissed me on the check and pulled me back in for a hug.

"We're going to get you out of here," I said, "don't worry." Three more gunshots came from down the hallway and another door was opened.

"Mom," said Dakota, sounding defeated. I glanced down the hall and found Dakota standing in front of a cell.

"I'll be right back," I told Mom. We let go of each other, and I walked up the Dakota by the cell just before my dad's. "What is it, Dakota," but I smelled it far before I got the answer. It was the worst smell I had ever experienced. It made me want to puke. A body lay in the cell in a pool of something dark.

"She's dead, Dakota," said the man in the cell to our left, who I assumed was Dakota's dad.

"Let's get away from here, Dakota," I said, putting a hand on his back.

"I'm sorry," said Dakota's dad.

"No, you're not!" yelled Dakota, walking over to his dad. "Don't you dare tell me you're sorry."

"I am sorry, Dakota. What makes you think I'm not?"

"Don't 'what makes you think I'm not' me," said Dakota mockingly. "You couldn't care less."

"Absolutely not! I loved your mother."

"You never loved her. You could have cared less for her; for me."

A group started forming around us. I made my way closer to Dakota.

"I am not going to start this reunion like this," said Dakota's dad. "Now, get me out of here."

"Don't let him out, Ash." Dakota held an arm out.

"Dakota, I'm not playing this game with you. Now let me out."

"Is that what you thought it was, just some game." Dakota took a step closer to the cell.

"What do you mean?"

"What do you mean? I mean the times you beat Mom!" Dakota hesitated a moment before replying in a softer voice. "The time you beat me."

"I did no such thing!" protested Dakota's dad.

"Are you telling me you don't remember any of that?"

"I would never do that, Dakota."

"You don't remember coming home drunk every night. And more often than not beating your wife. Oh wait, it makes sense now. You were too drunk to remember!"

"I would never beat my wife, and I would never beat you, Dakota."

"Are you telling me you never saw the bruises, the cuts, the scrapes, the burns? You didn't see any of that?"

"I told you I would never—"

"Look me in the eye, Dad! Look me in the eyes and tell me you didn't beat Mom! That you don't remember a single night that you came home and took your anger of work out on her. Look me in the eyes and tell me..." Dakota got quiet again, "tell me that you don't remember hitting me that night?"

Everyone was frozen in the room. No one made a sound. Cody came running around the corner, making his way toward us.

"Dakota..." started his dad.

"That's it," said Dakota, stepping back and raising his rifle.

"Dakota, no!" I screamed as I reached out for the rifle, shoving it upward as a shot rang out, the light from the shot illuminating the sheer terror on Dakota's dad's face. The shot echoed around us as I kept the rifle up, with Dakota struggling to push it back down.

"Stay out of this, Calvin," said Dakota through gritted teeth. The next thing I knew I was tackled and thrown to the ground with Dakota. The rifle ripped out of our hands with a scream from Dakota.

"Stand down," said Cody, holding Dakota's rifle toward him. I scrambled away from Dakota and stood up. Thomas and Megan were over by me in an instant to help me stand up.

"He should be dead!" screamed Dakota.

"Now's not the time to do that," said Ash, shooting away the lock and letting Dakota's dad out of his cell.

"What are you doing?" screamed Dakota.

"He doesn't die," said Cody. "Give me your side arm."

"Why would I do that when the Youth could come in here at any second?"

"Because you're not killing him." A second later, Ash came up behind Dakota and swiped the sidearm from his thigh holster.

Dakota put his hands up in fists. "You're making a mistake."

"You two," said Cody, pointing at Thomas's parents. "Stay next to him. Make sure nothing happens to him."

Thomas's parents cautiously eyed Dakota and his dad.

"Get everyone else out, we need to leave now," said Cody, running to open my parent's cells. I looked around at our new group. Thomas had his parents, Megan had both her parents, Dakota had his dad, and I was about to have my parents.

I wanted to say something, but I was at a loss for words. So, we waited in silence, eyeing Dakota as he stood back up, his eyes never leaving his father.

"Back to the doors," said Ash as Cody bolted past our group with my parents in tow. I went to pick up Eve when Dakota's dad offered to carry her. I obliged and thought it might help Dakota know that there was some good in his dad, despite what he may have thought.

"I thought we welded the doors shut?" I asked as we headed back toward the entrance.

"Just the one to the control booth," said Ash. "The other one we just locked."

"Can't the Youth get into the room through the window and disable to locks like Cody?"

"No," said Cody.

"How?" I asked.

"He disabled the locks," said Ash, "so we'll shoot the locks to get out."

We turned the corner with our exit in sight when the speakers suddenly crackled to life. "I'm almost impressed," said Paige. We all stopped dead in our tracks. "You nearly did it. But the Youth always win. So, I'll give you this one chance to surrender. It'll be easier on both of us."

"Like we'd ever do that!" screamed Ash.

"Cody, Ashley, and Calvin are to be captured alive for interrogation. Everyone else is to be killed. Teams, you may breach the prison."

"What!" screamed Megan

A muffled bang came from down the hall. We all went to investigate, finding a slew of Youth in the hallway just outside the prison entrance. Some of them even had riot shields.

"We need a new plan," said Ash. "Any ideas."

"If you hadn't saved their parents, we'd all be away by now," said Mason.

"Shut it," said Ash

"I'm not dying with him next to me," said Dakota, "What's beyond these walls?" Dakota pointed to the wall opposite the doors we came in.

"The emergency escape boat launch," said Ash. "But we need to get back outside to access it."

"How many explosives do you have?" asked Cody walking toward Dakota.

"I counted fifteen," said Dakota taking off his bag, "what's your plan?"

240

Prime Youth: Operation Turbulence

"Follow me," said Cody taking a few explosives and walking to the back wall.

"Do any of you know how to operate a gun?" asked Ash, stopping Dakota to grab the rifles strapped to his backpack.

"I do," said both my dad and Thomas's dad. Ash handed each of them a rifle and an extra mag.

As soon as my dad had his gun all set, he came to life. "Alright," he said. "Let's get out of sight of the doors."

"This way," said Cody, taking a right at the end of the hallway. We followed them with my dad and I bringing up the rear.

"Are you ready to use that?" my dad asked, looking at my gun.

"Yeah," I replied. "I've used it before."

"You have?"

"It's a pepper spray gun, not a real gun."

"What is that?" my dad asked as another explosion sounded. The last door blew open, and we rushed everyone around the corner. Bullets started flying toward us as my dad took cover behind the corner of the wall and started firing back.

"What's the plan?" I asked, backing up to the wall next to my dad, my mom holding my arm next to me.

"We need to keep them back," said Ash, running up behind my dad and firing at the Youth as well.

There was an explosion from behind us. All our parents flinched, and Eve flinched as her hands tried to come up and cover her ears. I looked down to see one of the solid steel door cells blow open at the end of the hallway. Cody and Dakota ran inside as smoke snaked around them.

"What's the plan?" I asked again.

"Take everyone down there," said Ash, nodding toward the door Cody and Dakota just went in. "Cody will show you what to do." Thomas's dad joined Ash and my dad as the rest of us made our way down the hallway.

Cody and Dakota came out of the very last door on the left of the main hallway, waving us to take a right at the bend, exactly like the other side of the prison where we found our parents. Cody shot the lock off the first door on the right, and we all piled inside. Dakota's dad set Eve down and I helped.

"Cover her ears," said Cody, pointing to Eve. Ash repeated the command to Thomas's and my dads as I took my hands and covered Eve's ears. An even louder explosion echoed through the prison, this one shaking the ground. Dakota's dad was standing up and started falling over, Dakota blatantly looking away as his dad caught himself on the wall.

"Dakota!" I yelled. I looked around at the crowded room for someone to stand in between Dakota and his dad. "Megan, you and your parents stand between Dakota and his dad. Please." Everyone shuffled around the room until Dakota was separated from his dad.

In the shuffle, Cody and Dakota left the room again. "Do we follow you, Cody?" I asked.

"Stay there."

"We're not going to make it out of here," said Megan.

"Yes, we are," I told her. "We're not done yet."

"They're right out there, Calvin. We have no plan, and Dakota and Cody are doing who knows what."

"Don't worry, Megan," said her mom. "We were able to escape before."

"Before we got captured again and you got taken."

"We'll make it out of this, Megan," said her father.

"Fall back! Fall back!" yelled Ash.

"What's going on, Ash?" I asked.

"They've pushed us back. You need to hurry whatever it is you're doing, Cody."

Cody and Dakota ran back inside our crowded cell. "Cover your ears," said Cody. I covered Eve's ears again as another explosion echoed through the prison, the ground shaking again.

"What are you doing?" I asked as Cody and Dakota ran out of the cell again.

"Don't say with the Youth this close," said Cody.

"I'll be right back," I said to Eve, getting up and peeking my head out of the cell.

"Calvin, where are you going?" asked my mom, reaching her hand out toward me.

"I'm just looking around the corner," I replied. I could see in the cell that was blown open there was a gaping hole in the back wall. I put the pieces together in my head, and it all made sense. They were blowing a hole in the wall to get to the emergency boat escape beyond the wall. Ingenious. I just hoped we had enough explosives to get through.

Bullets started littering the wall across from us, concrete chips flying everywhere.

"We're gonna die. We're gonna die," said Megan.

"No, we're not," I said, stopping her.

"They're right there, Calvin!" screamed Megan, pointing her hand toward the Youth.

"Would you calm down," I said, turning around and pointing at Megan. "What did I say before. Keep the negative thoughts to yourself. None of us want to hear them. And I will do everything in my power to make sure we get out of here. Which I know is true for Cody and Ash as well."

"My hands are unfortunately handcuffed, or I would be helping, too, not that I would have—"

"Are you done yet," I said.

"We need covering fire," said Cody. I turned to look back outside. Cody and Dakota were waiting inside the cell as a wall of bullets sprayed the hallway in front of them.

"Copy that," said Ash. More gun shots rang out, but the bullets stopped flying down the hallway. Cody slapped Dakota on the shoulder, and they both sprinted back to our cell.

"Last one," said Cody. "Everyone, cover your ears." We went through the motions again as Cody blew the third set of explosives. He stepped out of our cell as Ash, and Thomas and I's dads bolted around the corner, firing their guns the entire way.

"They'll be on top of us any minute," said Ash, as she ducked behind the wall, more bullets spraying the hallway.

"The hole's not big enough," said Cody. "We need one more run."

More bullets started littering the walls, forcing Ash, Thomas, and I's dads behind the wall.

"I don't know if we can get you a break," said Ash, trying to peek around the corner. She brought her rifle up before being spun around, a bullet catching her shoulder. She screamed as she went down, Cody pulling her back behind the wall.

"We're not going to make it." Megan was whispering.

We couldn't fail, not when we were so close, our exit in sight. I said a quick prayer when Megan got up, ran out of the cell, and yelled, "Stop, stop. I surrender, I surrender. Please don't kill me, please. I don't want to die." By the end, Megan was sobbing.

"What are you doing, Megan," I asked.

"Please don't kill me," said Megan through tears.

The firing stopped, and a boy Youth said, "Come out with your hands up, Megan."

Megan nearly sprinted out from behind the corner, throwing her hands in the air.

I prayed I wasn't making a mistake thinking the Youth didn't want me dead and bolted out of the cell in front of Megan.

"Calvin!" cried my mom. My dad also tried to grab me, but I dodged him, stopping in front of Megan and putting my hands up.

"Don't do this, Megan!" She tried to get past me, and I kept blocking her.

"We're dead, Calvin!" screamed Megan. "We have to surrender. Look," she pointed behind me.

I turned my head and at least ten Youth took up the entire width of the hallway, each with riot shields.

"You are more than welcome to surrender, Megan," said a Youth walking around a corner and coming up behind one of the riot shield Youth, not bothering to duck down to cover his whole body with the shield. "Megan, I can guarantee your survival, I just need you to do one thing."

"What's that?" asked Megan.

"Just come here. And Calvin, if you stop her, my men will shoot you. But not kill you."

Megan didn't even look at me and sidestepped me. I reached out my hand helplessly as she made her way to the line of Youth. "Please, Megan," I pleaded.

Megan walked up to the Youth behind the riot shield. He put his hand on her shoulder. "Mr. and Mrs. Nall," he said looking up. "Would you also come here. If you don't come out on your own, my men will come and drag you out here."

I turned around and found everyone lined up just out of sight from the Youth. I took a few steps toward Megan's parents when a bullet whizzed in front of me. My mom gasped and put her hands over her mouth.

"Not another step, Calvin," said the Youth. I was stopped just past the corner mid-step. Megan's parents looked back and forth at one another.

"Do you promise not to harm us if we come out?" asked Megan's dad.

"I promise my men will not harm you or your wife."

Megan's dad took his wife's hand, and they slowly walked around the corner.

"You can't do this," I pleaded.

"Looks like you're not as influential as you thought, Calvin," said the Youth mockingly. I turned my head to look at him, glaring behind my helmet. Megan's parents slowly made their way behind the line of Youth. All I could do was watch them, helplessly.

"Anybody else wish to surrender?" asked the Youth. "We promise there won't be any bloodshed tonight."

I turned around, taking in everyone's faces. No one looked like they knew what to do. We had our escape route, we just needed a minute to get through and we'd be free. That's when I noticed Cody and Dakota rush back inside the cell. A few moments later, they came out and quietly instructed everyone to move further down the hallway.

"Thomas," said the Youth. "I know you'd rather not die."

Cody pressed his mic-drop button and replied to us, "Don't say anything."

"Come on, Thomas," said the Youth. "We both know this is far more than you expected."

Cody dragged Eve next to everyone else and motioned for me to remain still. "Your mic-drop isn't on, Calvin," said Cody, "so don't say anything. On three, I need you to bolt toward us." Cody held up his statscreen, his hand hovering over a button.

"You have five seconds before I need an answer," said the Youth.

"One," said Cody.

"Five," said the Youth

"Two," said Cody.

"Four," said the Youth.

"Three," said Cody. I sprinted toward him. An instant later, bullets buzzed around me before an explosion shook the room. The blast of the explosion pushed me over, making me trip and fall, sliding across the floor. Cody slapped the side of my helmet, turning my mic-drop on, and pulled me up.

"Shoot the hole, shoot the hole," I barely heard Cody say. My mind was still trying to process what had happened.

Cody walked away from me with Thomas and I's dad. All three of them firing their rifles at the hole in the wall. Concrete chipped away, and the hole started to expand.

To the left of the hole, I found where the explosion came from. The cell everyone was just in had its wall completely destroyed. The rubble cutting off the hallway between the Youth and us, but not entirely. The smoke slowly started to dissipate when Cody yelled for all of us to follow him, motioning as well with his hands for our parents who didn't have helmets to hear him.

My brain finally cleared up, and I could comprehend everything normally again. My mom ran out of the cell and took my arm. "Let's go, Calvin," she yelled far louder than necessary, probably having lost some of her hearing from the explosion. Ash was cutting off the excess bandage over her gunshot wound while Dakota's dad carried Eve again.

Cody and Dakota were already at the hole, clearing away any sharp corners with the butts of their rifles before proceeding, Cody going through first. Thomas's mom ran up beside me as we made it to the turn in the hallway. I stopped everyone, holding my hands out and peering around the corner. There was a small gap in the rubble pile, enough for about one person to hop through. I could see the Youth getting reoriented, and Megan and her parents being pushed away. Megan glanced back toward the rubble, and our helmets locked view for a moment before she disappeared around the corner.

When the Youth didn't fire, I pushed Thomas and I's moms past the gap in the rubble.

"Here!" yelled Dakota, holding his hand out through the hole in the wall. Thomas's mom went first through the hole, my mom going next, with Dakota's dad and Eve following.

As Eve was passed through the hole, Ash fired into the gap in the rubble, allowing Mason past the gap and into the line that had formed to get through the wall.

The Youth started returning fire, and Ash was forced to duck behind the corner of the wall.

"That's everyone, Ash," I said, "come on!"

Ash looked behind her to check that everyone indeed was across. She pulled a grenade from her belt and launched it through the gap in the rubble.

"Grenade, get down," screamed a Youth, causing the returning fire to stop momentarily. The grenade went off, and an instant later, Ash bolted across the hallway, nearly running into me.

"Are you alright?" I asked Ash.

"I'm fine," she said. "Just got the wind knocked out of me."

"Good," I said as we joined the line to get out the hole. Thomas's dad just went through as Dakota's dad pushed Mason through feet first, Cody

246

and Dakota grabbed him by the feet and pulled him through.

The gunfire resumed through the gap in the rubble. Ash spun around and brought her rifle up, reading for anything that might come through.

"Hurry up," said Ash.

Mason was through, and Dakota's dad started climbing through.

"We can fit now," I said, grabbing Ash's shoulder and guiding her inside the cell. As we got in, she fired off a couple of shots, and Dakota's dad screamed, covering one of his ears. Ash fired a couple more shots before closing the door. Bullets pinged off the door, echoing inside the room as I climbed through the hole.

"Feet first, Calvin," said Dakota as I started climbing through on my hands and knees. I changed course and stuck my feet toward the hole, being careful not to cut my hand on any of the chipped concrete. I crab walked through the hole, and the second my feet were through, Cody and Dakota grabbed them, pulling me through. I nearly fell on my back as my hands slipped across the concrete.

I came out landing on my butt as Cody pulled me to my feet. "To the boat," yelled Cody, pointing to a couple of boats floating in a river of water. I glanced around at the concrete tunnel as I got my footing under me and made my way to the boats. A concrete sidewalk lined both sides of the river as I ran, looking behind me to make sure Ash made it through. She shot through the hole headfirst, diving out and rolling off the sidewalk straight into the water. Cody and Dakota immediately rushed down and pulled her out, taking her helmet off and letting all the water drain from it. Ash coughed and sputtered water while Cody picked her up and started dragging her toward the boats.

I turned around and followed the sidewalk just a short distance to the boat launch. The all-black boats were tied down to the beginning of the river, leading straight down the tunnel out into the ocean. Small dim lights ran the length of the tunnel with the moon shining bright against the water at the tunnel exit. Everyone had jumped in the closest boat that was long and narrow with a windshield covering the driver and passenger seat. Seats lined the sides of the boat with enough space for everyone to walk single file down it, fitting all of us with a few seats to spare.

There was no dock for these boats to get in. Instead, they had a small door on the back of the boat that opened, allowing you to walk on straight from the tunnel floor. And there were five boats total, each side by side taking up the entire width of the concrete river.

I went through the door with Dakota and Ash close behind me. When Cody came to the boat, he hopped the side, sliding into the driver seat, and fired the engine up. Ash closed the door on the back of the boat and instructed everyone to a chair. I sat next to my mom and dad, who were already sitting down.

Cody gave the engine everything it had, but it jerked to a stop barely away from where we started.

Cody spun his head around. "Ash, cut us loose!" cried Cody as gunfire started pelting the water and air around us. Our moms screamed as we all ducked to the floor of the boat, my dad covering my mom and I with his body.

Dakota stood behind Cody, and the two of them pulled their rifles up and fired over the windshield. Shots hit the windshield, but it was bullet proof; as more bullets peppered it, I was worried how long it would hold.

"We're free," yelled Ash.

Cody gave the boat everything it had, and we all lurched back, the front of the boat riding so high I was worried it would hit the ceiling.

"Stay down," said Cody as the boat came back down. I could see the Youth, but only their helmets, as we clung to the floor and sped past them, bullets knocking on the side of the boat. Stray bullets every now and then hit the boat as we flew down the tunnel. No one dared leave the floor as Cody was kneeling on the floor operating the boat, barely able to see over the control console.

I reached out and took my mom's hand as we continued to barrel toward the exit. Then in an instant, everything lit up around us by the light of the moon. Cody continued to go as fast as he could, glancing behind him for a moment, clearly looking at or for something. I followed his eyes and only saw a cliff face with the base barely creeping into view.

"Ash," said Cody, "blow it."

I looked behind me at Ash, who hesitated a moment before crawling over to Mason, who ended up next to me, and grabbed his statscreen.

"Look," said Dakota pointing toward the base. There was a helicopter lifting off from the base.

"Blow it now, Ash," said Cody.

Ash looked at the helicopter and without turning around said, "I can't. Not until that helicopter is clear."

I barely saw him move as Cody came over and pressed the detonate button on Mason's statscreen.

"NO!" screamed Ash as we all looked toward the base. A few second later, the entire base erupted in flames. Starting from one side and making its way to the other. The helicopter was hit by a burst of the explosion and started spinning before going down.

<u>Video and Audio Transcript Report</u>

Complex: 3
Camera: BSR-003
Room: Backup Security room
Date of Transcript: ████████
Time of Transcript: ████████

<u>Transcript</u>

General Johan stands behind two Techs sitting at the security console, both intently watching the security feed of the armory. YT305 cautiously enters the armory.

YT305: It's a pile of explosives wired to a detonator!

YT305 sprints out of the armory.

YT305: Evacuate! Evacuate!

JYT1 grabs General Johan by the shoulder and

shoves him toward the door.

JYT1: Fire up Youth 1! We're evacuating the general immediately.

JYT12: Copy that, sir.

General Johan turns around and points to the Techs at the console.

General Johan: I want everyone else evacuated immediately!

YT295: Right away, sir.

YT295 rolls to his right and turns on the speaker mic.

YT295: Attention all Youth. By order of General Johan, everyone evacuate. I repeat, everyone evacuate.

End Transcript

Video and Audio Transcript Report

Complex: 3
Camera: H-007
Room: Helipad Stairwell
Date of Transcript:
Time of Transcript:

Transcript

JYT1 bursts through the first floor door, taking the stairs two at a time. JYT2 and JYT3 enter the stairwell in front of General Johan, JYT4 and JYT5 follow behind the General. Everyone sprints up the flight of stairs.

General Johan: Make sure to wipe the mainframe if possible! The evacuation order comes first!

JYT1: Already working on it, sir.

JYT1 holds the helipad door open as everyone else sprints through.

End Transcript

———

Video and Audio Transcript Report

Complex: 3
Camera: H-002
Room: Helipad
Date of Transcript:
Time of Transcript:

Transcript

JYT2 slides the door of Youth 1 open as General Johan climbs inside. JYT4 follows behind with JYT1 getting into the passenger seat. Youth 1 takes off as JYT4 is still sliding the door shut. Four seconds after takeoff the helipad camera is blinded by a bright white light and loses signal.

End Transcript

———

Black Box Transcript Report

Youth 1 black box
Audio recording
Date of Transcript:
Time of Transcript:

General Johan: What was that!

JYT12: I've lost the tail, grab onto something!

JYT4: We have to bail!

JYT1: We're too low to jump, and not with that fire ball so close.

JYT12: Altitude dropping.

JYT1: You better save this bird!

JYT12: We're going down, sir.

JYT2: Surround the general.

JYT12: Brace for impact in three, two—

Connection Failure. Connection Failure. Youth 1 last know connection coordinates: ██████████

<u>End of Transcript</u>

We all watched in awe as the Youth Complex was engulfed in balls of fire. The orange light of the flame basked us all, creating harsh shadows that flickered over us and the water. I took my helmet off, pulling my balaclava down around my neck as I stared into the flame that was the Youth Complex. Everyone was frozen, unable to speak as we were mesmerized by the destruction.

When I could finally pull my mind out of its trance, I said, "We didn't need to do that."

A hand rested on my shoulder, and I looked behind me, finding my dad. "You didn't pull the trigger, Calvin," he said. "Don't take responsibility for this."

"How many kids died, though?" I asked.

"Thanks to you, not enough," said Mason. Ash was kneeling next to him, having taken his helmet off.

How bad I wanted to punch Mason for a comment like that. My dad must have known what I was thinking and tightened his grip on my shoulder.

I took a breath before asking, "Did you even care about saving our parents? Or was that just to convince us so we'd help you blow up their base?"

Mason laughed before replying, "This isn't about you, Calvin. Nor is it about your parents. But we have your trust now that we helped free your parents." Mason gave me a devilish smile.

"You didn't do anything," said Ash. "You're lucky you made it out alive, let alone us dragging you around when we could have left you."

"*He* shouldn't have made it out, though," said Dakota, eyeing his dad.

"Enough, all of you," said my mom, standing up behind me. She commanded everyone's attention as she said, "I don't know if this is the right time to say this, but I just want to go home." Dad stood up, putting an arm around my mom as she put a hand on my shoulder. "My family is all here now. Can you just take us home, please?"

"How are you going to break this bombshell to them?" asked Mason, looking at Ash and Cody.

Ash was probably glaring at Mason under her helmet as she turned and looked at him.

"You can't go home," said Cody not turning around from the controls, still taking us further away from the mainland.

"Why is that," asked my dad, beating mom to the question.

"Because you're dead," said Cody.

"Cody!" yelled Ash. She took her helmet off, pulling her balaclava down around her neck. She slowly stood up, looking me and my parents in the eye. I could feel everyone's eyes on Ash.

"You can't go home," said Ash, "because it's standard Youth protocol when recruiting someone to erase every thread of their existence once they arrive at one of our Complexes. This goes for the recruit," Ash motioned to me, "as well as the immediate family."

"But we're still here," said mom. "They can't just erase us."

"Unfortunately, they can," said Ash. "More likely than not, the three of you were in a car wreck on the way to the airport coming back from Rhode Island. You'll have a funeral, your house will be possessed, and your employers will pay out any insurance claims upon your death."

"But all we have to do is just walk back home," said my mom. "Then they'll see we're not dead. They couldn't have done all of that yet?"

"It's been over a month since you first flew to Rhode Island. You've been dead for probably two weeks now."

"No." Mom started sobbing and let go of my shoulder. Dad pulled her into a hug.

"What's to stop us from going back now and saying there was a mistake?" asked Dad.

"The Youth won't let it happen. They're far bigger than you realize. Especially now that they know you've escaped, you'll be hunted down until you're actually dead."

Mom let out a shriek and buried her head into my dad's chest.

"You can't go home," said Ash. "I wish you could, but you can't." She looked away from us. "I'm sorry."

I didn't really know how to respond. There was too much to think about. All my friends and family thinking we were dead. All the Youth we just killed in the explosion. And Megan surrendering to the Youth. Not to mention we were on a small boat in the middle of the ocean with no known destination.

"So, what's the plan then?" I asked.

"We're going to an island," said Cody, still keeping his eyes ahead of him.

"Where at?" asked my dad.

"That's classified," said Mason.

"It's better that you not know," said Ash, "for security reasons."

"Are you saying we can't hold our tongues if we get caught?" asked Thomas's dad.

"In the off chance that we are captured between here and the island, yes," replied Ash.

We all stood there in silence, no one quite knowing what or how to reply.

"Do you actually trust us?" I finally asked, looking at Ash.

Before she could reply, someone started throwing up behind me. We all spun around to find Eve puking over the side of the boat. Thomas's dad, the closest to Eve, immediately knelt next to her and pulled her hair out of her face.

"Oh, Eve," said Ash, making her way past everyone to get to her. She knelt next to Eve on the opposite side as Thomas's dad.

"Calvin, grab the clear vial from the med kit," said Ash, pointing to the front of the boat. Cody opened a door on the dashboard between him and the passenger seat. The door sat against the floor, so I had to kneel to look inside. I rummaged through various boxes and crates before finding a bright red case with a white cross on it.

I pulled the case out and set it on the passenger's chair. Inside, I found medical equipment stacked to the brim. After a quick glance, I found the vials, four of them stacked together. I pulled one out of the foam insert, perfectly cut for the vial to slot into.

I flipped the lid of the vial open and brought it to Ash. She grabbed it from me and poured something green from her other hand into the vial.

"What is that?" I asked, pointing at her hand.

"It's whatever Eve is throwing up."

I stood there dumbfounded, unsure what to say. "OK," I finally said, hesitantly.

Ash closed the lid and dunked the vial and her dirty hands in the water, everything coming out clean, the gloves stained slightly green.

Eve sat with her head dangling over the side of the boat, facing the back to keep some of the splashing water out of her face. Her shoulders heaved up and down from the ragged breaths I could barely hear above the sounds of the boat.

"Will she make it?" I asked Ash.

"We have a medical facility on the island. As long as we can take her there, she should be good."

"How long until we get to the island?" asked Thomas's dad. "She's not looking so good."

"That's classified," said Mason before anyone could reply.

"Would you quit it with that!" yelled Ash.

"If you want to survive and take down all the Youth, then it stays classified." said Mason, his voice rising.

"And where's that gotten us?" asked Ash, standing up. "With people that don't trust us," Ash pointed to me, "and a plan that failed because not everyone knew what the heck they were doing."

"You know full well they shouldn't have even been on the mission. And thanks to you, we lost one."

"Thanks to me? That was her decision, Mason, not mine. Megan made up her own mind when she decided to surrender."

"And who knows what they may pry out of her."

"You're acting like what she's seen of us will be detrimental to the cause. We know how to hide, how to disappear. That is not going to set us back."

"Just wait till they come knocking on our doorstep."

"What are you so worried about, Mason—"

"That you're a Youth ready to betray us at any moment!"

Ash darted toward Mason. I stepped in front of Ash who ran into me. and we nearly toppled over before my dad grabbed us and pulled us back upright. "Enough, both of you!" I yelled, looking back and forth between Ash and Mason. "Leave your bickering until we get to the island."

Ash eyed Mason a moment before turning around and heading for the back of the boat. Everyone was dead silent except for Ash's footsteps as she made her way to the very back of the boat, plopping down on the furthest seat away from Mason as she stared out into the ocean. The light from the burning Youth Complex started to dwindle as we continued making our way away from the mainland. It stayed dead silent until we got to the island, the only sound the chopping water and Eve throwing up.

Megan slowly woke up, realizing she was face down on the ground. She could taste dirt, grass, and blood in her mouth. As she struggled to push herself up, a hand wrapped around her waist and pulled her to her feet. Nearly vomiting, she put a hand over her mouth. Someone was talking beside her, but the voice was garbled and distant. As her eyes cleared, she could see her dad talking to her. Then her senses all came back. The roar of the fire behind her, the heat bristling her skin. The cries and screams around her. She looked around, and everything was in slow motion. Youth running every direction away from the blazing building, some helped by others that were clearly injured, but the majority unscathed.

"Megan, Megan, look at me!" She finally heard her dad scream. She slowly turned around and found her dad tugging her arm. "We need to go, come on!"

A moment later, someone grabbed her other arm, a Youth. Then the world sped back to life as she started running. The sounds around her became crisp and clear, along with a ringing in her ear.

Megan glanced over and saw her dad pulling her mom with them. She looked just as disoriented as she was herself a second ago. The three of them ran as fast as they could, following the Youth around them as they made their way toward a fire in the distance. The closer they got, Megan was able to make out what the fire was, a helicopter crash.

The ground was torn up around the crash, with one of the props having detached and stuck straight up out of the ground. More Youth continued to surround the crash and a car that was by the wreck.

"Follow me," said the Youth who had helped Megan up. He led them to the car by the wreck. As the crowd around the car parted, it revealed an SUV. The trunk was open, and something was happening that Megan couldn't see. The Youth opened the back door as Megan's mom got in first, followed by Megan and her dad, all three of them sitting on a bench seat.

As the door shut, all the noise from outside was funneled through the trunk. Everyone turned around as a man was lifted on a makeshift stretcher into the trunk. Two Youth hopped in, squatting beside the man, before the trunk was closed and there was quiet. Only the muffled sounds of the chaos outside made their way in the car. Megan's dad reached out and took his wife's hand as everyone tried looking at the man, but it was too dark in the car to make out much. The two Youth started tearing the man's shirt off before wrapping bandages around him in several places.

One of the doors opened, and the interior lights turned on briefly, everyone was able to see the burns that covered the man. Megan's mom gasped, putting a hand over her mouth and turning away, looking ready to vomit any second.

Megan couldn't turn away, even as the door closed and the lights turned off. The man seemed familiar, but she couldn't place him.

"What's his condition?" asked the driver. Megan turned around and found two Youth in the driver and passenger seat.

"He'll survive," said one of the Youth, wrapping bandages around the man, "just get us out of here." It all felt strange to Megan. The man she thought she recognized. The Youth talking through their helmets, sounding mechanical and unable to see their faces. The explosions and fire all around. Megan felt like she was in a sci-fi movie, at least what she could remember of the few she saw. Except, this was very real and very dangerous.

The driver started the engine, the dashboard lights casting a blue hue across everyone.

"Our apologies to you, Mr. and Mrs. Nall," said the Youth in the passenger seat. "We did not expect you to be in this kind of danger. Are any of you hurt?"

Nobody spoke, everyone just shook their heads. "Good." the Youth turned and opened the glove box. In the light, Megan saw the Youth had a different crest on his shoulder. It was the same YOUTH crest that every Youth suit had, but this one had a dark red background. These were clearly different Youth than the ones Megan had seen before.

The Youth closed the glove box and held out three black bags. "For your safety, please put these over your heads."

"What are they?" asked Megan's dad.

"They'll protect the identity of our base. Please put them on." Everyone hesitantly reached out and took one of the bags. There was an elastic opening on one side that everyone put their head through. As soon as the elastic opening closed around everyone's neck, it was completely dark and dead silent inside the bag. For Megan though, she could still hear the ringing in her ears.

Megan freaked out a moment realizing these were the same bags that had been used on her and Calvin back at the school. That was until her dad reached out and grabbed her hand. A few moments later, her mom grabbed her other hand. Immediately, her breathing started to slow back down.

But it was clear to Megan's entire family that when they had surrendered to the Youth, this was not what they were expecting. It was far more than they had signed up for.

After our adrenaline had worn off and enduring hours of Eve throwing up to the point of dry heaving, we arrived at the island. I barely saw the outline of the island until we were right up on it. It was about the size of a football stadium if I had to guess. Trees spanned the entire perimeter of the island from where we entered. A small dock jutted out from the beach that Cody expertly pulled up to.

Ash pulled a rope from the cabinet under the control console, tied it to a railing of the boat, and hopped out onto the dock. My dad and I hopped out to help pull the boat against the dock. Before Ash could get the boat tied to the dock, Thomas's dad carried Eve in both arms and hopped up onto the dock. As soon as Ash tied the boat off, she ran with Thomas's dad and Eve to the island. My dad and I helped everyone else off the boat.

The dock was only floating on the water, which made it shift every time we pulled another person onto it. Thomas's mom looked seasick and was not happy to still be on unstable ground, or she was upset her husband ran off to an island none of us had been to before.

Everyone was off now except for Cody and Mason. Mason still sat on the floor of the boat with his hands tied behind his back and his helmet next to him; Cody handed it up to me.

"Give me a hand, Dakota," said Cody, grabbing Mason under of his arms.

Dakota leaned down from the dock as Cody hefted Mason onto the side of the boat. Dakota started pulling Mason up onto the dock, and Cody hopped up from the boat and helped lift him the rest of the way.

The two pulled Mason to his feet and kept hold of his arms as they escorted him down the dock, but not before Cody grabbed Mason's helmet from me. I checked behind me at the vast emptiness of the ocean as Mason was dragged away.

"See anything," Dad asked, stepping up next to me.

"No," I said, carefully watching for any sign of the Youth.

"Let's get to the island, please," said Mom. "I can't stand not being on dry land anymore."

"Alright," said Dad as we all turned around and followed behind Mason and his escort, but keeping our distance from them.

"So, who is he and what did he do?" asked my dad, leaning into my ear so Mason couldn't hear.

By now everyone had made their way off the dock, and it was just my parents and I left.

"That's Mason," I said, watching him walk down the dock. "He was the leader that helped us escape the school in Rhode Island and helped break you out. That was before he nearly killed Ash."

"And who's Ash?" Dad asked, taking my mom's hand.

"She was the one that told us we were dead."

"Ok."

I glanced at Mom and could tell she didn't like me making that comment.

"So, walk me through everything that happened since you left for Rhode Island to now?" asked Dad.

"That's a lot to ask," I said, glancing at Mom a moment, "and probably not the best time."

"You're right," said Dad, putting his hand on my shoulder, "let's get settled in first."

"Hopefully they have some good food," I said.

"I could definitely use something more tasteful than the slop they fed us."

"It makes me gag just thinking about it," said Mom.

"I'd ask, but I don't think I want to know what it was they fed you,"

I said.

"It's probably best you don't," said Dad, taking in a deep breath. "I've missed that."

"Missed what?" I asked.

"The smell of the outdoors."

"I was getting sick of that stale smell," said Mom.

"There was also," said Dad before pausing. "No. I won't go there."

Mom and I didn't push him on it, but if it was related to smells, I think I knew exactly what he was talking about, and that was Dakota's mom. And now that I'm thinking about it, I don't doubt she was the one that was shot back at the school. When all our parents were gathered together in that big building, before I came crashing though the skylight.

And that got me thinking about the Youth, and about all they stood for, at least what they told me. You can't say you want to rid the world of all evil and in the next sentence gun down an innocent bystander, especially the parent of one of the kids you're trying to get to join your cause. And then try to kill us and chase us down when we say we won't join. I couldn't care less about what the Youth do, no matter how good it is. You don't do what they've done and expect me to join them. I'm running as far from them as I can.

By the time my brain took a break from processing everything the Youth had put us through, we made it to the end of the dock. There was no visible trail off the dock, but we followed the footsteps that Mason and his escort were following through the sandy grass.

It took a second for my parents and I to find our balance as we stepped onto solid ground. It was nice to be back on something that wasn't rocking sporadically and constantly.

We followed steps to the tree line, where there was a small break big enough for two people to pass through side by side. I went ahead of my parents, passing through very dense trees and bushes. If I had to guess, you wouldn't be able to see through them very far in daylight. The path weaved its way through the trees until a short walk later, we reached a clearing.

Several trees dotted the clearing with single story houses spread about. As I took a moment to gaze around, I noticed the moonlight dotted the ground. I looked up to find a ceiling of some sort above the clearing that wasn't treetops. Whatever it was, I couldn't identify it in the dark.

"Are we sure this place is safe?" asked Mom.

"Just stay close to me," said Dad, holding me back as he stepped in front of me.

"Over here, Calvin," said Thomas, waving from the porch of the closest house on the right.

We went toward the house as best we could in the clearing of speckled moonlight. If we weren't still slightly on edge about everything going on, I would have enjoyed the beautiful picture the moonlight painted in front of us; hearing the rustling of the plants and trees with the crashing waves in the background.

Instead, my eyes darted around the clearing, trying to take everything in. But I really didn't want to. I had been on edge since before we boarded our plane, and I was feeling it. I just wanted to rest. Not be worried about what was behind my back all the time.

"Are we safe here?" I asked Thomas as we approached the porch.

"Unless you're scared of beds," Thomas said, smiling. "Take your helmet off and stay a while."

I stepped up on the porch and checked my surroundings one more time before following Thomas through the front door with my parents.

The only light inside came from very dim lights under the cabinets in the kitchen. The kitchen was to the right of the door with a huge island. A dining room sat with two eight seat tables connected to the kitchen. To the left of the front door was a living room with three big couches situated around a TV against the wall.

"Not too bad, is it?" asked Thomas, walking backward to face us.

"I love the kitchen," said Mom. "It could use some more lights, though." Mom started making her way toward the nearest light switch.

"No more lights!" said Thomas, throwing his arms out. "Cody said no more lights."

"Why is that," asked Dad.

"I asked him, but he didn't have time to answer."

"There's no more lights, so we can keep the base hidden," said Cody. We all spun around and found Cody in the doorway with Dakota behind him, both of them still wearing their helmets. I hadn't even heard them walk up.

"And how would turning on a light do that?" asked Mom.

"A lit-up island sticks out in the middle of the night," said Cody, walking past us. "Your rooms are this way." Cody walked down the hall in the center of the room, motioning us into the first door on the left. We all looked at each other for a moment as we followed Cody inside the room.

It was a bunk room, four rows of six, forty-eight beds in total. Each bunk was a simple gray steel frame with a crate at the feet and the head. An empty mattress and pillow were all that occupied each bed. Thomas's mom was putting a sheet and blanket on the bed nearest to the door.

"There's more linens in the cabinet over there," said Thomas's mom, pointing to a tall cabinet against the wall to the left of the door.

We all headed for the cabinet, grabbing a set of sheets and blankets. Except for Dakota, who laid his belt and gun on the crate at the foot of a bed, took his helmet off, and flopped face first onto the bed, dropping his helmet on the floor next to him as his arm dangled off the bed.

"I'd get some sleep if I were you," said Cody, before walking off.

"And what's the plan now!" I yelled after Cody.

"Wait!" Cody yelled back.

"Wait for you to tell us the plan," I mumbled.

"We don't need a plan right now, Calvin," said Dad.

"Yes we do," I fired back.

"Let's get some sleep first and then we'll figure out a plan, together."

"And what if the Youth come in the middle of the night?" I stopped, turning around to face Dad.

"We'll deal with that if it happens, Calvin."

"But I can't go to sleep knowing that could happen." Everyone had stopped and was staring at me and Dad now.

"Then you need to pray about that, Calvin."

"I trust this place, Calvin," said Thomas's mom, walking up behind me and putting a hand on my shoulder. "We'll be safe here." Thomas's mom had always been a good judge when it came to safety. Both my family and Thomas's family believed the ability was spiritual in nature, something given by God. And that helped calm me down some.

"I'm just as concerned about the Youth as you are, Calvin," said Dad, walking up to me. "But if Lindsey says we're safe here," he said, looking at Thomas's mom, "then I trust that. And if something does happen," he looked back down at me, "then I'll do everything in my power to protect all of you. You don't have to protect everyone alone, Calvin." Without even seeing my interaction with Ash in the security room, without even saying anything, Dad always had a way of knowing what I was thinking.

"You're too good at that," I said.

Dad smiled his big bright smile that always managed to make me grin, even on my worst days. "Let's take that helmet off." Dad walked over to me and started pulling my helmet off. I unhooked the wires from the suit, and Dad pulled my helmet fully off.

I pulled my balaclava down around my neck and ran a hand through my hair, coming back soaked in sweat before wiping it on the leg of my suit.

"I don't want to know what that helmet smells like," said Mom. We all laughed.

When we all settled down, Dad said, "We should pray together, though. All of us, even—" Dad looked at Dakota who was fast asleep. "We can still pray for him, but everyone huddle up, kids in the middle." Thomas came and stood next to me; Mom, Dad, and Thomas's mom making a circle around us, their hands on us and the person next to them in their circle.

My dad started praying, and soon, everyone else was praying with him. Thanking God for our safety, our parent's freedom, our bravery to rescue our parents, for our continued safety and protection, and so much more.

By the time we all finished praying and praising God, we either had a huge grin on our faces, or tears in our eyes, which made falling asleep all the more easier as I was at peace about our safety on the island as my eyes closed and sleep overcame me.

58

Sydney stood in front of the window wall that led out to the balcony overlooking the ocean. She stood with her hands in her pockets, motionless, staring at her reflection in the glass. Rain beat against the window from a thick black sky.

"I liked our old room better," said Sydney, still staring at her reflection.

"I did, too," said her mom. "But I'm glad that none of us were hurt in that explosion."

"Yeah... I've never seen something that big before."

The two were quiet for a while as they watched the rain.

"Are you sure you don't want a wig?" asked Sydney's mom.

"That's why I have the bandanna, Mom."

"I know." Her mom gently rubbed her hand across her daughter's back.

After a moment, Sydney said, "I hope this is over soon."

"It will be, honey." Her mom hugged her tighter as her dad walked up and joined the embrace.

"How's my cute girl doing?" he asked.

"I will be when I have hair again," replied Sydney.

Taking her daughter's shoulders, he turned her to face him. "My daughter will forever be cute, no matter what happens to her. Don't think any less of yourself, ok?"

When Sydney didn't respond, her dad pulled her in for a hug. Her mom joined the embrace as Sydney began sobbing into her dad's chest, wrapping her arms around him

"We love you, Sydney," he said, kissing her head.

I woke up with the biggest kink in my neck. Before even opening my eyes, I was rubbing my neck. I either slept funny or my head did not like my pillow. Either way, I slowly sat up and hit my head. "Oww!" I said groggily, tearing my eyes open to find the bottom of the bunk above me. I looked around, only using the light that came through the door, as there weren't any windows, to find everyone still sleeping in their bunks. I frantically looked around, worried I had woken everyone up, but no one stirred. Everyone must have been beat from our escape.

I rubbed my head as it throbbed, slowly getting up and trying not to make too much noise. I carefully opened the crate at the foot of my bunk. I had put my belt and helmet inside, but ended up sleeping in my suit all night. I felt dirty and grimy everywhere. I pulled out a change of clothes from a little shelf in the crate, and headed out in the hall to look for the showers. There were four doors in the hallway. One at the end of the hallway that led to the other end of the bunk room. The other three were on the opposite side of the hall. I entered the door closest to me, finding a room with a dividing wall, only extending three-quarters the length of the room. On the right was what looked like a training area with mats and weapons. On the left was a barracks. I'd come back here later, so I tried the next door down.

Inside was the bathroom. A wall of sinks created a dividing wall for stalls, showers, and baths down on the very end. The baths weren't typical baths, though. They were feeding troughs like you'd find on a farm. Not exactly what those were used for, but I didn't want to think about that, I wanted a shower. I grabbed the closest shower and peeled off my suit, sticking to whatever exposed skin it could find. When I pulled my undersuit off, it was caked in sweat, the front part at least. Probably because I slept on my stomach. I threw everything on the floor and took a nice long shower, letting the hot water run over my neck in the hopes it would get the kink out.

When I stepped out of the shower, I felt like a new man, and some new clothes didn't make me feel half bad, either. I took a deep breath of the steamy air before grabbing my dirty and sweat suit. As I stepped out of my shower, there was an open basket against the wall. I assumed it was a dirty clothes basket and threw my clothes in, wiping my hands together before feeling the cool tile on my feet.

I headed back to the bunk room and quietly rummaged in my crate, finding a pair of socks and shoes. I carried them out to the family room, finding all the lights still off. I quickly put on my shoes and opened one of the blinds, only to find it still dark outside. I was hoping for a bright sun to have been shining. When I went to go turn on a light, I remembered what Cody had said, and avoided all the lights. Even the fridge light didn't turn on when I opened it. These guys were really concerned about our safety. I rummaged around and found an apple, not a green apple unfortunately, but an apple nonetheless. Finding a glass, I filled it with water and went out to the porch.

"Good morning," said my dad, sitting in a rocking chair on the porch.

"Not the morning I was expecting," I replied, sitting in the rocking chair next to him. "What time is it?"

"They took my watch," said Dad, holding up his naked arm. I looked down and realized I didn't have a watch, either.

"Guess we're not figuring out the time," I said.

"The sun set about an hour ago," said Dad, looking out toward the sky, or what little of it we could see through the fake ceiling that covered the clearing. "It's at least been a day. Or it could be more. I'm not that concerned about it, though."

I wish I could have said the same. I wanted to know everything.

Where were we, what day was it, what was the plan going forward. But I had to stop, because I clearly wasn't going to get those answers now.

"We're fine, Calvin," said Dad like he was reading my mind. "Trust me, I started overthinking this morning. That's why I came out here and took some time to pray. It helped calm me down real quick."

I breathed in the salty smelling air and took a bite of my apple. "So, what do we do now?" I asked between bites.

Dad took a moment before replying, "I really don't know. I think we're going to need lots of prayer before we make our next move. If we are truly dead and these… what do you call them?"

"The Youth."

"With the Youth after us to kill us, we can't make any decision lightly."

"Agreed." We both glanced around the clearing just enjoying the serenity. I looked up toward the sky to find the makeshift ceiling. "Did you see what makes up our makeshift ceiling?" I asked, pointing at it.

"It's a camouflage tarp from everything I can tell. They're all strung up at the tops of the buildings."

"Hmm… It must work at hiding this place if Ash and Cody trust us to be here."

"With the Youth chasing us now, I guess we'll see how well it really works."

The two of us sat there in silence for a while as I finished my apple. "Do you think they'd care if the animals took the leftovers?" I asked, holding up the core of my apple.

"Go ahead," said Dad. I threw the apple over the ledge of the porch before standing up, taking a big gulp of my water as I did.

"I'll be back," I said. "I'm going to take a little stroll."

"Be careful," said Dad.

"I will." I took a slow stroll around the perimeter of the clearing, checking around the tree line. Nowhere was I able to see through to the ocean. I continued walking, hoping to find some gap to the outside. As I did though, I finally had time to reflect on the events of the last almost two months. From attending the school that was really a recruitment center, to being chased across the country, captured twice by the Youth, held prisoner in a hospital for a month, escaped said hospital to skydive into a Youth base and save my parents before ending up on an island somewhere off the West Coast of America. And I shouldn't forget coming close to death a few too many times for my liking.

I held out my hand as it brushed against the bushes, trying to process as much as I could. And, of course, my brain went into overdrive, which actually, now that I think about it, hadn't happened much until that point. But my brain started thinking about all that could have changed, could have been done differently. What I could have done to change Sydney's mind, or reassure Megan we were going to escape. I nearly drowned in my thoughts and became overwhelmed when I stopped as a tear came down my face. I can't be crying! No, this wasn't right. Then I looked into the tree line and spotted a small clearing, one that you wouldn't see unless you were right up on the tree line like I was I made my way to the clearing and was bawling my eyes out before I even made it to the spot. I fell to the ground, unsure what was going on. Only later did I realize I was crying for the loss I had just experienced. The loss of Sydney. The loss of Megan. The loss of my home. The loss of my old life. And the loss of all the Youth who were inside the base during the explosion. All the souls who would never get the opportunity to live. To turn away from the Youth and their wicked ways. To grow up and start a family, have kids, be able to live a life. And now they wouldn't. They would be buried as teenagers. And I was right next to the trigger and didn't stop it.

As my soul grieved the loss it had just experienced, I had a conviction. I felt like I had forsaken God these past two months. Like I hadn't called upon his name enough, reached out to him enough, and a fresh wave of tears and anger aroused in me.

When I had no more tears to cry and the ground beneath me and my hands were soaked, I stood up, wiped my face off, and headed back to the clearing. I felt a lot better having spent some time with God, and the crying, of course, helped some, too. As I exited the tree line, Cody came out of a house just in front of me. He did a double take when he saw me.

"He wants to see you," he said, staring at me still in his helmet. He had his suit off, and the zipper unzipped down to his waist, the suit falling at his sides.

"Who does?" I asked.

"Mason."

"...Can you show me?" I asked.

Cody motioned to follow him, and I trailed behind him as we entered the house he just came out of. Inside it looked like an old western jail. There were prison cells along the back wall of the house with tables and chairs on the opposite wall. Cody led me to the far wall from the entrance and lifted a latch on the floor, pulling open a hatch with three rungs on the bottom. As I peered into the opening, a ladder ran down to a dark room below. Cody flipped a light switch on the wall by the door, and dim lights lit the room below, revealing an entirely concrete room.

I looked back at Cody who only nodded his head at the opening. I cautiously made my way down the ladder. I could barely see Mason as he sat in a concrete cell with a door made of steel bars with gaps wide enough to only fit your hand through. He sat against the back wall of the cell.

"What do you want?" I asked.

"I know you're the only one that will listen."

"Why is that?"

"It's what your God tells you to do."

"True," I said, taking my time before replying, "it's what *the* God tells us to do. Listening helps us understand."

"So, you want to understand me?"

"As much as I hate what you did, yes, I want to understand why you did what you did."

Mason stood up and only took a step before I could hear chains pulled taunt. "Ash is going to kill us all. But before she does, she'll reveal all of us, all the Renegades, to the Youth."

"And how do you know that?" I asked, crossing my arms.

"Because she's still loyal to the Youth."

"Again, how do you know that?"

"Of course," Mason started mumbling to himself, "you're not a Youth, you wouldn't understand."

"Then try to explain it," I said.

"When a child is growing up, they are more likely to take advice or suggestions because of their development stage. It can happen in adults, too, but it's always going to be present in kids. When you take a child and force feed them certain ideas, it's very hard to break those ideas and following habits. The YOUTH do this to all of us. The YOUTH being everyone involved in the entire organization. Not just the Youth like you and I."

"I'm not understanding the difference between the Youth's?"

"Ok, think of it like a department of a company. The YOUTH, all uppercase, is the organization as a whole. One of the departments is the Youth, only the Y capitalized. That's you and I. That's all the compounds we've been to, the train we were on, all of it."

"Alright," I said, becoming more engaged and wanting to find out more. "So, what other departments are there?"

"We only know of what they publicly display. All of us came to the Youth through the humanitarian department. They funnel their foster and orphan programs into the Youth. So, me, Eve, Cody, we all were brought in from an orphanage or foster home."

"So, you were more likely to be brainwashed by the Youth because you had no family?"

"Exactly!" said Mason, starting to sound excited. "You combine having no family and being a child and you have the perfect vessel to make into whoever your heart desires."

"But you clearly didn't take to their ideas?"

"Correct. Because I didn't put my identity in the Youth. But not all of us, the Renegades as you're now calling us, don't always put their identity in something else. They just want revenge for what happened to their parents."

"What happened to their parents?"

"Long story short, parents of the Youth were killed after they were funneled into the Youth program, if they were still alive. This was to ensure that there was nothing left for them if they ended up leaving the Youth, making them more likely to stay with the Youth, or return to the Youth if they ran away or escaped."

"And that's what you think is happening to Ash?" I asked, starting to connect all the pieces together.

"She doesn't have a purpose here." Mason's chains clanked taunt again. "If you keep her here, she'll expose us all."

I was trying to comprehend what Mason was saying, but it wasn't entirely making sense to me. "So, what reason made you think Ash turned on us?" I asked.

"When she activated the evacuate for the complex."

"So, saving people alerted you that she was still with the Youth?"

"Yes, because we went in knowing we would destroy the base with everyone in it. The goal was for there to be as few survivors as possible."

"Maybe Ash grew a conscious and realized blowing up a building full of teenagers wasn't a wise decision."

"If only you knew the Youth," Mason's voice started rising, "then you'd understand why they had to be killed."

"Nobody has to be killed, you chose to do that."

"I chose to save our future!" yelled Mason. "This is exactly why I didn't want you involved. Because you'd look at what we're doing as a sin instead of a favor. A favor that no one will ever know about, but one they desperately need."

"Ok, that's enough." I walked back to the ladder as Mason's chains pulled taunt again.

"Calvin, you have to kill Ash."

I spun around and pointed a finger at Mason, "Don't you dare say that about Ash!" I yelled. "I don't care who she is or what she did. She helped save my family, and I haven't seen any reason to take her life or question her allegiance. If she tries to take my life, you can come talk to me." I spun back around as Mason kept yelling my name while I climbed the ladder. When I got to the top, I slammed the hatch shut as it bounced once before settling into place.

I stared at the hatch a moment as I was breathing heavily. I looked up to find Cody staring at me. We locked eyes for a moment, even through Cody's helmet I knew he was looking at me, and I asked, "Do you trust Ash?"

Cody simply nodded his head.

"Where is she?"

"Follow me." Cody turned around and led me outside.

Cody led me from the prison house across the lawn to another similar looking house but longer and with double doors at the entrance. Inside was a small room with a few chairs and a window.

"She's in there," said Cody, pointing against the far wall to a stainless steel double door before exiting, leaving me in an eerie silence as I stared the down door. Clearly Cody didn't want to show me to where Ash was, just guide me as far as I needed. A muffled clatter of something falling came through the doors, and I rushed through them. Inside was a short hallway before another set of double doors. Between them on the right side of the hallway was a door that led to a small room containing various medial smocks and garments from gloves to gowns and so forth. No one was inside and the lights were off, so I continued through to the next set of double doors.

Inside, Ash was on her knees picking up vials and syringes from the floor and putting them on a tray, still wearing her combat suit but with her helmet off. She didn't even look up at me when I called to her and knelt next to her. It wasn't until I put a hand on her shoulder that she jumped back.

"Calvin!" she cried, dropping the syringe she was holding. "Where did you come from?"

"Did you not see me walk in?" I asked.

"You..." she looked toward the door and back at me. Then I saw how distant her eyes were when they looked back at me. "I'm sorry, but, but, but I can't talk right now." She grabbed the last of the vials and put them back on the tray before lifting it and struggling to stand up.

I helped her up, and she tried to shove me off. "I'm fine, Calvin." She took a heavy step and then another before she stumbled into a counter top, nearly spilling the contents of her tray before I grabbed her and steadied the tray.

"You are not fine," I said, taking the tray from her and setting it down. "What happened?"

"Eve is dying. I have to save her," Ash said with her eyes closed, leaning her head on the counter before shoving herself up. "Can't sleep, can't sleep," she muttered before slapping her cheeks.

"Have you slept any?" I asked Ash, as she stumbled down the counter and nearly fell had I not caught her.

"Can't sleep," Ash muttered again, her eyes growing heavy.

"Why can't you sleep?" I asked, helping Ash stand up as she tried to stumble further down the counter. She came to a small device and flipped a clear cover up to reveal several slots for what looked like vials. Ash, clearly thinking she had a vial in her hand, grasped her hand around nothing and set that nothing in one of the slots. She closed the cover and pressed a button, the device started spinning rapidly inside the cover.

"You didn't put anything in there, Ash," I said, spinning her around to look at me.

"What, I put the vial in there," she said with her eyes closed.

"What do you need to do that you can't sleep, Ash?" I said, raising my voice.

"I have... I have... the blood. Her blood. I have to fix it."

"How long will that take?"

"Time... time will... need to get blood fixed."

I glanced around the room for the vial Ash thought she put in the device when I found Eve. She was on an operating table. All kinds of machines and tubes were hooked up to her. Her body was still green. Her veins and arteries a bright green against the pale green of her skin.

I shook Ash, and her eyes opened up wide. "Ash! How long until she dies."

278

"Death... death is... projected for, for... for..." I shook Ash again.

"Projected for when!" I yelled, hoping to keep her awake as her body started drooping and falling into mine.

"Projected for... a later date. But the effects become... expo, expo, exponentially worse the longer... the longer. The longer without... getting... it... out." Ash's body became limp, and she fell against me, her head falling against my chest.

I grabbed her, putting an arm around her back and under her legs as I picked her up, being more than I could manage. I quickly walked to the nearest open bed, and with a grunt, lifted her up over the side rails and into the bed. I leaned against the bed railing as I breathed in deep breaths, taking a moment to rest before adjusting her into the bed properly. There was no blanket, so I searched around, but before finding one, I found Thomas's dad passed out in a chair near the door where I had first come in. His head was slumped to his chest, and his arms hung at the side of the chair. I finally found a blanket in a cabinet and threw it over Ash.

As I situated the blanket over her and pulled the blanket up to her neck, I noticed some strands of hair that were covering her face. I gently pushed them to the side and used the back of my hand to wipe some sweat from her forehead.

I stood there for a moment looking at Ash and admiring the work and dedication she had. I don't think I could push myself to the point of exhaustion. I think I'd have fallen asleep long ago like Thomas's dad.

Then I slowly turned around to look at Eve. Tubes were hooked up all over her arms and mouth. Various liquids were being pulled and pushed into her body. Several of them green. Eve was asleep and was breathing normally from everything I could tell, and the heart monitor beeped a quiet beat. I didn't even know how to begin processing all of this. So I did only what I knew how to do. I gently laid my hands on Eve's arm and said "Hi, Eve. I don't know if you can hear me, but I'm going to pray for you. I serve a God who does miracles, and since I can't understand anything that's hooked up to you right now or how it works, it's going to take a miracle to save you." I started smiling and then laughed at myself before praying.

In the middle of my prayer, I felt a hand on my shoulder. I stopped praying and looked to see Thomas's dad. "Don't stop," he said. I just nodded my head and continued. And the two of us prayed there for a while. I don't know how long, but a while.

When we finally finished, I took a deep breath and looked over Eve, wondering what in the world the Youth had done to her.

"You're a good man, Calvin," said Thomas's dad.

"Why do you say that?"

"Not everyone is willing to believe and do what you just did."

"Really?" I asked. "That's all I know how to do in a situation like this."

"And it's what you should do. Not everyone is as brave or faithful as you are, though."

"I'm sure there's lots of people better than me out there."

"Some. But I would argue not many."

I stood there letting what Thomas's dad said sink in. "I just do what I know how to do, and that's trust in Jesus."

"And that's all you need to do in this life."

I smiled at him before asking, "So I take it you were here with Ash?"

"For a time. I couldn't help much, let alone understand anything that she was talking about. I probably know about as much as you do right now."

I turned around to look at Ash. "Once she gets some rest, we'll have to see what's going on. From everything I can tell, she's stable."

"I would agree." Thomas's dad patted me on the back. "And we have to trust that God will keep her stable until Ash wakes back up."

"Yes."

"Let's not stay in here, though, we can't do much."

"Yeah…" I trailed off as I stared at Eve in pure wonder as to how this could be done to a human.

"Let's go." Thomas's dad pulled my arm, and I followed after him.

As we made it outside, Thomas's dad said, "It's still night?"

"It's been a full day since we landed on the island."

"A full day." Thomas's dad just stared up at the night sky, or what little of it he could see through the covering. Then he started sniffing, "Is that…" he smelled his shirt, "oh my, that is me. There isn't a shower here by chance is there?"

"I'll show you," I said, taking him back to the bunk house. He and my dad shook hands on the porch, and I took a seat next to my dad again.

"You were gone for a while?" asked Dad.

"Yeah… I talked with Mason some and then found Ash and prayed over Eve."

Dad just gave me a big smile and looked out beyond the porch. "You remind me a lot of your mother. She's praying over there right now," he said, pointing to her in a clearing between the houses. She looked like she had just finished as she looked up at us. I waved to her and she waved back. She went back to praying, and as I sat there, a question started forming in my mind.

"Dad?"

"Yeah."

"Back in the prison. How could you... How could you so easily pick up a gun and shoot the Youth? Shoot those kids?"

Dad looked out beyond us. I could see the gears turning in his head.

"I've come to find, Calvin, that war is never pretty. As much as I didn't want to kill these kids, they were shooting at my family; my wife, my son, myself. As much as I would have loved to just run away, when someone threatens to take the life of myself, those I love, and those around me, I'm doing everything in my power to defend their lives. To ensure they can live tomorrow. Unfortunately, it doesn't matter who's pulling the trigger, it's a matter of stopping whoever is pulling the trigger.

"But hear me out, stopping them doesn't always mean killing them. Though in most situations it normally does, purely because situations like this require split second decisions. You don't have the luxury of trying to find an alternative. Does that make sense?"

I wanted it to make sense. It made sense to my dad, how could it not to me? On one hand, I understood the concept of war being messy, but when actually faced with those decisions that you're responsible for...

"I'm not sure," I finally said.

"And that's perfectly alright."

I looked over at my dad a little dumbfounded. "Really?"

"Yes. If I had my way, I'd keep you from ever having to go to war. From ever having to make these decisions, from having this conversation. But here we are. And all we can do is rely on God for guidance and ask for help." Dad stopped and had a look on his face like he just realized something.

"What is it?" I asked.

"When... I just, I didn't expect your life to turn out like this, let alone mine." A tear fell down Dad's face before he looked away from me.

"Dad?" I reached out and put my hand on his shoulder. That's when he leaned over, putting both hands over his face, and cried.

I didn't know what to do. I had seen Dad cry before at church, and sometimes when we prayed, but never like this.

I looked out and saw Mom pacing back and forth with her head down. She glanced up at me, and I waved her over. She came running, concern all over her face.

"David," she said, kneeling in front of Dad, "what's wrong?" I rarely heard my mom call my dad by his name. As she put her arms on his shoulders, I took mine off.

"It's all my fault," Dad said through tears.

"What is?" asked Mom.

"Everything. From letting Calvin come here, to being in this mess—"

"It's not your fault." Mom pulled her head closer to Dad's. "We both vetted everything before sending Calvin to Rhode Island. We could have never known this would happen."

"And if I had," said Dad, "we wouldn't be stuck here, away from our home, away from our family with no one and no way to contact anyone. We have no one."

"No," said Mom, firmly. "Don't say that. We have God with us, and that's all we need, no matter the situation we may be in."

"But if I—"

"We both know that we can't change the past. Don't beat yourself up for your past, again."

Dad's back started heaving up and down as he cried. "I'm sorry," he said between sobs.

"You have nothing to be sorry for." Tears started to run down Mom's face. "Please, don't cry."

Mom pulled Dad into a hug, holding his head to her chest, both of them now sobbing.

I didn't really know what to do, but I felt compelled to stay. All I could do was stare at Mom and Dad. And it was then that I realized how much they loved each other. How deep of a relationship they shared. How much they cared for each other. I hoped I'd have a relationship with my future wife like this, if I ever got married.

I couldn't just sit here doing nothing, I was a part of this family. I may not know Dad like Mom did, but that didn't mean I couldn't encourage him. I got up and hugged both of them.

"This isn't your fault, Dad," I said. "If it wasn't for you, I don't think I'd be here today."

Dad sat up and wiped his eyes. "Really?" he asked, looking at me.

"Absolutely," I replied.

Dad looked over at Mom, and even with red eyes, she gave Dad a look of "I told you so." A grin broke out across his face that turned into a smile. "Thank you. I love you both very much." He pulled us in for a hug, a hug I didn't want to end. Just sitting in the peace that God had blessed us with. Not thinking about tomorrow, not regretting yesterday, just enjoying the moment. The now.

When we finally pulled apart, Dad pulled Mom in and kissed her. I looked away until they finished, then said, "I love you, Dad, but-but please don't kiss me."

We all laughed.

I gathered everyone together the following afternoon in the living room. Ash was the only one not there, still sleeping in the medical ward from the previous day. My dad, Thomas and his dad, and Cody, were all standing while everyone else sat on the couches. Cody still wore all his armor and helmet. I stood in front of the TV at the head of the couches, more than a little nervous for what I was about to say, not sure if I fully understood what I was about to suggest. But I knew in my soul, it was what needed to be done. Even if it didn't make sense, or whether I liked it or not.

"Hopefully, everyone has had a chance to calm down and take everything in from the last few days." My crowd definitely didn't look like they had even begun processing. The men in the room, at least, were looking at me. The women were a mix of looking at their hands in their laps or blinking from puffy tear-stained eyes.

"I-I know it's not been the easiest having to deal with what's happened to-to all our lives." Thomas's mom started quietly sobbing as my mom put an arm around her. "From not knowing where our families are, losing our homes, having an army after us, and a friend with something we have no idea how to cure. And as much as we may want to just sit here and let Cody and Ash solve all our problems, I'd like to pr-

propose a new idea."

"Calvin…" my mom said, hesitantly, worry all over her face.

"Hold-hold on," I said as reassuringly as I could. "Clearly two people can't take on all the Youth, no matter how good you-you may be." Cody's hands tightened on his crossed arms.

"I don't doubt your ability, Cody, just trying to be realistic."

"Did Mason teach you that?" asked Cody.

It shocked me a little that he responded. "No, I just needed to be reminded that I can't always be the hero, and the same goes for you. We can't just rush into danger and expect to return every time. We need to take the time to think and plan before we move. Especially after talking with Mason, and confirming it with Cody, the Youth are far bigger and more powerful than we realized."

"How powerful?" asked Dakota.

I waited a very long time before replying, working up the courage, nervous of the reaction. "They want to take over America."

The second I finished, the whole room erupted, their questions directed at me or Cody.

"Quiet!" I yelled over everyone when I couldn't take it anymore. Everyone looked a little shocked at my outburst, but everyone quieted down immediately. I spoke softly but confidently, "If the Youth are willing to do what they've done to us… then they need to be stopped."

"Agreed," said my dad.

I gave him a grin and continued. "And correct me if I heard wrong, Cody, but we're on our own when it comes to stopping them?"

Cody nodded his head.

"Alright. Cody informed me of all the allies the Youth have in the police and the government. Making it impossible to get support without alerting the Youth to us. Which means, we're on our own when it comes to stopping them." Murmurs scattered the room. I waited for them to settle before continuing.

"The odds may be against us, but with God on our side, we have His power on our side. And I'm going to do everything that I can to ensure not a single person more has to experience what we have. And I'll do it alone if I have to." My mom and dad gave me big grins, though my mom looked more sad. Though I'm confident they were proud in that moment to call me their son.

"I understand what I'm about to ask is a lot. And it means putting

E.E. Cooley

your life on the line. But men and women laid down their lives to give us what we have today, the freedoms and blessings we get to experience. And the Youth want to take that away from us. So, don't feel obligated because it's a heavy burden, but who will join me in stopping the Youth, whether you can fight or not?" And as I asked the question, I wondered if I could fight or not? The comment Ash made before our plane ride banging around in my head, that the only resort with the Youth should be violence. Was that right though? Before I could doubt myself anymore, the responses came in.

"You're not doing this alone," said Thomas, immediately, "I'm with you." We smiled at each other, and I felt ten times lighter knowing I wasn't doing this alone.

"I'm with you, Calvin," said my dad. We gave each other a nod.

"Do I get to blow stuff up?" asked Dakota.

"Probably."

"I'm in." Dakota raised his hand. The rest of the dads raised their hands, too.

"Cody?" I asked. He replied with another nod.

When no one else replied, I asked, "Mom, what are you thinking?"

She turned around, looking at my dad before replying, "I may not be able to fight. And it makes me sick thinking about what we're getting into. But I'm not leaving my family behind. I'll help how I can."

"Me, too," said Thomas's mom, having regained her composure and some confidence as well.

And with that, everyone minus Ash was with me, which I was not expecting to happen. Though I was confident Ash would join us.

"Hey, Calvin?" asked Dakota.

"Yeah?"

"What was that name you picked out for us again?"

"The-the Renegades."

"The Renegades... yeah, I really like that name."

"Me, too," said Thomas.

"Then we'll be the Renegades from now on." I said, smiling along with everyone else, having gained some confidence back. And in that moment, I made a decision. One that I didn't know how it would be accomplished or what would come from it. But without a doubt, I know it was what needed to be done "Alright then Renegades, let's go save the world."

286

More Books by E.E. Cooley

Prime Youth

Prime Youth: Prisoners of the Masquerade

The Nameless Man

Bondage to Freedom

Sign up for my email list at eecooley.com to be notified before anyone else about my latest books, new merch, writing updates, event updates, and more!

If you enjoyed this book, please consider leaving a review on Amazon. They help me out immensely!

Acknowledgements

This acknowledgement goes out to the fans. Specifically, the fans who waited. If you're reading this soon after the release, you'll know you had to wait a little longer than I would have liked for the book to make it into your hands. *Prime Youth: Prisoners of the Masquerade* was published in May of 2022. This book was published in October of 2025. That's a long time to have to wait for a sequel in the book world, where most sequels come out the following year. So, my biggest apologies to you dear reader that this book did not come out earlier.

But now you have it. You stuck out the wait, and I hope you were very well rewarded with a story you enjoyed if not loved. Thank you for coming on this adventure with me, and I hope you not only bring yourself but others along for the ride as well. Enjoy!

E.E. Cooley
July 2025

Photo by Rylee Schneider

After dropping out of college to pursue a career with less textbooks and debt, I published my first book *Prime Youth: Prisoners of the Masquerade*. And since then that decision worked out far better than anyone could have imagined. But when I'm not writing I always have a list of books to read that's a mile long, play video games, and enjoy hiking.

Website: eecooley.com

Instagram: @e.e.cooley

Facebook: E.E. Cooley

Twitter/X: @EECooley

www.ingramcontent.com/pod-product-compliance
Lightning Source LLC
Chambersburg PA
CBHW020602110726
47899CB00002B/329